Morag is magnificent!

Shirley Barr

A profound sense of the beauty of place and the community bound to it. If the setting is a thousand years in the past, the underlying themes are quite contemporary.

Br Daniel OSB, Pluscarden Benedictines

A book to encourage those who teeter on the brink of claiming their place within the whole.

Romany Buck

Moves the reader beyond 'good and bad' and allows a common humanity to be seen, even in 'villains'.

Cornelia Featherstone and Sylvia Robertson

Thought-provoking. I was captivated by the characters, the landscape, the Celtic spirituality.

Ann Barr

Imbued with the author's love of nature and its wild and elemental forces that shape and govern Island life, *The Priest's Wife* makes for compelling reading and leaves the reader impatient for more.

Benedict Thwaite

THE PRIEST'S WIFE

The second book of the Trilogy
The Seaborne ⌘ The Priest's Wife ⌘ The Shareg

A. G. RIVETT

Pantolwen
Press

Published by Pantolwen Press, an imprint of
Bryn Glas Books, Llandysul, Ceredigion, SA44 4LD

This edition is available through UK bookstores
printed litho by Gomer Press, Llandysul, on Carbon Balanced Paper;
or set digitally, print-on-demand, from various sources worldwide.

First edition 2023
www.brynglasbooks.com

A CIP catalogue record for this book is available from
the British Library.

ISBNs
Hardback: 978 1 73936 230 0
Paperback: 978 1 73936 231 7
eBook: 978 1 73936 232 4

Edited by Gillian Paschkes-Bell

Cover design by Karl H

Body text typeset in Charter 10.5 pt

The publisher acknowledges the financial support
of the Books Council of Wales

CYNGOR LLYFRAU CYMRU
BOOKS COUNCIL of WALES

To my daughters,
Cat, Jen and Hannah

Tha mi ar slìi na fìrinne;
Tha mi ar slìi mo fise

I am on the path of truth;
I am on the path of my vision[†]

Contents

Author's note

The Priest's Wife continues the story begun in *The Seaborne*, and so it occupies a world that is both like and unlike our own of a thousand years ago. This is a world where the head man of the town is the shareg, the big roundhouse where people assemble is the rondal, and their version of what, in a church is called a service, or in a temple, a puja, is known here as the Tollach. In *The Seaborne* the main character, whom the Islanders call Dhion, is a present-day Londoner, washed up in the medieval world of the Island. The story of how he adapts to Island life and how his host community adapts to him was told in the earlier book. Now, in *The Priest's Wife*, Dhion is a secondary character but remains singular in that he alone has lived in our world and retains much of our knowledge and ideas.

The Islanders speak a Celtic language entirely their own. For readers interested in such matters, many words have similarities with Gaelic spelling, but the name of the town at the centre of the story, Caerpadraig, has a mix of Brythonic and Gaelic elements, while the name of the nearby village of Fisherhame has nothing Celtic about it at all. My main aim in these matters has been to keep a balance between English language readability, the need to keep a Celtic setting alive in readers' minds, and the constant hint that the world of the Island is both similar to and different from our own. So the main town of the Island is called Mhreuhan, which the Islanders pronounce something like 'Vroon.' But this is not typical of actual place names in Scotland or Ireland. On the other hand, the beings of Otherworld who play a part in the story are referred to as the Sidhe, which will be very familiar to readers of Irish mythology. Similarly, the chant and some liturgical words are in true Gaelic.

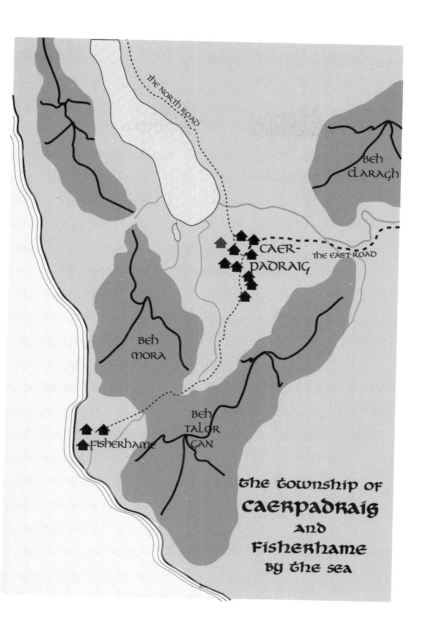

THE NORTH ROAD

BEh CLARAGh

CAER-
PADRAIG

THE EAST ROAD

BEh
MORA

BEh
TALOR
GAN

FISHERhAME

THE TOWNShIP OF
CAERPADRAIG
AND
FIShERhAME
BY THE SEA

Prologue

You cannot see me. And I cannot see across the water to the mainland. This is my charge, this Island; this patch of rock and earth, of heather, rush and moss. Indeed, this is my body, that you can see and walk upon; where you live your lives. Myself you do not see as I hover, high above the mountains of the Northland, the dunes and flower-meadows of Midland, the rich pastures of Caerster.

My people, too, mostly you do not see. But maybe, sometimes, you catch a glimpse that *there* a Sidh had been, a moment before you looked. One of the fey folk of mountain and lough, of bog and rock and tree; or a diva of the wild peoples: the wolves, the geese, the deer. Long ages we served Sky-Father and Earth-Mother, ever and again making love in the rain and the mist and the dew, refilling the world with their ever-varied children. Then Rortan came on the backs of whales bearing the gospel of compassion and the name of Ieshu the Chrisht. And we saw that Ieshu knew us, so we danced together in the service of the Chrisht.

But more and more, people are closing their minds to us. In the meadows of Caerster they no longer bless the fields on Bride's Day. We are forgotten, or denied, or denounced, and so we lose our power and fall dumb. We slumber in the hollow hills, where we will remain until the time of man fails. Then we will rise again, and terrible will be the thunder of our voice.

Now, as I fly, I see the rocky headlands and white beaches of Westerland. Lower I stoop, to look down upon the two peaks of Beh' Mora by the sea and dark Talor Gan, the low pass between them, and the little hamlet of Fisherhame nestling by the shore. I see the town, inland from the pass: Caerpadraig at the head of its shining lough. Lower still, my gold-brown and green wings invisible to your eyes, and below are the houses: some so close two women crossing on their way must squeeze past each other; some set around broad green spaces where sheep and cattle graze while children play.

There is the priest's house. That one, larger than the rest – almost as big as the shareg's next to it, where a dozen or more men could sit and hold council together. The thatch of a roof is no barrier to me. I see through, into the dark space below, the faint red glow of the fire-bowl, the point of light where the lamp flickers. The two figures asleep on the bed platform in their alcove off the living-space: the priest, and the priest's wife.

THE FIRST PART: THE MADMAN

Chapter 2

Morag was up at day-break. She heard bleating, and the soft rustling sound of many delicate hooves. Duigheal was leading his flock out to pasture. Now that winter was past he would take them onto the mountain slopes, leaving only the ewes still in lamb on the town meadows.

'Duigheal – God be with you.'

'Ghea keep you, A'Phadr,' he replied. He bowed his head in that measured way that was so much the shepherd.

'Duigheal, you heard that the – ' she was about to say *madman*, but checked herself ' – the prophet, Gormagh, was here yesterday?'

For a while he stood, silent. 'Ah, that one. He's well touched by the Sidhe.' He went on gazing at the ground.

'It's just that – ' She felt suddenly embarrassed. 'If you see him – if you hear where he's resting – would you let me know. Or tell the Father,' she added.

He raised his eyes for a moment to glance at her from under his brows. 'I will, Lady.' He turned, gave that odd little call to his sheep, and trudged on.

Hugh was out, visiting. The house was silent. Gormagh's question lay before her: who was she? These many years such a thought had not troubled her; but now?

'I am Morag,' she told herself. 'Wife of Hugh, priest of Caerpadraig. I am Morag A'Phadr.'

She paused. Went on.

'I am Morag, daughter of Murdogh, son of Conor, the son of Cormac. I am a daughter of Kimmoil in the Northland. No mean township, a proud people and strong.'

She recited the genealogy of her forebears. She knew it by heart. The maternal line they had taught her was the ancestry of her father's mother. But it would not have satisfied most men, most men's families, that the line of her own mother was a blank. Hugh's great step in setting this aside and asking her to marry him had persuaded her she could put it all behind her. And now here it was, staring her in the face.

She looked into the glowing heart of the fire and let her eyes close. She began to drift, sinking into a world of memories that seemed to be below, deeper than the world of here and now; that held this world like a mother with her child. She journeyed back to the time when she and Hugh were still young. Lingered on the long months, the years of waiting for the baby she'd never borne him. A silent regret.

And then, after so many changing seasons, had come the completely unthought-of thing: a grown man, come from who knew where, brought to them to raise like a child. They had been charged by the shareg to teach him their speech and their ways. In the end, they had adopted him as their own, to give him a lineage among them. So now she who was barren had a son: Dhion, called the Ingleeshe from his first word to them, and the Seaborne from the way of his coming – plucked, like a great fish, from the sea.

Back further she journeyed, to her own childhood. The town looking out onto the long northern lough. Her father, dark, silent; his house, not her home. And the absence of a mother. Her grandam and granda were good people, and loving in their way. Their house was warm, holding. But they were not her mother. And what was it about her mother that led, for a time, to the other children's taunts, so that she had to play alone – until they forgot whatever it was – until they remembered it again: *Who's your mother? Don't you know?*

What had she been like, this mother of hers? They would tell her nothing. Why? As a small child, she had accepted how things were. It was only as she grew older that the questions came. But why, when she started asking them, would the subject change? Suddenly there would be something else that must be attended to, or she was not to ask at that moment. In the end, they said her mother was not of their people; was a foreigner, not to be trusted. That she had gone away, no one knew where. And that was the end of it. *She's a bad woman*, one of the children blurted out – her mam had said so. Yet somewhere, in a deep recess past conscious memory, lingered an impression that was sweet and warm. It was the world around her that was hard, and sometimes bad; not that. She clung to it.

She made a further effort, and behind closed eyes sank towards that realm where all things are known, seeking for the sweet, warm place. A picture began to form. A stone-built crofthouse in the arm of the mountain. And a presence. Not a vision, not a face, but a feeling of motherness around her. She was there. Just a fragment of realness, and no more.

She let herself float upwards, back to everyday reality. She opened her eyes. The fire flickered and glowed, the pot simmering over it. But a tinge of the Other was still in her. Checking that all was well to leave for a little time she put another stick on the flames, rose and, smoothing out her skirts, opened the door.

The rondal was quiet. A lingering memory of incense, a coolness on the floor as she slipped her feet out of her shoes. She closed the door behind her and the shutters on the windows made the darkness almost complete. Only chinks and glimmers of light through crannies in the eaves; in one place a narrow shaft of sunlight falling through the drifting motes.

And the lamp. Under the far wall, in the sanctuary, its yellow flame.

She drew closer. Her feet felt the hard earth of the floor change to rustling reeds as she entered the sanctuary. The lamp lit the wooden cross that rose behind it and threw its shadow on the rough wall: four broad arms held in a circle. Four arms, signifying the four directions and the four elements; the upright, piercing, penetrating the cross-piece, as Otherworld pierces and penetrates the world of things. And all around, sunlike as a halo, the encompassing circle, gathering all together, enfolding all in eternity.

Fire was present in the lamp above, and Air in that slight scent of incense, all around. On one side stood the font; to the other, the outcrop of bedrock round which the rondal had been built: Water and Earth. The great stone rose, its dull redness touched by the light of the sanctuary lamp, speckled and sparkled with tiny crystals of quartz: the rock they called the Mother.

She knelt before the Mother and invited Her presence, curling forward so that her lips touched the stone. Straightening again, she raised her hands to her breast in salutation.

She thought of all the mothers who had ever borne life – birth, and hatching egg and swimming spawn; seed of flower and seed of man; seed of grain, ground, leavened, baked and eaten. Fruit, dark juice running, dark blood flowing; held, fermented, matured, drunk. Here, in the holy place, all life held.

She reached out and touched the cold stone. She leaned forward and rested her brow upon Her body. She sank lower, her face to the ground. Now she was weeping, she who had never known what it was to give birth to a child; whose own childhood was marked by the absence of a mother.

❧ ❦

The week passed, and Morag grimaced wryly at the cooking pots. *Why didn't you – you could have – you should have. He was here, right here, in your house, and now – who knows?*

The shepherd brought no news. No one had seen Gormagh. He had vanished.

First-day Eve, and first light. Morag jumped as a vigorous knocking resounded from the door. She had already risen and was blowing up the fire, but Hugh, sitting on the side of the bed, stood and reached for his cassock. 'I'll go.'

She heard the shareg's deep voice, but couldn't catch the words. She saw Hugh nod. She heard him say, 'I'll get the Sacrament.'

As soon as Micheil had gone Hugh turned to her.

'Who is it?' she asked. She heard her own voice, edged with anxiety. Someone in the town? There was no one sick that she knew of.

'It's our prophet of the other day. It seems he found his own quarters in the ruined bothy at the head of the glen – you know the one.' She nodded. 'Duigheal Shepherd discovered him this morning while he was climbing up to his flock. Duigheal said even then he sounded as if he was taking his last gasp. Micheil doesn't expect us to find him alive.'

While Hugh finished dressing she brought him his boots. 'Here,' she said, handing him a bowl. 'Take a spoonful before you go.' He gulped it down gratefully, took his cloak and opened the door.

As she went about her work, Gormagh's face filled her thoughts. Gormagh, staring at her. His words: 'Don't you know who you are?'

It was nearly noon when Hugh returned. He ushered in Micheil, and the two men sat by the fire, unlacing their boots. Morag brought a little water and mixed in the brown crust that had formed on the porridge. She lowered the trivet until the pot began to bubble.

'Micheil, I'm sure you're hungry.'

She ladled out two bowls, root vegetables mixed in with the oats, and a little salted meat. She set them down and folded her skirts to sit on the bench beside her husband. 'Well: what news? Were you in time?'

'We went as fast as we could,' Hugh replied, 'but not fast enough. When we reached him, he was already cold. Stretched out on the floor. I closed his eyes and said the prayers – it was all I could do.'

She met his gaze. All he could do was still good to do. But it meant that her question would never be put to the man. Disappointment flooded her. She felt the unworthiness of caring so little about his passing; so much about his no longer being there to be asked.

'But there was blood.' Micheil's voice sounded weary. 'We both saw it, from his mouth and on the floor. I shall have to hold a speaking.'

'Surely it was the white sickness? I've seen it before.' Hugh had sat by countless sick-beds; witnessed death in a multitude of forms.

'Blood was shed,' Micheil repeated. 'And the man was alone. I'm sure you're right, and there was no foul deed. But still, I shall have to call a speaking. There's nothing more to be said.'

'Then – may we bring the body down for burial?'

'Yes, of course. I'll ask Murdogh to take some men up there.'

All week the weather had been unseasonably cold, but that day the wind turned, blew the clouds away and wafted the faint scent of bluebells from the lough-side woods. By mid-afternoon it was warm, and Murdogh and his men looked hot as they set down their heavy litter before the rondal. Morag took the few steps to the shareg's house to ask Aileen to help her prepare the body. A'Shar'g came, along with her sonswoman, Doirin. It would be First-day tomorrow, so Gormagh would be lying through the Tollagh, a silent symbol of his fierce God in a community gathered in peace for prayer. Morag hoped it would do his troubled spirit good as it set out on the long journey.

They brought him behind the priest's house and worked outside, benefitting from the fine weather. Some of the filthy clothes had to be cut away from the stiffening body. Doirin, small and pale, the white skin of her neck and arms seeming almost transparent, worked quietly.

'Look at these,' remarked Aileen. 'None of it's fit for anything! Doirin, bundle these up and …' She glanced over the roofs of the town and caught the thin blue column of smoke from the smith's forge. 'Ask Shean Blacksmith if he'd put them on his fire, would you.'

Morag noticed the young woman's eyes flicker under her brows towards her mansmother. She smiled at the thought of how the peppery smith might receive such a present.

'Hugh! Hugh: you must get up. It'll be time for the Tollagh soon.'

He groaned. Then slowly sat up, swung his legs out of bed. He stood, swayed, reached a hand out to steady himself on the wall.

She looked at him in the morning light flooding through the windows. He looked grey. Alarmed, she saw dark marks under his eyes. Shadows under his cheek-bones.

'Hugh, love: you're not well. Shall I ask Micheil to take the Tollagh, and you can get back to bed?'

His mouth cracked open. 'No, no. I can manage. He can't give the Sacrament, and they'll expect me to be there.'

'But he does it when you're travelling. Isn't there more reason now, if you're ill?'

'I'll be all right. Look, there's only a few steps from here to the rondal. I'm not dead yet.'

Don't say that, her heart screamed.

He coughed, and tottered past the curtain to the kaleyard beyond.

She helped him to dress. How, such a change in just a week? He was not slim: he was thin. She could count his ribs. She put his bowl before him. He pecked at the porridge.

'Hugh, love … Really, you're not well. Let me …'

'I'll be all right.' He turned on her the warm brown eyes that had won her all those years before. Those dear eyes, now sunken in his face. 'Come on.'

It was as the Tollagh moved towards its climax that it happened. Hugh was lifting the bread and the cup before the altar. All at once he dropped his arms and placed the sacred vessels on the table before him. He produced a white cloth from his scrip and coughed into it. Morag heard a deep rattle as he finally drew breath. She watched from her bench among the women as he clutched at the holy table and sank down on his knees to a collective gasp from the assembled townsfolk.

She jumped up and ran to him amid the mounting hubbub, her bare feet slipping on the crushed reeds that floored the sanctuary. She knelt beside him. Behind her, the shareg's solid presence.

She lowered his head into her lap.

Hugh was struggling in her arms. 'I must …' he began.

'No, you mustn't.' She was now utterly firm. Micheil had already picked out three men who were making their way through the benches towards them. 'You're going back home, and that's the end of it. Micheil will close the Tollagh and send the people on their way.'

The men came. Strong as they were, they lifted him carefully from where he knelt on the ground. Reverence for the priest awed them.

She took the hem of Hugh's chesible, the short outer robe, richly-embroidered, that he wore to celebrate the breaking of bread. She pulled it gently over his head. Then she stood, and laid it reverently on the altar. Straightening out her skirts, she took a step back. She bumped into something. Turned, off balance. Before her, Gormagh's dead face stared blindly, impassive above his shroud.

Chapter 3

For three days Hugh kept to his bed, his appetite gone, his chest shaken with coughing. Then slowly he improved: much of his strength returned. But to Morag he was thinner, more drawn, a shadow hovering beside him. He made himself attend Micheil's inquiry into Gormagh's death. 'After all,' he said, 'I was one of the first to find him dead.' As Morag expected, no one came forward with evidence of foul play.

But as summer ripened and the fruits swelled on the brambles, Hugh no longer visited the homes of his people. First he returned, defeated, from attempting to reach Fisherhame. Later, he found he could barely walk to the smithy. Micheil sent to the neighbouring towns to see if there was a priest who could come from time to time and help with the Tollagh. Inveraerd was nearest, just up the coast, and replied first. The next First-day Eve their priest, Mungo, appeared.

After the Tollagh Mungo sat with them in the priest's house, having given Hugh the host. 'Listen,' he said, 'I have heard this from the wise. After the sun-darkening they took counsel. This is what they say.'

Morag leaned forward, keen to hear what Mungo had to tell.

He pushed his long hair out of his eyes. His hooked nose, like a hawk's beak, thrust forward. Morag listened. Hugh listened, propped up in the little bed where Dhion used to sleep when he lived with them.

'They say that Atain is sad. The Lady of the Sun has passed her hand across her face, to hide her tears from the Earth.'

Morag considered. What had happened since that time? Gormagh, horrible yet compelling, had come among them, seemingly only to disturb her, and had died. And now Hugh. His sickness affected the whole township and beyond. Four months now he had been ill, and while sometimes he declared himself a little better, after a few days he would sink back, if anything, lower than before. She still hoped. But while she hoped, she also feared: more and more, with each repeated back-sinking. While those two voices struggled within her heart, it was a stark clarity that was gaining the upper hand: he was beginning to leave them. And, strangely, what came with that knowing was the ability to bear it. A kind of peace.

But still these must be only the little, nearby out-workings of something greater.

'What is it?' she asked Mungo. 'Why is Atain sad?'

'They do not know clearly. There is a rumour of murrains and blight; of fighting on the mainland. But that is always so. They say it is a time to watch and wait. To prepare to withstand what is coming. The lords and ladies of the heavens have sent us a warning. And that may be of things we have not seen before.'

It was not only Hugh who ceased visiting the people during those four months. Morag, taken up by his care, had also stopped her visits to the households of the town. Slowly, almost silently, the women of Caerpadraig presented themselves to offer help. This one brought a dish of food; that one carried water. Sometimes Aileen would sit, watching Hugh, sometimes silent, sometimes sharing the town gossip, while Morag took herself out to walk a little way along the loughside, grateful to stretch her limbs and feel the light wind in her hair. More often, Shinane sat with him. Hugh seemed to rest more deeply in her presence. In the evenings, Dhion would appear and, sitting quietly, take Hugh's thin hand and hold it in his strong one. And, day after day, Morag would sit beside him, sometimes reading from the Book of Caerpadraig that he himself had kept, recording the people and their events. Over the weeks they went right through it from the day he had made the first entry, remembering their years together in the place he had been sent to, the place they had made their home: rich years, filled with so much, both of gladness and of sadness.

The sun set, yellow and watery behind Beh' Mora and, as the sky slowly darkened, the new moon showed himself, slim and silver. The moon after Lammas, and the summer was dying. But in the arms of the crescent, faint and round, lay the ghost of the old moon. Duigheal brought his flock down to the town to fold them for the night.

'The peace of God, Duigheal. It's not often you bring your little ones down so soon in the year.' Morag was standing by her open door, breathing the last of the day's clear air.

'Aye. But look at yon sky.' He nodded his head towards the west. 'Yon's muck comin, an I no want my wee ones out in tha. God's peace, A'Phadr.'

He strode on towards the tiny hut where he dwelt alone beside the folds.

She watched the star-folk come out to step their nightly dance. Hugh was asleep, and she could breathe for a while. But among the little lights of the stars, the greater light of Brother Moon was slowly covered over as a mass of darkness arose like a great blanket out of the west.

Moon, she thought. What had Dhion said about Brother Moon, those months ago, when the morning sunlight had darkened? That Little Brother Moon had come between them and the Lady of the Sun? Well, why had Moon seen fit to do that? Mungo the priest had told a different story.

She watched as Brother Moon disappeared behind the murk. Mungo's words and Duigheal's mingled in her. She shivered, and went within.

It was dark, dead dark, when she woke. Hugh was calling.

She went to him. He was too weak to do more than turn on his side.

'I'm sorry to wake you. The bed – it's wet.'

'Have you …' Her caring was weighed down with tiredness.

'No – it's all over me. It's as if I've been sweating. Only, so much …'

She touched his brow. It was clammy like a fish straight from the sea. 'Let's see what we can do,' she said, and kissed him.

Carefully she lit a lamp from the little rush-light and went to the press where she kept fresh linen. As she rolled him to strip away the damp sheet, she was aware of how she could feel every bone of him. She must be so careful.

At length it was done. There was fresh linen on the bed and the sweat-soaked sheets were piled up ready for washing. She must be down at the washing pool tomorrow. But, no! She must be here. By Hugh's side.

Her own bed – their bed before he became so ill – was cold and unwelcoming. She lay upon it and gazed up through the darkness. A wind began to shake the shutters. It found cracks and chinks and sent little emissaries into the house to cause mischief where they could. Soon the rain began. At first a sporadic patter, it grew steadier. Then, as the wind rose to a howl, it flung itself against the shutters in huge handfuls.

There was no sense in trying to sleep. She rose and crossed the floor to the little shrine in the wall where they said their daily prayer. She lit a tiny candle and began in a whisper: 'In the name of the One, without beginning, without ending. In the name of the Highest Intention.'

As she repeated the invocation, she became aware of a faint echo. Hugh, also wakeful, was joining in, as best he could.

The dawn was hardly brighter than the night. She supposed it was day, from the grey apology for light creeping round the shutters. It was no time to open them just now, though: the rain was still rattling against the wooden panels like fine pebbles.

She lit the lamps and prepared their first-food. She took a bowl to Hugh. He was too weak to hold it. Balancing the bowl on his flat belly, she raised his head with her left arm and, in her other hand, brought the spoon to his lips. He took a little, and again. Then he turned his head away, staring up at her with huge hollow eyes.

'Love, you must eat. You're as thin as bone. Try a little more.'

'I cannot. I'm sorry. I can't.'

She cleared away the bowls and went outside, behind the house. The swaying and creaking fence gave her a little shelter as she crouched.

An owl. Brown and speckled, a brindled owl, huddled under the kale-tops, its bedraggled feathers ruffled by the wind. He swivelled his head around to stare at her with great yellow eyes. Again he turned and, with an effort, took a couple of hops and jumped into the air. The wind caught him at once and whisked him away, half flying, half blown. He vanished.

She shook out her cloak as she reached the door and went back into the house. She grasped the pot-stand, her head bent over the dully-gleaming pans. She realised she was weeping.

It was Moira Ag'Olan who took the pile of washing. 'I'll ask my man's mam to put them in her tub. She'll grumble, but she'll do it.'

Catrean was one who would not deign to go with the other women to the washing pool. Morag could never have imagined their own bed-linen would find its way into her hands.

That afternoon, while the house was still and no visitors appeared and Hugh slept, she turned again to her embroidery and, as before, found the steady stitching a comfort to her soul.

It was in the late afternoon that he stirred.

She looked up. 'Are you awake, love?'

His nod encouraged her. 'Do you think you could manage a little broth?'

'I'll try.'

When she returned to his bedside, a warm bowl cupped in her hands, he was staring up at the roof with his hollow eyes. She helped him to sit up, and brought a spoonful to his lips.

He sipped, and swallowed. 'I'm dying. You do know that, don't you, Mora?'

The voice of hope lay down and covered its head. But the other voice did not crow over its victory. It became a quiet peacefulness. 'Yes, love. I know.' She gave him another spoonful. He took it. 'Are you afraid?'

He turned his head to look at her. 'Yes, I am. More than afraid …' Again he gazed upward. 'I'm terrified.'

He said the words. But, looking at him, she did not see terror in his eyes.

She sat on the bed. A silence grew around them. She listened to the wind outside, swirling around the house. Somewhere a slow dripping signalled that rain had found a way through the thatch.

He began, 'I am not a good man.'

She knew to say nothing. There was a long pause. At last, slowly, haltingly, he went on, 'I hope I am becoming better than I was.'

Still *becoming*. It struck her deeply.

Hugh stopped speaking and after a time she wondered if he had fallen asleep. Then his eyes opened and he whispered out of dry lips. 'And, if I have become anything at all, I hope … it will not be lost.'

He closed his eyes and she sat on beside him, listening to each rasping breath. Daylight, the thin daylight under the storm-wrack, began to fade. She had kept the lamps lit since morning. She rose to bring more oil, but he opened his eyes again. A hint of the old liveliness shone from them.

'I go on the Great Adventure,' he whispered, with a gleam. 'Where would the adventure be if we knew what was coming? Eh?'

His words, but even more the look in his eye, warmed her heart with a sudden rush beyond anything she had felt for a long time, and broke through in a glorious smile.

'Only … be there with me,' he added, suddenly. 'Hold my hand as I begin … I know you will.'

'You know I will.' There was a lump in her throat, but her eyes were dry. 'I'll be here as much as I can. So don't go slipping off while my back's turned, will you?'

Another gleam. 'I won't,' he promised.

Chapter 4

Night came, and she dozed on the floor beside him. In the small hours he woke, and again the sheets were wet. Again she changed the bedding, and slept fitfully.

She was woken late by a tapping at the door. She realised it was morning, and she had slept in her clothes. Her gown was crumpled. She quickly shook out the creases, and answered the call.

A thin sun leaked through high cloud. The world looked bedraggled. And there was Aileen, her little dancer's body straight as always, but her eyes full of anxious care.

'How are the two of you?'

Morag brought her into the house.

'Hugh – Aileen's here.'

There was no answer. The two women crept to the bedside. Morag could not help but watch his chest, to assure herself it still rose and fell.

'He's asleep still. Come to the fire.'

The embers of last night still glowed weakly. Without a word, Aileen took down the shutters to let in the wan daylight and set to mending the fire. Morag sank down thankfully into her chair.

Aileen gave her a penetrating look. 'You haven't eaten, have you?'

'It's … it's not been easy. It was a long night.'

'Sit you down and wait there. I'll be back right away.'

She did as she was told. Aileen slipped out, and it seemed no time before she pushed open the door again. She held a dish in her hands from which wafted a scent of sweet herbs, warmth and savour. In spite of her fatigue, Morag's mouth watered.

'The goose has been laying for you.'

Her mood lifted a little with the tasty food. The two women talked.

After a while Aileen glanced towards the pile of crumpled sheets. 'You've got some washing there. I can take that.'

'Thank you,' Morag answered, humbly and gratefully. She knew she was exhausted.

There was a knock on the door, but before either could rise it was pushed open. 'Mother …?'

Morag looked up, startled, to see Shinane's face appear, pale, round the edge of the door.

'Come in, child.' It was Aileen who answered.

They sat together. After a while Aileen looked across at Shinane. 'I'm going to leave you with your mansmother, if I may. I've a wee bit to do.' She scooped up the pile of damp bedding and disappeared.

The morning passed. Shinane cleared away the bowls and beakers from the first-food and swept the house. They talked of this and that.

Hugh stirred. Morag went to him and knelt by the bedside. She reached for his bony hand. He opened his eyes and turned his head towards her.

She looked at him as she knelt by the bed. So shrunken, his cheek-bones stretching the yellowish skin; his eyes sunk in the skull, strangely bright.

The eyes caught hers. He opened his mouth and whispered. 'It is time. Go for the bread and wine.'

Her heart beat faster.

'My love – are you sure?'

He said again, 'It is time. Go now and bring the bread and wine … from the sanctuary.' It was less than a whisper.

'I'll send for Mungo. Can you hold out, till he comes?'

She could see him summoning himself to speak; the effort it caused him. He could not hold out long enough.

'Just … bring the bread and wine.'

She studied him again. His face was intent. She reached for his thin hand, lying lax on the blanket, and squeezed it.

She called to Shinane. 'Love, would you sit with Hugh a moment. I'll be back straight away.'

Outside, autumn leaves swirled in a sudden gust. The air felt warm, and she looked up, half-expecting to see thunder-heads forming above the town. But the sky was clear, blue between the creamy white and grey clouds.

As she returned, Shinane rose from the bedside and retired to a stool. Morag's own hands were full with the little pewter box that held the unleavened wafers, the precious crystal flask of oil, the plain fired-clay bottle of wine. The linens hung over her forearm.

'Shinane love, pull up that other stool, would you? … There now: take this linen – no, the big one underneath – and spread it on the stool. That's right.'

She put the holy vessels down on the white cloth, all the time aware of Hugh's eyes upon her, his wry humour somehow surrounding her.

'You haven't brought the chalice and paten. Nor the stole.'

She looked across at the sunken eyes. 'I was leaving them for Mungo, when he gets here …'

He summoned what strength was left him. His husky voice filled the air. *'I don't want Mungo.* Please – bring them now.'

She looked from the sick man to the young woman, and back again. Shinane had half-risen, expectant.

'I'll go, love. You sit down again.' She saw the questioning look the girl gave her. Resolutely, she stood, and made once more for the door.

Hugh had, of course, often given himself the *Beannach* – but only, ever, in the course of giving it to others. She would take it with him now. They would all three take it. Entering the rondal again, she dropped to one knee before the Presence. Returning, she put the cup and the plate on the stool with the other vessels. Last she laid the stole beside him on the bed.

He looked up at her. 'Pick it up. Put it on.'

She took the length of white cloth that she herself had embroidered for him, with intricate knot-work in the shape of the equal-sided cross standing in the circle; below it, two entwined fishes, and above, a bird taking wing. She made to pass it around Hugh's neck.

He raised a hand to ward it off. 'Not on me. Put it on *you*.'

She stopped, motionless, the stole held in mid-air.

'Hugh, I can't.' The thought shocked her. 'I'm not a priest.'

'You are,' he said. 'And I'll make you one.'

'But … I'm a woman … and … the Rule: you don't have authority.'

'Fuck the Rule. And I know you're a woman.'

The sudden coarseness shocked her, from a man who would not have said *damn*.

She hesitated. There had been times – several times – when Hugh had been travelling or was ill, when Micheil had presided over the *Beannach*, using bread and wine that Hugh had already consecrated, only leaving out the holy words that the priest alone could say. Dael Fisherhame had done so once or twice. It wasn't the same, but it was enough for the time. Always, it had been a man. And they never wore the stole.

'Put it on. Please. I haven't much time. And bring me the oil.'

She looked at him, and blinked back the tears. Through his wasted face he was smiling.

Clear as a mountain stream, Shinane's voice broke through: 'Please, Morag. He's right. He needs you to do this. For him.'

She glanced round. Shinane was leaning forward on her stool, her eyes bright and moist. Morag had entirely forgotten her.

She took stock of herself. She trembled. The rules were crumbling, crashing down within her.

Then the door burst open, and a gust of wind swept through the house. It ruffled her hair and surrounded her, perversely, with a warm fragrance. Somewhere deep within her, voices were still chanting: *Who's your mother? Don't you know?* With her mind's eye she saw the taunt curl up like autumn leaves and flee before the swirling eddy.

Morag stood. She picked up the stole, let its length unfurl and, as she had seen Hugh do many times, kissed the little cross at the back of the neck. Her lips tingled. She bent her head and hung the white linen over her shoulders.

'The oil … ' His voice, husky with effort.

She reached for the bottle, pulled out the stopper, passed it to Shinane, and cupped her free hand. She poured out one golden drop. A new fragrance filled the air, mingling with that brought by the wind. She handed the bottle to Shinane and extended her cupped palm towards her husband's hand as it lay, gaunt, upon the bedcover. Trembling, he extended his forefinger and dipped it in the sweet-smelling oil.

'Bend down … '

She bent her head. With evident effort, he raised his trembling hand and touched her brow, moving his finger in the sign of the encircled cross.

'In the name of the One, our Father Mother. In the name of the Chrisht, who is one with the One. In the name of the Sacred Spirit … who dwells in all … servants … of the One.'

The effort it cost him was clear. He breathed out. His hand dropped back on the bed. He lay. He took another breath.

Morag raised her head. Now authority came upon her and settled around her like a cloud. She trembled a little at the feeling – the responsibility that weighed massive yet gentle upon her like the sweetest new-mown hay. The power that lay in her hands. She picked up the flask, poured a little wine into the chalice.

Hugh watched her every move. His sunken eyes glistened.

She knew the actions her hands must make: she had seen Hugh often enough. He mouthed the opening words. She spoke them, firmly, softly, with awe. Then words came flowing through her from a deep well that rose up within. Had she not heard such words again and again down the years?

She took her hand away from the plate. The fragments of bread looked no different than before. But now, in her heart, they meant a universe.

Shinane had dropped to her knees. Morag picked up a morsel of bread and held it to Hugh's lips. '*Corp Criosd.*' Shinane was holding up her hands. '*Corp Criosd.*'

Then the cup. For Hugh: '*Fuil Griosd* … ' Shinane: '*Fuil Griosd.*'

She took, and ate, and drank. On one level, nothing had changed. On another, everything was different.

She felt she was carried on a wave of power and a majesty she had not known possible. She pronounced the blessing, making in the air the great, equal-armed cross that signified the world made sacred; the sacred, breaking into the earth; dust and dung and mud, made glorious in the Divine Mystery.

Hugh was asleep. A thin, contented smile hung upon his yellowing face. She watched his chest rise and fall.

She removed the stole from her neck. With care she folded it, laid it on the bed. She let out a sigh. She felt small again, no more than herself.

Shinane was on her feet. Morag looked at the younger woman: there were tears standing in her eyes. The girl bent down, collected the sacred vessels, straightened herself. A willow in spring.

Morag turned away. She crossed the room to where the unshuttered window gave onto the rising slopes of Beh' Talor Gan. Past the shareg's house, up the cleft of the burn, the yellows and russets and earth-greens of the mountain, the dun and grey of its rounded crest.

What have I done, she thought. Yet she didn't feel guilty: she felt, in all humility, that she had done what compassion demanded. How to reconcile her thoughts and feelings?

There were clouds over Talor Gan, high and thin in the sky. A pair of eagles soared and circled, dark and tiny in the vastness. A tear wetted her cheek.

Shinane left, promising to come back with some supper. Micheil called by, smelling of cattle, and stood a long moment gazing down at Hugh, a little awkward in the presence of illness.

'Thank you, dear friend,' he muttered at last. 'I don't know what I'll do without you.'

At last, Morag was alone with Hugh again. With the dying man, once her lover; always her foil. Behind Beh' Mora the sun set and the house darkened. Morag put up the shutter. She lit a lamp. Little and yellow, it threw a circle of warmth around them.

He coughed. She brought a bowl. There were flecks of blood. He lay back, sighed. His breathing settled. His gaze seemed fixed at a point behind her shoulder, but when she turned to look, there was nothing but the bare wall.

Shinane came back and with her, Dhion. She made way for them, and Dhion knelt beside the bed. She saw the tenderness as he held his father's hand. Could any natural son be closer?

They sat all three together at the bedside, watching, while Hugh slept. They told stories. Mostly, the stories of their own doings together. Of Dhion's coming to the house dressed in his clothes from another world. Of his shameful clumsiness at harvest with the scythe; of the day when Hugh discovered the newcomer could write. And of Shinane's coming, later, to learn to read the few and precious books they had.

From time to time one or other would rise to feed the fire or trim the light; bring a bite to eat or a cup to drink. At last, they fell into silence. Then Morag began to sing: a long, low chant, matching the cadence to the slight rise and fall of her beloved man's chest. It was a wandering chant that made it easy to match his ragged breathing. Again there was silence. They watched, and waited. Morag held Hugh's hand and felt him holding hers, his grip strangely firm and sure.

The sick man's face changed. A beatific smile broke through the gaunt features. Morag saw it with amazement. *What are you seeing, my love? What do you see that I cannot?* She did not know if she asked the words aloud or only in her heart.

There came no answer.

Outside, a bird sang. A few essays of broken whistles, little fragments – as if the bird had fallen out of practice since nest-building – then came the full-bodied song. A thrush. A phrase, liquid and mellow. As though the sound was sufficiently pleasing, it was repeated. And another bird, fainter, further away, joined in.

Hugh sighed. He was still. They saw his chest rise again. Another sigh, and a pause. His lips parted to admit the breath, then long, slow, let it out again. A sigh into silence.

They waited. Stillness.

She felt Dhion's arm around her. She allowed herself to be drawn against him, and laid her head on his shoulder. It was Shinane who quietly rose and closed Hugh's mouth and eyes. Then she crossed the room and opened the shutter. The birds sang, and a dim grey light heralded the dawn.

Chapter 5

The priest was dead. Swiftly, relentlessly, the news seeped through the town and beyond. Shean took a load of his wares over the pass to Fisherhame, and with him the tidings. Duigheal shepherd, crossing the path of other shepherds from the out-crofts on the high grazings, carried the word. A runner was chosen to go to Midland to tell Hugh's family. And Micheil sent Euan Ma'Challen from Fisherhame a day's sailing round the Island to bring word to the new archpriest, Feirgas, in his great High House of stone: his priest is dead.

Those days were a muddle of comings and goings, of people saying things – things Morag could not keep to mind – and doing things around her she scarce noticed.

The morning Hugh died she sat on, holding the thin hand as the day brightened around her. His breath was gone, but his presence felt near. Dhion rose quietly and tended the fire. Dimly, she could hear Shinane busying herself; a clattering of pots. They were leaving her alone with Hugh for the last time. In the space that opened, she bent over to kiss the silent lips. 'Thank you,' she whispered. It was all she could find to say. Someone softly opened the door. In a little while Shinane returned with Micheil, who stood looking down on the still body of the man with whom, through long years, he had carried the leadership of the town. He shook his head. After herself, Morag saw, he was the one who would feel Hugh's loss most keenly.

As the news passed to the craftsmen and the landsmen and around the washing pool and the dairy, the little family sat with their loss. Shinane placed porridge on the board, and Dhion came gently to bring her from the dead towards the living. At last Morag rose. She had never felt so stiff. She wanted no food, but just to sit by the fire, wordless, spent, letting the others be and do quietly around her. She sat, while the sun rose in the sky. And then she heard, softly, raggedly at first, and then stronger, the chant from outside: *The blessing of God on the soul of the dead.*

Many times she herself had chanted thus for those she knew: knew and missed, or knew and quietly found relief in their passing.

And now? She felt like a piece of flotsam, standing by as the people began to mourn the loss of their priest. But were they not also mourning the loss of her own quiet service to them? For had they not worked together, she and Hugh? Until, as his sickness took hold, not only he, but also she, had ceased to move among them. With the priest, it seemed the priest's wife had also died.

Then: 'Aileen's come to help you wash him, Mother.' Shinane was the one who was finding her strength and taking charge. 'Will you put out what he should wear.'

'Yes …' Morag made an effort. 'He must lie in the rondal.'

'Micheil is arranging it.' It was Dhion who answered. 'There's his two boys and Olan and myself to carry him. Olan will bring a board.'

Morag looked at him. She took his hand. 'You're a good son.'

He smiled. 'No more than you deserve.'

The door pushed quietly open. For a moment the chant swelled, and the small round figure of Fineenh was silhouetted against the light outside. As she came forward across the house her bustling body was lit fleetingly by the wan sunlight from the unshuttered window. Then, as she passed further in, only the glow of the lamp shone dimly on her face, throwing it into lines and shadows.

Morag rose, but before she could straighten, Fineenh's arms were around her. 'Mora …' she choked. And then, pulling herself together, 'I've come to help lay him out.'

The intensity of the embrace and the intimate name took her by surprise. Fineenh had never called her anything but 'A'Phadr.' She felt the social distance between them shrink. Morag bent her head and submitted to being kissed by the other woman. She tasted tears on Fineenh's cheek.

Fineenh leaned over the still form on the bed. 'Dear soul,' she said. 'Ye're in a better place now, I'm sure. Go wi God. And look after us from there, won't you …'

Father Mungo came that same day, First-day Eve. He heard the news at Fisherhame as soon as his boat was landed and came at once to the priest's house. Morag liked the wiry Northerner who looked her straight in the eye. He took her hands as she opened the door to him and held them silently for a long time.

'How was it with him, at the end?' Mungo asked. 'I feel his soul still present. It would not be too late for me to give him the sacrament.'

'He has taken the sacrament,' said Morag, carefully. 'All that he asked has been done.'

And so she told him, and did not tell him, how it had been. He did not press her further.

As soon as he had finished his ale and bannock, he rose. 'Will you take me to him?'

The evening was beginning to darken. The half moon hung in the western sky. There were candles alight in the rondal and Morag looked towards a figure seated on a stool by the head of her husband's body.

It was Dhion. He stood as they entered. Since they had brought Hugh for his lying in, dressed in his cassock, his sandals laid across his thighs, the townsfolk had taken turns to accompany the body, usually two together for fellowship. But Dhion had taken two turns to every other's one.

Mungo looked into the dead man's face. 'He was a good man. He served you well.'

They stood, the three of them, looking down at the pale, unspeaking body.

Mungo turned towards her. 'Where is his stole? A priest should carry his sign of office.'

'I am keeping it.' She said it softly, keeping her eyes down. 'He has asked me to keep it. For him.'

'Has he now? Mmm.' She felt him look keenly at her and made herself meet his gaze. It was hard to know his meaning. Was there a twinkle? His eyes darted at the tall man watching behind the corse, and back to her. 'It's no usual,' he commented. Then he added: 'I don't say it might not be right.'

Silence.

She took a breath. 'Will the archpriest come for … the burial?'

'Feirgas? He may … he may. But more often I've heard he sends a depute. He doesn't travel often – no like the old one.'

She turned and gestured towards Dhion. 'Our son, you know: Dhion.'

Dhion bowed his head, and simply said, 'Father.'

'Come: a priest's son need no be so stiff. Give me your hand.' And Mungo took the other's forearm in the Island greeting.

'You'll lie at Shareg's as usual, Mungo?' enquired Morag.

'Aye, that'll be right. I'll take m'sel there.'

☙❧

41

The Tollagh the next day passed in a blur. People came up to her, one after the other, saying they were sorry for her loss. The words bounced off her as if she were covered by an outer shell. They could not touch her. She remained unreachable. Fineenh could not cross the unseen barrier now. Only Aileen and Shinane could draw near. And Shareen, who gave her a shy smile as she shepherded her two children out of the rondal.

After the Tollagh, the priest's widow sat in the priest's house, her own house, and then, in twos and threes, people came and sat with her, bringing gifts of food and drink. They talked among themselves, sharing their own memories of Hugh, and shaking their heads, for all felt his loss. No one expected her to do anything, and always, either Aileen or Shinane or Shareen would be there to provide for them.

But two days after First-day Fineenh called again, subdued and a little distant.

'You'll come and sup with us at the smithy? The girl and her man will be there. Ye're family, after all.'

By adoption and marriage, this was so. She had no blood family.

It seemed strange to leave the house in the gloaming. 'Goodnight,' she whispered into the empty darkness. 'I won't be long.' He was so much more there than with his body in the rondal.

The evening was dark. People spoke around her while she sat alone with her loss. She had never felt such a sense of just being. Nothing to attend to. Nothing to be done, except to sit, to breathe, to eat a little; to go on living.

It was as they were finishing the meal that the silence outside was broken by an unfamiliar sound: horses' hooves, and the jingle of their gear.

Shean rose and went to the door while they sat, listening. Two men. With Midland voices. Like Hugh.

Shean returned, followed by the strangers. They all rose. It was long since Morag had seen men dressed so fine. The first was cloaked like a shareg. In the lamplight a jewel flashed from his brooch. The second was hardly less remarkable, and both had neatly-trimmed beards framing their angular faces.

The first man spoke. 'We are come for the funeral rites of Hugh Ma'Cholm. We called at his house, but none was there. We were told we could find his widow here.' His eyes swept them, and rested upon Morag. Commanding eyes, that held her own. It had been many years, but recognition kindled. Hugh's brothers had come.

She stepped forward. 'I am Morag.' She met his gaze, held it.

The man paused. Weighed her. Considered. His chin, held high, dropped level. 'Madam, we bring you our consolations. We have ridden from Midland today.' He turned to the others. 'Malcolm Ma'Cholm of Tridrochad am I, shareg of that town. My brother Finn Ma'Cholm, merchant.' He nodded towards the other man. Morag's eyes darted towards him, and she felt her heart pause a moment. There was Hugh's brown beard, his brown eyes sparkling back at her from an only slightly thicker-set face. But it was a cool sparkle. She knew what they thought. She had dragged their brother down.

Malcolm was still speaking. 'Is there an inn where we may stable our horses?'

'We don't see many horses hereabouts.' It was Shean who answered. 'There's a rail outside, an you can hitch them there for now.'

Morag found her voice and spoke firmly. 'Our shareg will expect to give you and your horses lodging.'

The brothers exchanged glances. Finn nodded.

Shean glanced across at her, his black brows furrowed. 'I'll take ye to him,' he said. And led the two brothers out into the night.

Tridrochad – Three Bridges. It was the town where Hugh had been brought up, where he had taken her, before travelling on to Mhreuhan to receive his priesting. It had been a long time.

Dhion walked with her, back to her home that night. It was dark and starless and the light he carried flickered in a fitful breeze. She kissed him at the threshold, and watched the torch-light until it disappeared.

She was trembling. What was it? She knelt at their little shrine to say the night office. Her childhood home in the Northland. Her journey with Hugh, newly married, into Midland. That sojourn with his parents. Hugh. His brothers. And Hugh's face …

Chapter 6

Another night alone. Even though through Hugh's illness they had not shared a bed, yet always there had been his presence; a breathing, warm presence somewhere close in the closeness of the house. Now that his bodily presence was gone, somehow his ghostly being was more evident. She slept only lightly; woke early.

Making her first-food for one made the absence more keenly felt. It was as she was rinsing her dish that there came a knock on the door.

Drying her hands, she opened. Her heart jumped. Hugh. There before her once more she saw his living face. But not quite. A fuller face, richer clothes. Hugh's brother, Finn. And behind him, Malcolm the shareg. She stood back to let them in.

'Madam,' Malcolm began, as the three of them stood beside the fire. 'Your husband, our brother, will be much missed.'

She bade them sit.

Finn leaned forward. His shrewd brown eyes had a kindness in them. 'Will you be well provided for here? Life in the Westerland …'

She did not know how to answer him.

She glanced down, suddenly unable to meet those eyes. 'The people here look after each other. Our shareg is a strong friend. And I have my son. He is good to me.'

'Your son? We thought …'

She looked up at them.

'Hugh and I, we adopted him. Last spring twelvemonth. Where he came from, none can tell. Not even he.' She looked from one to the other. 'It is not that he hides his memories, nor that he has forgotten. It is that what he remembers does not join with what we know of the world. You saw him last night at the house of the smith. We call him Dhion, and he is still known as the Seaborne.'

The two men exchanged glances. 'Some time past,' Malcolm began slowly, 'did we not see a certain coat that was sent around the Island – was it three years and more – from a seaborne castaway. Sent to find if anyone had seen the like before?'

'And what a strange coat it was,' Finn recalled. 'Our weaver had never seen such. Smooth. Only beneath could you see it was woven at all. And with that metal fastening – so intricate!'

'That is Dhion's coat. It is of a piece with his tales of where he came from.'

Shareg and merchant looked at her. A frown gathered over Malcolm's face.

'And Hugh adopted this … seaborne, as his son?'

She felt the particularity, and the exclusion.

'We did,' she said firmly. 'After we had come to know him deeply. After he had lived with us in this house nigh a year before going to be apprenticed to the smith. So that he could take his place among us. For there was no going back.'

She read the doubt in their faces. She had met it before. 'He has gone through much and proved himself,' she insisted. 'As to where he has come from and how, neither he nor we can explain. In this, as in many things, we live in mystery.'

The archpriest sent word: his depute would be with them by the sixth day, and on no account was the burial to take place without him. Almost a week since Hugh had died, and the year was still warm; they would have to cover his body with rushes and fragrant herbs. They sent messages up and down the coast. The burial would be First-day Eve.

46

The depute was a short, red-faced man, mounted on a pony. His chaplain followed on another, leading a pack-pony. Their escort of three men-at-arms camped in the town meadows, their horses picketed beside them. Micheil came knocking at Morag's door.

'I understand,' she replied to his question. 'They must have this house. Fineenh will give me Shinane's old bed. I've already asked her.'

'Good,' replied the shareg. 'The best place for you.'

She knew he meant it kindly. Everyone meant kindly. But she received the words bitterly. The best place for her was near Hugh, whose presence lingered in the house they had shared.

Still, she knew this was the only thing to do, in the little town suddenly thronged with dignitaries. Yet, as she left their home after welcoming the two priests into the house, she felt she was deserting the one with whom she had shared their board, their bed, their life for so long. She walked to the smithy, a hollowness in her legs, in her belly. She did it, because there was nothing else to be done.

The next day dawned grey and damp. The day. The burying. Fineenh was bustling about and calling her *Pet*. Strange, Morag reflected. *A'Phadr* had died along with the priest. Soon it will be *A'De*, like Shareen – wife of God. Should it not be the greatest honour to be a Wife of God? Instead, the title was heavy with the expectation of want. Of being a burden.

She walked up to the shareg's house, where Hugh's brothers were leading their horses out to graze. They had not come to visit her again, but left for her a small bag filled with coin. 'In case of need to come,' Finn said.

Now a ragged procession was coming slowly down from the Pass of the Sea: an unusual mixture of seamen

– those who could, dressed in their best plaid – and the brown-cassocked priests who had come ashore at Fisherhame.

She stepped into the rondal and caught the subtly sweet scent of death. She looked at the body, only the face showing among the green rushes. This was no longer her man. And yet he was somewhere near; still somehow connected, more and more thinly, with this flesh. It was not he whom they would bury today. He would be watching, smiling his wry smile, somewhere very close to her. She turned away without touching his empty flesh.

The depute's chaplain came in, and she knelt before him. He bade her rise. His eyes seemed kind, but they slid away from hers. 'The body must be uncovered. You must take those reeds away,' he said. 'He is cassocked, with his sandals and stole?'

'I am keeping his stole.'

'That may not be.' The chaplain frowned. 'He must wear it.'

'I am keeping his stole. It was his wish.'

The man's face reddened. 'Well, take those reeds away. But the depute will tell you, he must wear it.'

'I am not talking about it.' She said it quietly, keeping her eyes down. She felt as cold as iron.

'A'De, the depute stands in the place of the arch-priest. You must do as he says.'

So there it was – that was the first time: *A'De*. Meant to put her in her place.

He paused. She saw his lips tremble. 'I will speak with the depute.' He turned and hurried out, passing Aileen and Shinane at the door. As they entered Aileen looked at her keenly. 'You're shaking,' she said. 'Are you all right?'

'I will be,' Morag replied. 'Let me just catch my breath.' Then, quickly: 'Can we take those reeds off him now?'

As they gathered the wilting rushes in their arms, she felt their eyes watching her. She waited, tense, for the archpriest's depute to appear. But as Hugh's cassocked body emerged from its coverings, no one came. They carried the armfuls of reeds out of the rondal.

The bare trampled earth outside was filling with all kinds of people. Townsfolk and fishwives, crofters from the hills and gaunt shepherds who scarcely said a word, knowing better how to tend their flocks than hold converse with other humans. Malcolm and Finn, Hugh's brothers, stood a little apart, their dress and carriage signalling that they were strangers. And, in a group keeping to themselves, the priests. Only Mungo was chatting with a well-to-do hill farmer.

The door of the priest's house opened and the chaplain came out. He caught sight of Morag.

'A'De: the depute will see you.'

A shiver passed through her. She raised her chin the smallest bit. The chaplain led her into the priest's house: her house. Lamps had been lit by others and the fire lent a yellow light. The depute was seated on what Dhion used to call her teaching chair. The fire behind him cast his face into shadow. Shareg Micheil sat on a bench, his face lined in the lamp-light.

She knelt and kissed the plump hand held out to her. The ring, a large topaz set in silver that Hugh once told her a depute would carry from the archpriest, bore with it his authority and power. He motioned to her to rise and she stood before him. She set her jaw.

He raised his eyes. But meeting her cold steel, they dropped again to examine his hands folded in the lap of his cassock.

'A'De, we are come in the name of the Chrisht and of his servant Feirgas, Archpriest of the Isle Fincara, to close the affairs worldly and ghostly of Hugh, priest of Caerpadraig.'

Worldly and ghostly – the language the man used! She listened as he continued, describing the nature of the Tollagh for Hugh and how she was to conduct herself in it: 'You shall be quiet and lowly, as befits a goodly matron …' Then he went on to speak of the house: 'You may continue to dwell in the house of the priest as in your husband's home until the festival of Bride next, or such time as a priest be appointed and established to the cure of this place, whichever is the sooner. Excepting that you shall not use it for any purpose unworthy of the servants of the Chrisht …' Really. What did the man think?

So that was it. The feast of Bride next: early spring, and she must leave this place. She allowed her eyes to take in all that the walls held, all that she must relinquish. The good dark furniture, the pots she had scoured to a shine, even the covers on the beds. The tapestry in its wooden frame, in the design of a map of the Island: that was hers – she had poured herself into it. She would gift it to the people to stand in the rondal. And Hugh's stole? After all, he had not mentioned that. A lightness filled her and she smiled. She glanced towards Micheil, who seemed to be looking steadily at nothing at all. Had he been her saviour? Who knew by what means he must have persuaded them. She was dismissed. Before she turned and walked out into the thin sunlight she caught the eye of the chaplain, standing behind his master. He looked down in confusion.

And through the Tollagh, and the ritual wrapping of Hugh's body in its winding-sheet, and its carrying to the graveside, and the dull thud of the clods falling onto the pale shape, the thought stayed with her: *I can leave all that was you here, for what I have is of your essence. What you have given me you do not need. And that I have, and will carry for you.*

Chapter 7

Slowly the year died. The first of the autumn storms brought the sheep down from the shielings, and the bleating of grown lambs from the town meadows accompanied Morag's prayer morning and evening.

'The long nights are coming,' she said to Shinane. 'I will curl up like a beast in her lair, and stay close to Hugh in our home through the winter. When Bride's Day comes and the new year starts to waken I must leave this house. Then truly I will feel alone.'

'But you'll come and live with us at the smithy, won't you? You'll have the lean-to Dhion and father are building on to the forge. You'll be warm there, and we'll be just alongside. And –' Shinane's voice dropped to a whisper. 'I think I'm carrying. I feel it. I've missed two months now.'

It was to be expected, yet it came as a shock. This simple, common miracle that had been denied her, coming to her sonswoman. But it was hard to embrace new life while she still lingered with the life that had been. Yet she said, 'Good news, then!' and kissed her. 'Be patient with me,' she added, wistfully. 'I'll be getting ready, bit by bit. Just as you will.'

She began to picture a home full of children. She could not see herself there.

Now, daily, Morag would go to the smithy for the midday meal. She knew she must get out, see people and stretch her legs. And she was grateful to be cared for. But she liked to be home, sitting alone through the gathering twilight, the in-between time when the worlds met and merged.

One day at the smithy, as she was talking with Fineenh and Shinane, Dhion came from the forge for his meal with something particular to say.

'I've been thinking,' he began.

The three women looked up.

'About what?' asked Shinane, a shade cautiously.

He put his head to one side, his eyes sparkling. 'The burn of the Pass of the Sea – there's power there that we could use.'

Morag immediately felt anxious. Her son had got into trouble before with his ideas. But he moved on too quickly for her to interrupt.

'We could build a water wheel,' he announced. 'If the town hasn't seen one, at least the craftsmen have heard of them.'

Yes, even she had heard of such a thing, through Hugh. But still it sounded strange – unIslandlike. There was silence.

'And for what purpose would your water wheel be turning?' Shinane asked. 'What is it we lack, that this water wheel will bring?'

'Well, it could grind corn. Two stones, one on another.'

'We can do that by hand well enough. And it's companionship. We women talk at the kern-stones.'

He hesitated.

'Don't try to make us something we don't want,' Shinane pressed.

But now he seemed to be looking somewhere behind her. 'Well, to tell the truth,' he began slowly, 'what I've really been thinking about is a lathe. Something to turn wood on. With a lathe, a man like Olan could make all kinds of things.'

'Turn wood?' questioned Shinane. 'What does that mean?'

Morag wondered too. Wood was something you hewed or sawed or split or carved.

But Dhion's eyes shone. She saw he was far away in a world of his own picturing.

'Olan would love to work a lathe. I see it in him. I've watched him, when traders come up from Caerster with their nicely-turned woodwork from the mainland, looking at the pieces, holding them in his hands.'

'And your water wheel could help him make those? Better than he can carve?'

Morag looked from Dhion's eager face to Shinane's anxious one. He was right about Olan, she thought. He would be ready for something new if it helped him fashion a thing of wood. She looked at her son through the half-darkness of the house. His eyes were alight.

'Olan would help me get the timbers I need from his father,' he was saying. 'He'd help me build the wheel.'

'So, this wheel. It would help you follow your will. And Olan follow his dream. But would it help the town? Would it?' Shinane fixed him with her gaze, and fire leaped from her, challenging him.

Fineenh cut in: 'Talk it through with Shareg first and get his aye.'

Dhion smiled. 'All right,' he said. 'I will.'

Shean came through the door into a sudden silence. He looked suspiciously from one to another. No one said anything more. He shook his head and held out his hand for his bowl.

Samhain came, the thin time between the old year and the new; the border time, when the veils between the worlds grow thin. Without Hugh, who would lead and hold the night watch? It crossed Morag's mind to offer to do it herself. She even felt eyes turning to her, as if she might. But when she looked within she knew she was too deeply in mourning. For her, it was a time of sitting and being, and little else. In the end it was Micheil who led the watch in his businesslike way, so out of

53

keeping with the time. Morag helped him close as the last folk left in twos and threes and took their lamp-lit paths home. She and the shareg blew out the light and he saw her to the door of the priest's house.

'Good night, A'Phadr,' he said. He had never stopped calling her that. It gave her back the dignity she felt slipping away.

'Good night, Shareg,' she replied, equally formally.

She settled herself for sleep. Only a little rush-light flickered near the fire, adding its tiny flame to the dull ruby glow of the fire-pot. It had not been a good vigil: the veil between the worlds might have been of leather for all she had been able to pass through.

Her eyes closed.

Looking back, she could never quite grasp what woke her; nor indeed whether she had indeed wakened, or if it was all a dream.

It was as if honey-coloured light filled the house. Not bright, but warm, like a bees-wax candle. It seemed to be all over, not coming from any one place. She sat up, made as if to rise. And then she saw him. He seemed to be formed out of light itself. He seemed to be shimmering …

'Father Hugh?' Shinane's face was pale.

It was the afternoon of First-day, after the vigil, and Dhion and Shinane had come to sit with her in what was still her house.

'Hugh – yes. It was he.'

There was quiet while they took this in. A fly buzzed in the rafters, and was still.

Then: 'How did you feel? Were you afraid?'

'My love: how could I be afraid of him? And yet, in a way, I was afraid. I was trembling. Like, when you go among the hills and look up, and there above you is the highest peak, and you feel… You know it's not going to fall on you, or that any harm will come, yet you feel …'

'You know your own smallness.' Shinane supplied the words.

'Yes, and – the otherness of it all.

'Then he spoke. Not in words, exactly. But what he said stays with me. He said: *You don't know who you are.*'

'Just that?' This time the question came from Dhion.

'Just that, son. *You don't know who you are.*'

'What did he mean?' he asked.

Morag shook her head.

'I don't know. That was all he had to say. He seemed to fade then. There was just the dark house, as ever.'

She stopped. Looked from one to the other.

'There's something else I'd like to tell you,' she went on. 'Those words Hugh spoke: they reminded me of other words. Words that were shouted out at me not so long ago.'

For a moment her eyes roved around the little house: its stones, the cracks between them packed with moss. The bookstand, with the precious volumes nearby on a shelf. Her tapestry.

'You remember the day that man, Gormagh, came?' They nodded. 'Hugh brought him in and asked me to give him food. He stared at me in a most strange way, and then he cried out, *Do you not know who you are?* He shouted it at me: *Don't you know who you are?*'

Again, she paused. Looked at them. 'It was most strange and disturbing, I can tell you. His face kept coming back to me after he was found dead. And those words. Now this.'

She lowered her head.

Dhion leaned forward. 'What does it mean to you, Mother?'

She hesitated. 'When a word is spoken twice, it carries urgency. I dare not ignore it. Yet, I don't understand what it means. Do I not know who I am?'

They fell quiet in the fading light. It was Shinane who spoke into the silence.

'Mother, you remember just before Father Hugh died?'

She turned to her husband. 'I haven't told you this: I felt it was something private, between the three of us there.'

She turned back to Morag.

'When you put on that stole – when Hugh insisted you put it on – I saw you change. You grew. As if something inside you was set free. I've thought about it since. You were like a butterfly just come out of its case, and it clings there on the grass-stem, its wings like little crumpled bags. Then slowly, as you watch, its wings stretch out to their full size and it basks in the sunlight. Until suddenly it flies away.'

'What are you saying, child? That I should be a priest – a priestess, perhaps? We don't have priestesses here.'

She looked at Shinane. Her sea-grey eyes. *The sea will always win in the end,* she thought.

'There's something in you,' the girl was saying. 'I can't see it fully yet. But I'm beginning to know quite plainly that it's there.'

Morag gazed at her thoughtfully.

'Well then,' she said at last. 'My way is clear: I must find out who I am. But – how am I going to do that?'

Chapter 8

She pushed open the door of their house. A full week had passed since the showing, as she now called it, when Hugh had formed before her, made as it seemed of light itself, and she had heard his words. The puzzle he had left her with possessed her. She had work to do and she wanted to get on with it; but how to go about it remained dark. An expectation grew in her whenever she entered their house, whenever she blew out the light, whenever she woke in the night. Not that she would see him again, but in some way she would sense his presence. A feeling, maybe. A voice in her imagination. Perhaps only a particular arrangement of household things: a plate and a beaker set as he might have left them, a feather lying across the pages of the book that stood on its stand, as he might have laid it down.

'Are you there?' she whispered into the darkness of the house.

Of course I'm here.

She crossed to the dully-glowing embers of the fire, felt for a spill from the kindling-basket, and blew up a little flame to light the lamp. When she once more had a cheerful blaze burning she sat back on her haunches, still in the pool of lamp-light, her hands in her lap.

After a long moment she spoke into the silence.

'I don't understand. Do I not know who I am? The people in the town know. *Here's Morag, the priest's widow,* they say.'

There are many ways of knowing. There are more ways than one of seeing.

'So who am I? I am Morag, wife of Hugh, the son of Colm, son of Finn, son of Malcolm. I am Morag, daughter of Murdogh, the son of Conor, son of Cormac.'

Is that it? Are you only you because of the men in your life? You know who is missing from those lists.

'All right. My mother. Who was my mother? I doubt she still lives. What was she like, this woman I have never known? That's what you mean, isn't it?'

You might find that a useful question to begin with.

'No one would tell me of my mother. How can I find her out?'

Silence.

'Targuid. Blind Targuid of Kimmoil. My home in the Northland. He knows – he knew – the life-lines of everyone. He used to recite them by heart. He would know, if anyone does. But he was old when I was a girl: surely he will have passed long ago ... Must I go back? Find who holds the lines from him? Go back to Kimmoil?'

There was a pause, a hush. A settled feeling. Was this, then, what she must do? But when? She knew she could not go now, with the weather closing in as winter took hold. And how? Dhion might walk with her in the spring. Except ... was that not when his child would be born? Then – could she go alone? The idea began to grow within her.

Aren't you forgetting?

What? The wind moaned round the shutters. The lamp-flame shivered. Of course – it was time for the evening prayer. She turned and knelt at the shrine. Composed herself for the wordless prayer of contemplation. But her mind was churning. It took some time.

'In the name of the One, with no beginning and no ending ... the Intention behind all life.'

A few big, floppy flakes of wet snow drove past the houses of the town. A brisk nor'westerly was blowing straight up the lough, its eddies playing with Shinane's cloak as she hurried to Moira and Olan's well-built house near the saw-pit, not far from the rondal. She heard Moira's voice answer her greeting with a tired note.

As she pushed open the door there was little Bran bawling as he sat dumpily on the earth floor. Moira looked up as she entered, relief in her eyes.

Shinane knelt before the babe. She reached out with both hands, placing a single finger in the red palms of the little one. She watched Bran's face change from crimson fury to mixed anger and wonder. Then the chubby fingers closed around her own. Slowly, gently, she raised her arms, and Bran followed her. Cautiously the babe straightened his knees and stood. A huge grin spread across his face. The tantrum was forgotten as swiftly as it had come.

She and Moira always found plenty to talk about as they sat together peeling neeps. Little happened in the town that came neither to the carpenter's shop nor the smithy. And now there was Shinane's own babe growing within her, hoped for in the coming year.

Moira opened the subject that concerned them both. 'Olan's so excited about your man's idea. He's already tried working a pole lathe. But this …'

Shinane's mind swung away from her friend's talk. She wondered vaguely what a pole lathe might be, but asked the question that was foremost in her heart. 'What does Carpenter think of it?'

Moira tossed her head.

'Oh, you know what he's like. Shareg came and talked with him. He was grumpy as usual after, and came and talked with Olan. Asked why he wasn't content with the work his da had done and his grandas before him. And at the same time you could tell he was itching to see what his son might do.'

'What did Shareg say?' But already she knew the answer. Dhion had come bursting in with the news only the day before.

'Well, Shareg started off about the water and the burn and so on. A'Shar'g says it's a big thing to take a free stream and enslave it like a paelht. But he's goin to talk wi some more people, and on the whole, he's moved to say Yes. You can guess how Olan was when he heard.'

Darkness came early in that eleventh moon. For Morag, the thought of returning to Kimmoil had reawakened memories as she sat in the yellow lamp-light.

A girl, standing on the shores of the lough. These are not the soft banks of Lough Padraig. This is Lough Moil, reaching in from the cold and restless waters of the northern sea, its shores brown with wrack and dark with tide-washed sand.

The girl's dark hair is plaited down her back, over the wool of her gown. In those days her gown was the colour of oatmeal, just like everyone else's. She looks up as the honking of geese calls her gaze. Watches them as they cease their flapping and curve their wings downward, gliding lower, to the surface of the lough. The birds' pink feet come down as they skim the wavelets. Each one leaves a short wake of white water and then sits still, wagging its pointed tail a few times in satisfaction.

Morag smiled. There was always something splendid about a flight of geese: both splendid, and a little ridiculous. Had she appeared ridiculous to them, she wondered.

Once more the memories pressed in on her.

There stands the door. If once it had been well-made, strong and tall between its jambs of stone, now it is more than elderly. Its boards have shrunk apart from each other, have worn round at their corners. She loves its cracked and fissured face.

She has no need to knock. Softly she pushes it open. Calls into the gloom of the single lamp.

'Brother!'

The daekin will be there, waiting for her; waiting to give her a writing lesson. He shares the house with Father Callen, priest of Kimmoil.

The Father had said to her once, 'Child, I am hoping that this day or the next, or soon, a man will be coming to help me. A daekin come from the School to share my work. I would like him to teach you from time to time.'

'Father, may I ask? What is a daekin?'

'When I left the School in Sharilland – and that is a long way away, across the Island and then two days' sailing until you reach the hills of Mueill – they sent me back here, to the land I love, and to an old Father who taught me the art of priesting.'

'Did they not teach you at the School, Father?'

'They taught me many things, child. And I read many books, and listened to many men of learning. But to be a priest you cannot learn from books. You must come and live among the people you serve, and learn how to be priest to them. That is what a daekin is – he is one who is learning how to serve. And when his time is come and his priest thinks him ready, the archpriest at Mhreuhan will lay his hands on him and he will be made priest. Then he will go and serve a township in his own right.'

'So … is this man another Father?'

'When he is made priest he will be called Father. But while he is a daekin and with me – while he sees what priesting is and learns to serve – he will be called Brother. He is Brother Hugh.'

Brother Hugh is there, mixing his ink in a small wooden bowl. The wooden board, ready for their lesson, has been washed clean of the ink from her earlier attempts. He looks up as she calls. It is not every girl in the township who has this privilege: none but she, and very few boys. Only because of her grandfather. He had insisted: *It is still a noble line she is from, and if she will, she may.*

She would. She is keen to understand this magic, of how spoken words become marks of ink upon parchment: how ink once more becomes words.

And there is more. It is something in his eyes, this daekin who has come across the mountains to her northern folk from his home in Midland. Something that laughs gently at the waywardness of people. That knows her line is a noble one and her birth a shameful one; who knows, and still laughs. Gently. Kindly.

They sit together and he writes a line. She must read it to him and then copy it below his neat, careful script. His hand touches hers to guide the quill and she glances up at him. His eyes are already on her. Father Callen sits by the fire, carefully not watching.

The pot bubbled, and she reached out to stir it. Peas, and a good mutton-bone. Good fare, and better than many in the town. Hugh had given her much; as if his love and his wit had not been enough.

They are walking together on the lough-shore. It is midsummer night and the air is deep blue around them, the water black before them.

'And your mother? You say nothing of her. Have you lost her?'

'Yes,' she replies. 'I've lost her.'

She straightens, stops walking, looks him in the face. 'I am expected to be ashamed of her.' She pauses, hears again what she just said. 'I feel ashamed when my father's wife looks at me, when I cannot walk into my father's house. When …' At last it comes out. 'When people tell me she was of no account, or flighty, or bad. Because they do not know her kin.'

The water laps, laps, by the shore edge. A bat, a trembling blackness against the night, passes low over their heads.

'Are you any less, for what you do not know?'

The water laps.

'I do feel less. I feel a hole in my heart where my mother's love should be. And because I know ...' She stops herself.

'What do you know?'

She pulls her hand away from his. She looks away. Her voice is over-loud. 'I know that, without the mother-line, no man can wed me.'

He reaches for her shoulders and turns her towards him. She resists, makes to shrug his hands off her. And yet she wants those hands to hold on.

He looks at her. There is mischief in his eyes once more. 'Perhaps you are wrong in that, Morag Mi'Mhurdogh. Perhaps you are wrong.'

She feels tears coming. She never cries. She has taught herself not to. She turns her head away, hiding her eyes. He must not see.

She feels his hands either side of her hair, gently turning her face back to his. He would look on her tears.

Then his face draws closer to hers. And, lightly, he kisses her.

Chapter 9

The days shortened and darkened. Brother Moon waxed and waned and waxed again. The time for Iulgh, the mid-winter festival, drew near. Life waited, quiet and still under earth, in seed and womb, in sleeping beast and slumbering tree. Gales came and went, snow fell and melted and fell again and more fell, until the hills were covered and the strath was a waste of white, studded with greys and browns. And into this waiting world the Chrisht-child was born, like the sun returned, brief and weak, but with the promise of more and yet more.

They met in the rondal as always for Iulgh, to watch out the longest night with song and story. They heard the tale of Coll the tailor and the giant Bica: how Bica kept to himself a great crock of porridge which gave him strength to move the mountains as children play with pebbles on the beach. How Coll decided he would take that crock and let the mountains stay still so that men could settle between them. Then Coll sat before the giant and told him many tales, until Bica's head nodded and he made as if to sleep. But always a giant hand would rest upon the crock, or a giant's arm would fold it in its elbow. Then Coll crept up to the crock and tasted the porridge, but he could not move it without waking the giant. So he waited, and when the giant woke, Coll shouted, 'Bica, quick! A mighty hero crept in while you slept and tried to steal your crock of porridge! Run to the door – you might yet catch him!' Dazed from sleep and too many stories, Bica ran to the door, and stood there looking to see where this hero had gone. Seizing his advantage and strengthened by the porridge, Coll picked up the crock and leaped with it out of the window before the giant could return. And Bica, bereft of his strength, lay down and never rose again.

He lies still, the great ridge that cuts off Westerland from the Midland, that men now call Beh' Bhica.

Aileen told again the tale of Bride on Ioua, the Isle of Yews; how she had sat long into the darkest night secretly watching the druids at their sacred rites. How she had been carried over land and sea and had mid-wifed Mother Mair and learned from Her Child the way of compassion. How she was carried back to Ioua in darkness, as if no time had passed, and set down on its peak, Dun-I. And how the oyster-catcher, the shore-bird with its piping call, had guided her down through the dark to the world of men, and ever after had earned for itself the title of the Ghilliebride: the servant of Bride.

The story-teller finished. For a few breaths' space there was silence. Then a single voice rose, strong and earthy, in a chant that was rare among them, yet all knew it.

Tha mi ar shli na firinne; tha mi ar shli mo fise. I am on the path of truth; I am on the path of my vision.

Morag felt as if her heart missed a beat. All her waiting, her anxiety to be gone as soon as may be, her frustration that the winter prevented her, her grief and her loss, changed into sudden energy. She joined the chant in a wild harmony as it repeated again and again. Other voices came in: Shareg Micheil roared the bass drone. Like a whirlwind it gathered energy and whisked them in and together and up, until there were no longer a hundred hearts but one only, beating in a hundred bodies.

When at last it came to an end, it left her filled. She felt her eyes were shafts of light. This is it, she said to herself. I am on the path of truth, to find at last my vision.

She did not notice, as she pushed open her door in the deep darkness before dawn and peered into the deeper darkness that surrounded the remaining embers of yesterday's fire, that she did not ask if he was there. He did not remind her.

'But what the archpriest says in Caerster and what happens here in Caerpadraig are two quite different things.' Micheil was sitting on the bench in the priest's house. 'When you are still here after Bride's Day I will certainly not be turning you out.' He took a gulp of the beer Morag had brought him. 'I don't know by what authority the depute says who should or should not stay in this house. It's we have provided it for his priest. And I say you can stay – until, of course, the new priest comes.'

So she could stay a little longer. Something in Morag eased. And the idea formed in her that it would be from the home she had shared with Hugh, with his spirit behind her and with her and blessing her, that she would set off on her quest. That this was right and must be so. When she returned – well, that was all unknown. 'Thank you, Shareg,' she said.

'I know Dhion is preparing a place for you. Is it ready, yet? He glanced across to where Dhion sat, confident of his answer.

'We are making ready for that time. But, Shareg, there's something else my mother wants to talk about.' Dhion turned to Morag.

'We want to ask your advice, Micheil,' she said in a voice that suddenly sounded small.

Why did she feel so diffident, so unsure? She hardly wanted to say what came next. She pulled herself together.

'I need to make a journey to the town of my birth. Back to Kimmoil. I want to set out soon after New Spears.' The Feast of the New Spears came in midspring, as the days were quickly growing longer and the sun daily rising higher in the sky. It still seemed far off today, as snow was driving against the shutters before a fierce nor'wester.

Micheil opened his eyes wide. 'Kimmoil? That's a way! I've never been there mysel,' he added, and shook his head. 'Met the shareg now and then. Fierce sort of a man. You'd need an escort.' He looked at her shrewdly. 'Dhion, of course. I might send my eldest with him. It'd do him good to see the world. But why do you want to go?'

She drew herself upright on her stool by the fire. 'I want to go by myself, Micheil. This is something I want to do alone.'

The shareg stared as if he had never seen her before.

'Alone? A woman, walking the muir alone? It's out of the question.'

'Coghlane lived up on the mountain all alone, did she not?'

The thought rose in her like a flame. Hugh used to climb up to Mother Coghlane's bothy when he needed advice, or refreshment for his soul. He would climb to the hollow in the mountain where she lived with her sheep and the creatures of land and sky and the vast silence. But Coghlane had died, and also Hugh. As must all. She found the thought strangely comforting.

Dhion leaned forward. 'We've talked it through, Shareg. There's nothing I can say to make her change her mind. It's been all I could do to stop her leaving before now.'

The shareg brought his hands down on his thighs with a slap. 'No! I can't condone it. I can't stop you,' he added. 'But … you don't know what you're facing.'

'That's why we're asking you,' Morag insisted. The steel in her was beginning to shine again. 'You know the roads across the wild better than we do. Help me. Help me prepare.'

But Micheil turned now to her son.

'For God's sake, man, talk to your mother. Are you head of your household or no? You can't allow her to go. Certainly not before the good weather and the time of plenty comes. It's madness!'

It had not struck Morag before that when Hugh died, she had come under her son's cloak. What a turn-around! She and Hugh had never worked like that. They had shared a yoke and borne it equally. That was how, in those astounding months when Dhion had learned the Island life from them, they had brought him up. She had seen then that this seemed natural to him.

'Shareg …' Dhion spoke slowly, weighing his words. 'In the few years I've been with you, I've grown to love this woman, not only as a mother. I have grown to respect her for her wisdom and insight. If you cannot give her your blessing for this journey, please at least help her with your knowledge.'

Morag watched Micheil's response. The shaggy black brows drew together. He drew in his breath, held it in his red cheeks, let it out with a sigh. He raised his hands, and let them fall again into his lap. He glowered at Dhion, then, from under his brows, at her. She felt herself become still, all her senses alert as he spoke.

'All right,' he said slowly. 'But first, hear that you go against my advice and without my warrant. And that you risk your life in this. It is not just the dangers of the road. In the wild, there are wild men who live outside the sharegs' rule. Men who would knife you for a bag of corn. I know Hugh used to go visiting his wise woman in the hill. But his cassock still gave a little protection. And just because every time he returned safe and well, it doesn't mean it will be the same for you. Morag, please think again.'

'I also have protection.' The words seemed to come not from her, but through her. 'I go in the protection of Heaven. If I live, I live. And if I die, we must all die some time. I have seen Death, and he has taken away my best friend. There is nothing worse he can do to me. But …' She glanced down at her hands. 'I hope I will live a bit longer.'

'Hmm.' Clearly Micheil was not comforted. Then he said, 'Dhion Ma'Phadr Seaborne. We have been through much, you and I. I have come to respect you, and I like you. And this woman I name as my friend, and the widow of my very dear friend. I have told you what I think. I called it madness.' He paused. When he continued, it was in a steadier tone. 'It is not wise – not by my lights.' He turned a grim face towards Morag. 'But what help I can give, you know I will. I want to see you come here again. I will … I would miss you.'

The coming year grew big in the womb of the earth. A pair of grebes on the water's face bowed and postured to each other. The hazel's hard little catkins opened into delicate tassels that sent puffs of yellow into each gust of breeze. And as Morag drew a supple twig towards her where it leaned over the lough-side path, she sought for the hidden crimson threads in the leaf-angles that would catch the drifting pollen and grow secretly into the nuts of autumn.

Shinane's child was growing, too, she thought. When would be its time? Not long. This child, her own grandchild, would grow, and in time, God willing, have children. And they, theirs. She looked down the long view of the strath. Who she was was not a question for her alone: she owed it to all those generations still to come, that they might know who they were in the long, long line; the line that reached from unremembered ancestors past, to unguessed-at descendants still to come.

And not only to them. She reached out her hands to either side, touching the bare twigs of hazel and alder and oak. She owed it to the people amongst whom she lived. She longed to be more to them than just the priest's widow. But before she could become anyone more, she knew she must go back; take up the quest offered. And the quest would be her becoming.

She turned, and followed the little path that climbed the brae. Above the tops of the trees of the wood that fringed the lough, where townsfolk had coppiced the hazel and the alder and the oak for unguessed years, she went. There she looked back and saw the town, crouching by the head of the water, nestling among the meadows dotted with sheep and cattle. Hugh was gone. She was preparing to leave. Yet she knew this was still her home.

Chapter 10

A small cluster of townspeople gathered to see them off. Micheil still looked grim, but Aileen kissed her warmly. Dhion carried his targe and spear, with his knife like a short sword at his side. Shareen was there, and Fineenh, while Shean stood at a distance by his forge door. At Dhion's request he had provided Morag with a proper hunting knife instead of the kitchen tool she had proposed. When she made to tuck it into her pack he had her thread its sheath onto her belt. She felt it hanging there, an awkward, unfamiliar sensation.

It was a fair mid-spring day. A gentle westerly was blowing small puffy clouds over the summit of Beh' Mora. They took the eastern shore of the lough, through meadows where the wet grass, just beginning to grow, darkened their boots. The blackthorn was starred with white, and the apples were covered with tight buds of deep rose. Oonagh's bees had stirred from their skeps and were busy in the flowers.

They travelled for a time in silence as the sounds of the town faded behind them. They splashed through a little stream that came tumbling down into the lough.

'Now, tell me about this wheel of yours.' She looked at him sideways. 'I hear only pieces of your ideas, without ever making them whole.'

'You want to hear about that, do you?'

She waited while he chose his words.

'Olan and I, we've looked carefully at it all,' he began. 'We'd dam the burn with a weir, and then cut a channel to lead the water along the glenside. We know where we'd like to build the mill, opposite the shareg's house, where there's that patch of flat ground. But we'd have to find a way to bring the water to the wheel-head. We'd make a waterbridge.'

71

It sounded like another word Dhion had made up, for an idea that didn't yet have a name. She asked him to explain.

'The land slopes steeply above Shareg's, which gives us room for our water-wheel. Picture a long wooden trough raised on trestles higher than a tall man, standing out from the slope. The water flows along it, then out the far end, over the top of the wheel. It's the water falling over the wheel makes it turn. Then the channel we cut at the bottom takes it back to the burn.'

Morag pursed her lips. 'Micheil – he's happy with this?' She could think of some people who would not be. The idea of blocking the running water, of leading her as you would! 'Water should be free to find her way.'

'And she will find her way freely. I do not take from that – I cannot. I just offer some of the water a new route for a little part of her journey. The water is happy enough to take up my suggestion, and give me a helping hand. Then she rejoins her old course a bit further down.'

He did have a way of putting things, Morag reflected. He had learned this, at least. She felt almost persuaded, listening to him. Would his words persuade others?

'The shareg wants to hold a council about it,' Dhion added. His gaze was down at the path before them. Now he turned his head to look at her. 'That makes me a little anxious. But I know the people better than I did. I know what I will say. And when to let Olan do the talking.'

They walked a few paces in silence. 'So, you're sure?'

'Yes,' he said. 'I am.'

They came to the foot of the lough, and the Padraig River fell over a lip of the land, down to where it met the big river in a green triangle of lush herbage. A wide ford lay just upstream of the watersmeet. Dhion showed her, as Micheil had shown him before, how to use her staff to buttress herself against the push of the water. Her gown was already hitched to her knees for treading through the long grasses. Now she hitched it higher. The water was ice-cold almost up to her knees, numbing her.

They sat on the far shore where the path stepped up through low banks of sandstone. Fineenh had provided them with buttered oatcakes in a greasy linen wallet. They allowed themselves one apiece, then bent to put their boots and stockings back on.

'Thank you,' she said, taking Dhion's hand and giving it a squeeze.

'For what?' He raised a quizzical eyebrow.

'For showing me.'

'I think I gave you a rough lesson,' he replied, ruefully. Then, with concern, 'The current is strong, and there may be other rivers to cross. I can come on further with you.'

She squeezed his hand again. 'Enough,' she said. 'I told your girl I'd be coming back for my grandchild, and I shall!'

They went on. The path was climbing steadily now, onto a great dun-coloured moor. The sun on their backs had the first touches of warmth in her.

'Mother,' he began. 'You say you will come back, and I long to believe you. Mostly, I do believe you. But – have you truly faced the possibility you might not?'

Morag sighed.

'I know what I must do, Dhion. It doesn't help me to think how I might fail to do it.'

She walked on a few paces, then added, 'Anyway, if I die doing what gives purpose to my life, what better can I ask?'

'Brave words,' he said. He added, 'I came from a place that wards off death as far as it can.'

'Yet you yourself have risked it,' she flashed back at him. 'Death will come to all of us, soon or late.' A little wood was rising before them, and beside their path a single primrose showed its hopeful face.

'Were you accepting, then, of Hugh's death?'

'Not willingly.' She spoke a little sharply. 'If there had been a herb that could have cured him I would have walked the earth for it. We gave him what we had. Oonagh did what she could with her herbs. But we know the white sickness. We knew there was little we could do. I accepted it because I had to.'

She paced on, a feeling of annoyance running through her. Then she relented. Added more gently, 'Still, for me – for us – death is not the end of life: death is the other side of life. The dark side of the circle.'

'The dark side?'

'Yes. Flowers die. They rot into the ground. But their seed lives on, hidden in the earth. And when the sun comes back, they spring up again. So it goes round: winter, and spring, and summer and autumn. Life, and death, and life again. Ever repeating; never the same.'

Morag loved Dhion dearly, but she knew this talk was not what she needed. She looked away, up at the rocks patched with grey and orange, clumped with spikes of heather. She sighed. From away on their right, where white cotton-grass grew amongst the lank yellow blades of last year's sedges, a curlew called. Long, thin, thrilling, other-worldly.

Dhion had dropped back a little, but now he caught up with her again. 'All right,' he said. 'But let me ask you something else. When you get there, to this town of yours, who will know you, Mother?'

Who indeed? It was more than twenty years since she had left this place. Many who had known her would have died. And what of those who might remember? Her brothers and sisters – half-brothers, half-sisters – how would they greet her? She was not at all sure.

She was already a growing girl before the eldest of them was born to her step-mother. Then her father had kept them away, as if she was somehow infectious. She thought of her grandmother; her grandfather's hall, as big as the shareg's. But they had passed on years before, and likely her father too, though she had heard no word of it. Unless he lived still, she thought it unlikely that any of her kin would know her. Even if they did, would they own her? Then she thought of the girls she used to play with, when they would let her. Some of those must still be there. They would all have changed so much, but …

'Someone will remember,' she said, firmly. Surely that must be true.

'That doesn't sound like much of a welcome to me.'

'I don't go for the purpose of being welcomed!' she retorted. 'I go because this is my quest. And, now it has begun, it doesn't help me to think of these things!'

The true beginning of her journey, she thought to herself, would be when at last she was alone.

Now they walked what was unknown ground for both of them. For a long time they travelled in silence. She was grateful for it.

The sun circled round to their left and slowly climbed down the blue bowl of heaven. Gradually a thin white sheet of cloud formed above the two figures that trudged, now in single file, along the narrow, stony path.

'I don't know that the weather will hold for you tomorrow.'

Morag looked up, felt the air. It lay still upon the moor like a shroud. She replied. 'I don't think there's rain on the way. It looks more like a fog setting in.'

Dusk found them in a little cut in the northern edge of the high moor. The silence pressed all around. The clatter of stones rattling under their boots rang and was quickly hushed in the thick air.

Here the path led under a small cliff, boulders strewn across the narrow glen. They found a shelter under a stone facing away from the weather, mild though it was, and unwrapped their cold supper. There was water in a little burn, and they washed their faces. Neither moon nor stars came out, and they had no fire. In deep darkness they rolled themselves in their cloaks, found themselves a spot where stones did not press too hard, and the banked earth, cushioned with dead bracken, gave them a little warmth, and settled for sleep.

She woke, cold and stiff, some time between night and early morning. The sky was scarcely less dark. Her cloak was wet and heavy, and a fog hung thickly around them. Dhion lay still, his back to hers.

A movement. Barely seen, but a deeper darkness against the black. Cautious, silent. A low, slinking shape, coming a little nearer, stopping, coming closer again. She dared not move a finger.

And there it crouched: the long muzzle, a pair of yellow eyes that seemed to shine with their own light. The pricked ears over the high, powerful shoulders.

The wolf was little more than a long pace away. She lay motionless, barely breathing. There was fear, yes; but something else lay under her fear. Awe. She felt respect.

'Brother wolf,' she whispered.

He sprang back, his forepaws straddled on the ground. A low growl escaped between his white teeth. Then he turned, glanced at her over his shoulder, and padded silently into the blackness.

Chapter 11

'You can't go on in this!' Dhion held her hands, his face close to hers, his eyes anxious under the dark brows.

The morning had lightened slowly, but the light made little difference. They could see barely twenty paces through a whiteness that was clammy with cold. She'd said nothing of her visitor in the night: she sensed it would be a betrayal of something entrusted to her alone.

'Then, what do you suggest?' She watched him, guardedly.

'Come back with me. The weather has turned against you. It's telling you not to go on. Two pairs of eyes will have a better chance of following the path than one. If you stumble, I'll be there.'

Morag shook her head.

'You must go back. That is what we agreed. But if I do so, I fear I will not set out again. Shinane will beg me to stay and the moment will pass. I will go on.'

'But you can't. Look – you can't see your hand in front of your face!'

'Don't exaggerate, son. It will be difficult, but not impossible. And I must. That's all. I must.'

'Then I will come with you. I won't let you go alone.'

'No!' The argument felt like a battle of wills, a battle for survival. In the end, Morag simply said no to everything. No. No. No.

'Mother …' He peered through the mist from one side to the other as if seeking an answer from the rocks. He took a breath, but found no voice.

'Dhion, come and sit down. We'll share our first-food; then we'll go our ways. It does have to be, love. Doesn't it?'

'I won't sit, thank you. Everywhere's cold and damp, and so am I.' His voice was flat and low.

They ate in silence, the two of them standing, miserable in the dank fog. They shared out the food left over in their packs. Then there was nothing more to do. In a moment they would walk away from each other until the mist swallowed them.

She drew him to her and hugged him. 'Don't worry about me, son. For my sake. Worry won't help. Your place is to look after that girl of yours. I will come back to you – I don't know when. It may be a week; it may be a year. But I feel it. I will come back. In *this* life!' She smiled at her own levity, and kissed him.

He broke away from her, squared his shoulders. He sighed. 'I wish I could feel your confidence. I couldn't live with myself if I didn't argue with you. But I see your resolve. In the end, it's your choice. I must give in.'

Then he held her again and kissed her. 'Go with God, Mora.' No one had called her that since Hugh had died. Except, that once, Fineenh.

'Ghea carry you,' she whispered.

She sensed rather than saw the glen widening and deepening as she picked her way down into it. A little burn flowing to one side guided her steps. Even before the fog had covered Dhion's shape, grey and bulky under his pack, the water's chatter silenced his steps.

The fog showed no sign of lifting, and she could only imagine the height of the mountains on either side. But the feeling that rose in her she could name as exultation. She was alone, and the thought thrilled her. The raw world, untamed by man, stretched all around. It filled her with an awe that might have made her tremble if she had stopped.

Around midday – as well as she could guess – the valley floor steepened. The sun was still not to be seen, was no more than a soft whitish light that might have come from anywhere. The little wandering burn beside her became a fast-flowing stream hurrying over a stony bed. Then, quite suddenly, it fell over a rocky edge in a tumbling fall. Her guide, having signalled the danger, had abandoned her. Her path disappeared in a jumble of stone steps. Her stomach clenched. But at the same time a breeze sprang up and lifted the fog in rags around her, and through its tattered skirts she could catch glimpses of another valley below.

The rocks were slippery with wetness. The thought flashed through her: *What if I fall and break my neck? Why was I so stubborn?* But hard on its heels came another: *You promised them you would return.* She must be very careful. She cast around for her best way and began to climb down. As when she forded the river, she hitched her skirts higher to give herself the freedom of movement she needed.

At times she found herself crossing the fall of the burn and re-crossing it, as she sought her path first this side, then that. Her heart was thumping in her ears: *Don't let me die! Don't let me die! Don't let me die!*

Now the burn was no longer a waterfall. From the brown pool beside her it rushed down a grassy slope pock-marked with stones. Then the slope flattened until it formed the bank of a small river. The far side of the river, clearly-marked at last, was her path.

Rough stepping stones had been laid, and she crossed the river without difficulty. Sheep were grazing on the coarse grass and after a while she passed dry-stone walls laid out as folds. The fog now rolled above her as a featureless grey cloud, shedding on her a thin grey drizzle. She pulled out her skirts and brushed them down. She was reaching the end of her journey, and the thought of what she would find pressed upon her. She tried to picture a familiar face. But – twenty years! Almost half a lifetime ago.

A sound. Broken, but clear in the distance ahead: a reedy pipe. She stopped and listened. Now her heart began to sing. It was an air she had forgotten, yet it lived still, somewhere deep within. A song of the land of her girlhood.

Weary though she was, her step quickened until after a little while she came upon the piper: a boy, not yet a man, his chin with the first downy growth of beard. He sat cross-legged in a tiny bothy that held the smallest patch of dry earth. He was wrapped in a grubby, patched cloak. Around him ewes, big with lamb, were grazing. He looked up as she approached, and his charges huddled closer to him. He lowered the pipe from his lips.

'The peace of God,' she called to him.

'Aye.'

'Are these your sheep?'

'Aye.'

'Is this the way to Kimmoil?'

'Aye.'

'Is it far to go?'

'Naw.'

She paused, taken aback by the youth's shortness. Well, what welcome had she been expecting? 'Thank you,' she said. 'Ghea stay with you.' She turned and walked on.

Her road led into a small wood of stunted oak and ash, bare branches still. It entered a clearing, and there, a tangle of roots reaching out into the empty air, a larger tree lay on its side. It would have taken a great storm to topple this. She stopped before it, shock running through her. Was this the oak? Her mind wheeled.

She went back: saw herself a young girl again, barely a woman, and her mind filled with thoughts of the young daekin prenticed to Father Callen. A great oak had stood in the middle of a clearing where they had met. But no living oak soared above her now. Instead, this lean grey skeleton lay before her. Was this the tree? She reached out and placed her hand on the bare wood and tears welled up for her memory. She closed her eyes.

Midsummer. The oak tree, tall and green. Musicians on the lawn. And Brother Hugh, looking out of place in his long cassock, but for the pipe in his hands.

The sound of the bodhran, a simple steady rhythm. Then the drones starting with the shrill little chanter, the drum bringing in its cross-rhythms. In the player's hand the stick, a blur. And her young self tall, motionless as a standing stone. Slowly she had raised a foot. And then, as Brother Hugh's flute began, at the same moment she leaped.

Whether Hugh caught the movement of her body and wove it into the song he played, or whether her limbs were answering moment by moment to the music that wrapped her round, she did not know. She did not hear the music: it took her over, as the air takes the soaring gull and carries her, its pulses and her pinions one. Only to dance and dance and dance; to rise above the scent of crushed grass and woodsmoke, to whirl until she was nothing and nowhere and only was, everything and all and nothing more. And there was no time. Every time was now and now was all. On and on: arms, legs, gown, hair, feet on grass and feet in air, and hands wafting the scents of evening, on and on and on and on and on.

She had stood on a low summit of the eastern hills. The whole town was there, gathered to watch for the first sliver of burning gold to appear beyond the eastern mountains and bring in the midsummer dawn. She was empty, very peaceful, almost as in a dream; the last to leave the peak, to thread her way down the little path that twisted between rocks.

In her infolded state she had not noticed that other who followed. As she turned her head, he spoke. His words came back to her through the vanished years.

'I thought it not good to leave you alone. If one falls, another can help them up. Pity the one who falls and has no help.'

She threw her reply over her shoulder. 'And though one may be overpowered, two can defend themselves.'

'You have found me out,' answered Hugh. 'I see you know the Book of the Wise.'

'Indeed, brother. And it is the cord of *three* strands that is not easily broken.' She looked at him sideways in the gloaming.

He chuckled. She dared, and reached for his hand. His fingers folded round hers, firm, warm.

'A cord of three strands,' he had answered. 'You and me and the midsummer sun.'

It had been this path. This path that ran on between the twisted trunks of oak trees, still bare from winter. This same path, where the first primroses were putting out their early blooms, pale in the grey light.

A man leaned on his axe to watch her pass. He barely nodded at her greeting. Then the smell of wood-smoke was on the wet air. She emerged from the trees to see walled meadows and little fields, brown from the plough and not yet green from the springing grain. Across the river a yoke of oxen was turning the heavy soil. These were the fields where her grandfather had sent his men to plough, to harrow; sow them, harvest them. These were the fields where she had played as a child. Kimmoil.

Chapter 12

In the little house behind the smithy, Shinane lay once more with her man. 'I'm glad you're back.' She turned, shifting the bulk of her belly off her back, and put an arm round Dhion. The darkness of their house was warmed by the low glow of the embers. 'I couldn't help worrying while you were gone.'

'Me too,' he returned. 'About both of you. I'm sure Micheil had right with him when he tried to stop her.' He pursed his lips. 'I hope she's found her way. I hate the thought of her sleeping out alone in the wild tonight.'

The wind keened through the thatch. A cold drop of rainwater splashed on her bare arm.

'I feared you might stay away. Not come back in time.' It stung her that his thought seemed more with Morag than herself. She went on: 'Dhion, Morag has asked us not to worry for her. Now we must do what she asks. There's nothing more we can do. We must wait, with trust, for her to come home among us again.'

'But will she? I keep going over all I've said to her, feeling I could have found a way to turn her. Should have.'

'Do you think so? She's following her destiny. Didn't you feel it? Nothing could have kept her from going, except force. Not even … the little one who's coming to us.'

He turned his head towards her face, hidden as it was in shadow.

'How have you been while I've been away?'

'Oh.' She tightened her lips. 'It's heavy work, lugging your child around, you know. You men – you have it all, don't you?' Nonetheless, she kissed his nose.

'It can't be much longer now. Have you felt anything?'

'Off and on. Just little cramps. Rhona tells me to drink more water – but then I want to piss and that makes them worse.' She gave him a squeeze. 'I want to see her again tomorrow. Mother keeps telling me I'm awful big.'

Shinane called at the potter's house the next morning. She could see Padragh in the lean-to, hard at work. A heavy-looking wooden tub lay at his feet while he pounded the clay within.

'Peace of God, Padragh. Is the wife within?'

It was between grunts that he answered. 'Aye. Go you in, girl.'

Rhona A'Phadragh was a big woman, and seemed bigger with her sleeves rolled up on her red and freckled arms. It looked as if she was preparing to go to the washing pool with a great pile of laundry. With four growing youngsters and her man's messy trade, it must be a frequent journey. Her greeting was brusque.

'Shinane, girl! Surely it's not your time yet. Don't tell me ye've started so soon?'

Shinane glanced at the birthing stool in the corner. It belonged to Rhona, and was the town's resource.

'No, no, not yet. I just called by to make sure all's well.'

'Aye, you'll be fine. How're the stones going?'

Rhona had given Shinane a bag full of tiny pebbles soon after she knew she was carrying. 'Take one out every First-day,' she'd told her. That morning she had taken the second last from the bag. There was only one left.

'Well then, let's hae a look at ye. Lie you down on the bed there.'

She did as she was told while the birthing-woman pulled at her gown, wriggling it up above her waist. She felt naked lying in the strange house with only her shift covering her nethers. But Rhona's big hands held a reassuring quality. They arched over the top of her belly.

'Well, I'd say ye're big enough for two. The babe's movin fine?'

Shinane nodded.

'So let's hae a feel of ye.'

The hands ran down her sides. Up again. Carefully feeling.

'Well, I'll be – '

'What is it?'

The words came out more anxiously than she intended. Rhona took her hand.

'Nothing to worry about,' she said. 'But feel you here.'

She took Shinane's hand and placed it beneath her own.

'There – feel? That's babe's back, curlin up to his head, there.'

Shinane felt the firm roundness under her hand.

'An then –' She took her hand and laid it on her other side. 'There's the other's back, goin down the way.'

Shinane stiffened. She looked up into the puffy face that hovered over her, framed with a storm-cloud of red hair. 'What's it mean? Two backs?' She felt confused, alarmed, terrified. A succession of wild visions flashed through her mind.

'Nothin to be fashed about, dear. It's twins, that's all.'

'Twins? Isn't that …?'

'Nothin to be fashed about,' Rhona repeated, firmly. 'I've birthed 'em afore.'

'But isn't it more dangerous? I've heard tales …' Shinane's voice died away.

'Well, if ye want tales, go an talk wi A'Shar'g. Look at her boys. As big strong louts as ye could wish. An she nae looked back on the birth naether.'

It was true. Micheil's wife was as trim and lively as a dancer. It was a mystery how she had ever birthed those two sons of hers. But another tale came also to her mind. She said nothing. She left it, like a crow of ill omen on the thatch.

Her hand was still on her belly, wondering at the feel of it – that these two – two! – were there, curled up inside her; her children, and she could feel them. One made a movement.

Again the wave of terror. 'Where's the other's head? You said we can feel both their backs, but I only felt one head.'

'Oh, that's way away down there. Firmly seated between ye're hips, just waitin for the door to open.'

The relief. 'Soon?'

'I think so. I'd say they'll be with us, mebbe afore we expected. Any day now.'

But the crow in the thatch sat on. It had all happened years before, but was still there among them, a story of the town, and still known to her in a living person.

As a child, she had grown up thinking of Oonagh as the herb-woman, the bee-woman. She kept a herb garden in a protected spot beside the town meadows, and in it, half-a-dozen skeps for the bees. If you had a sore throat or a belly-ache, or were in agony with the cramps of your monthly flow, Oonagh could usually find something for you. Even with worse ills, sometimes the herb-woman could stop the fever.

Then, one day, after a visit to the healing woman with her mother – she had been, what? fifteen or so – Fineenh had told her Oonagh's story.

The shoemaker had been a big man. Black-haired, strong-jawed, blue-eyed. He had grown up in the trade in Mhreuhan, the big town, where there was more quality to wear leather shoes. But when his father had passed him skilled as himself, he chose to wander off to see more of the world. In time he had journeyed out to Westerland, where he fell in with Tearlach, the leather-worker of Caerpadraig, and began to teach him to fashion shoes. Then he saw Oonagh.

The daughter of Ranal was as lovely as he was fine – and what a pair they made! It wasn't long, in the way of things, before she was carrying, and the time came for her. Four days she was in labour – four long days. At last the babe was born, though she screamed with the agony of it. But the child was dead, its skin grey and scaly. A boy-child it had been. But there was more. Still she laboured, and the breech appeared. The sweat stood on her brow and ran down her face, but it took from first-light until midday before the head was delivered. And that child, another boy, was also dead. Then Oonagh bled until they feared for her life too.

But she was strong. Slowly she healed, though it was a month before she could walk. The old birthing-woman who saw her told the shoemaker: she must never have children more. At this he grew angry, and maybe in part it was because he felt he had brought evil upon her. He could not bear to stay in the same house as she and not lie with her as man and wife, so he put her away and she went and lived alone. But the shoemaker could find no peace, and soon after they could not find him. Some said he ran away to another town; but others say he found a secret thicket and there, in desperation and grief, opened his veins. But Oonagh stayed where she was and began to learn the lore of herbs. Maureen A'Dhael from Fisherhame took her under her wing and taught her, and in time Oonagh grew wiser even than she.

Shinane had not known how to hold the two together: a tale so dark, and Oonagh, as she saw her in the town, firm and steady and wise.

꩜꩜

It was a long afternoon. Dhion was working, but for her there were light duties. Fineenh was taking all the heavy work on herself. Still, there were always the neeps to prepare, and more needlework. Now all her preparations must be doubled. She waited through the long afternoon until at last he came and she could unburden herself. Dhion listened as she poured out what she knew of Oonagh's story and her tormenting fears.

A log slipped in the fire and subsided into a crazed red glow.

'We'd not looked for twins, had we?' he said.

He looked deep into her eyes. He touched his forefinger to the tip of her nose.

'Do you remember, when I was out on the ocean. You called me home. That was not for no reason, was it?'

'I don't know, Dhion.'

'Love – there is Oonagh. And there is A'Shar'g. I think we had better choose one, and fix our eyes on her. Which shall we choose?'

'You mock me.'

'I mock you not.'

Tension stretched taut between them.

'Shinane. Life is a chancy thing, and the way is hazardous. But when I was preparing for my ordeal at sea, the wise woman taught me that where we set our thoughts and our mind has power. We're going to think on something, so let's choose what it will be. I'm sorry for Oonagh's tale. And I admire her, for what she's become. But I say we think on A'Shar'g. What do you say?'

She drank in his words like a medicine, stilling her anxious thoughts. At last she returned his gaze.

'Very well,' she said. 'A'Shar'g.'

'Let's ask her to come and speak with you. Would you like that?'

She nodded.

'Good girl.'

'This is my ordeal.' But her voice was small. She stared into the embers.

His arm slid round where her waist had been. 'Show me how to hold you through it, as once you held me.'

She looked up at him, his bearded face in the firelight, picked out red against the darkness of the house. 'And you, Husband. Teach me how to be held.'

Chapter 13

Morag stopped. Before her, a high stockade and the roofs of the town. And piecemeal, through the open gate and in thready gaps between houses, the glint of water where the lough curved its arm into the dark northern sea. Lough Moil. She had returned.

She remembered now how shocked she had been, when first she came to Caerpadraig and found it unwalled. Her northern home had always been fenced, even though the raiding Northmen in their longships were now distant memory, and one high shareg after another had ensured peace between quarrelling townships. Coming to a town as undefended and open as Caerpadraig, she had felt at first vulnerable, too much exposed. But now the sight of the high fence, the heavy gate, the two armed men before it, seemed somehow childish, as if they might be afraid of the dark.

The men had seen her. Recognising her for a stranger, they jumped up and reached for their spears where they leaned against the fence.

They really are young, she thought. *They can't distinguish a lone woman from an approaching war-band.* She greeted them. 'In peace, and in God.'

'In Ghea, and in peace,' the elder of the two replied. His voice was flat, and she felt no welcome in it. His auburn beard jutted forward from his jaw like a fist.

'My name is Morag. I am a daughter of this town, returning after many years.'

'What is your business here?'

'I come to talk with Targuid the Blind, or whoever follows him.'

The men exchanged glances. 'Targuid son of Tarshan has been laid in the ground these many years.'

'Whose daughter are you?'

So. It was as she had thought. She answered, 'I am daughter of Murdogh, the son of Conor.'

'Murdogh Ma'Chonor we know. It is three years since he died. Did no one send to give you word?' The question fell upon her like a challenge. When each of her grandparents had died, word had worked its way round the coast. It may have taken a month or two, but it had reached her. No one had brought her news about her father. She knew why: because, to her father, she was of no account. It was like receiving a blow. Now the guard was asking, 'Is there another who will speak for you?'

Morag hesitated.

'His sons or daughters may remember me. I married a priest, Hugh Ma'Cholm, who was once daekin to this town. I went with him into the Westerland, to Caerpadraig. That is where I have come from. I am tired from my journey, and wet and cold. I hoped to find hospitality in my own town.'

The older man seemed to soften a little. He turned to his fellow: 'Run to the shareg. Tell him how she has answered.' Then, to Morag, 'Come, sit you down. Shareg won't be long. But we may not let any enter whom we do not know.'

'That was not always so,' she replied, folding her skirts beneath her as she took the proffered stool.

'It is so now. There are men in the wild who do not follow our laws. Shareg has spoken.'

Who were these men, she wondered. She had seen none. Still, she was glad to find this man more approachable now.

'What is your name?' she asked.

'I am Coll Ma'Lennish. And … you came from Caerpadraig in Westerland?' He leaned forward with a sudden eagerness. 'Is not that where the marvellous Coat came from? The coat of the seaborne one, who came from an unknown land?'

91

Morag stared. It seemed that not her father, but her son would give her standing here.

'It is,' she replied. 'And that same Seaborne, whom we call Dhion Ingleeshe, is now my son. My husband and I adopted him when he had no family here of his own.'

Coll gaped at her. It was, she realised, as if a legend had walked into his life. He recovered himself. 'But where is your husband now? Why do you travel alone? Had you come with him we might have given you a friendlier welcome: women do not walk alone in the wild.'

'My husband has died. He was long priest of Caerpadraig. He died between Lammas and Samhain last.'

'I am sorry for you.' Coll paused. For a breath there was silence between them. 'I remember when our last priest died. His wife and family had to leave their home when the new priest came. Is that why you have come?'

But before she could answer, the young guard came running back. 'We are to bring her to the shareg.'

'Come,' said Coll as he rose. 'I will take you.'

They came to a stone-built house that seemed both strange and familiar at the same time. Morag found herself comparing it with the house where Micheil and Aileen lived. This was a little smaller, lower, more dour. Would she recognise the shareg when he appeared? He must have been in the town during her girlhood.

Coll had her wait outside. The drizzle had stopped and the cloud was less evenly grey, as if it might soon break; but Morag, in her woollen cloak and gown with the wet of the fog still on them, began to tremble with cold.

She did not wait long before the shareg came out. At once she could see he was younger than herself. He must have been still a lad when she left. She saw his strength of character. He had a fine, chiselled face upon broad shoulders, his black beard neatly trimmed along his jaw-line, his eyes grey and hard. With him was Coll, and another man, taller, his eyes steel-grey.

There was no greeting. 'Who are you?' he asked. His voice was firm, short, efficient.

'The peace of God be with you, Shareg' She recited her lineage another time. As a woman, custom required her to keep her eyes down when answering a man. But another voice within her said: *Look him in the eye*. She did.

For a moment a line of fire burned between them.

'Do you know this man?' the shareg said suddenly, indicating the grey-eyed man. His eyes held Morag's until the last moment. Then he turned: 'Eoghan, do you know this woman?'

Eoghan was the name of her eldest half-brother, several years younger than she. Kept from her father's household as she had been, Morag had never taken much interest in him. But she had known who he was. She looked hard, saw the lad he used to be, hidden in a face leathered by the years. Had she also changed so much? But Eoghan said, 'No, Shareg. I cannot say I know her.'

'Shareg, I have only now come here,' she said, swiftly. 'After more than twenty years. Many of those I knew must have died, and others, including myself, may be changed out of all recognising.'

Keep your eyes up, repeated the voice. *Remember who you are.*

'I was born to my father by a woman not his wife. I was raised in the house of Conor, my father's father, away from my own father's family. I have been living with my husband in the Westerland more than twenty years. I do recognise my half-brother, though I find him much changed. He was not much more than a boy when last I saw him.'

'Shareg.' Steely-eyed, Eoghan spoke. With an arm on the shareg's shoulder he steered him towards the door and whispered.

They turned back to her. The shareg searched her with cold discernment. 'It seems you may be speaking truth.'

'I do speak truth, Shareg.'

'Why do you come here?'

'I seek after my mother. It has come time for me to find out who she was.'

'Where do you make your home?'

'My husband, Hugh the priest, and I, we made our home in Caerpadraig in the Westerland. To there I will return.'

'Where is your husband today? Do you have his leave to wander alone in the wild?'

'My husband died last year. But he it is who told me to come here.'

'And your shareg? What had he to say?'

'He … foresaw difficulties, dangers. But he saw too that my mind was firm. In the end he gave his blessing.'

'You would have done well to have heeded his counsel.' The shareg paused. 'Tell me, Morag Mi'Mhurdogh, is your town of Caerpadraig so rich that they do not feel the time of year?' She felt his cold eyes on her. 'Or are they so poor that you come here hoping for better? The winter stores are nigh gone, and this year's provender still awaits the season. We have little food, and none for wandering women. My advice to you is to return where you came from. You may rest here the night, and be gone tomorrow.'

'Shareg,' Morag returned. 'I am a woman grieving her husband, who follows his command to seek after my own mother. I have been on the road two days, and I need to find the one who follows Targuid.'

For a long moment the shareg stroked his beard. Then he spoke, and his tone was measured. 'Hear this,

Morag Mi'Mhurdogh. You have ventured on this journey and must take what the path offers, whatever it may be. Here, we have scarce enough food to feed our own. If someone of the town is willing to feed you, for three days you may stay here. After that, you shall go.'

There was silence among them. Morag's heart was beating fast. She turned to face her half-brother, but he shook his head. 'I would betray my father to help in this matter,' he said. 'You must find your help elsewhere.'

A cold feeling settled round her heart: one she remembered from the years before Hugh.

The shareg turned to Coll. 'Take her to the rondal,' he said. He turned back to Morag. 'They stand there who seek shelter, until someone passes by.'

Trembling, but not only from cold, she followed Coll, who left her at the rondal door. In her heart she felt the justice of the shareg's words, hard though they were. Why had she not waited until the weather was kinder and food more plentiful, as Micheil had urged? Well, now she was here and, as the shareg had said, must meet whatever came her way. She swallowed hard.

She waited. Men passed, not looking at her, or looking, as it were, through her. Women passed, some carrying loads – a sack of flour, a bundle of firewood. All the time she wondered when she might meet someone she knew. A woman who looked as if she might be of an age with herself passed by and gave her a smile. It was the first she had received. She smiled back. But the woman walked on. Morag looked after her. That smile. Something about it stirred memory. Or was that wishful thinking?

The western hills, walling the left-hand bank of the lough and marching up beside the narrow strath above the town, hid the setting sun. The broken clouds were lit by yellow-grey light. Dusk began to deepen.

She sat on the ground, and waited. A young girl, ragged clothes barely hiding the thinness of her limbs, appeared, stared at her with big eyes, and wandered on.

Then the woman who had smiled returned. 'I see ye're still standing here. Is it a bed for the night ye're seeking?'

'For a night, or three.'

'Well, we can manage one night at least. Come with me. Is that your pack? Oh my dear, it's cold ye are.'

With an exclamation of thanks and relief, Morag struggled to her feet, picked up the pack and followed. The woman led her deeper into the town, then pushed open the heavy timber door of a substantial-looking house.

'Wait here,' she said.

Morag waited. How long must she endure? Then the door, left ajar, opened wide.

'Come in,' said the woman.

'In the name of God, and in peace.'

Morag stepped inside.

'In peace, and in Ghea.' A man's deep voice answered.

The sense of being under a roof and within the warmth of a fire flooded Morag's being. Gratitude rose within her like a shout. She looked around. Several lamps were lit, and she took stock of where she was. The man who had greeted her sat by the hearth. He did not rise, but swept an arm as if to indicate his house. 'You are welcome,' he said. There were two other men, much younger – almost boys still – and a young woman with a distaff and spindle, who regarded her with curiosity.

'You are a stranger here,' the man continued. 'I am Finn Ma'Mhoran. My sons, Moran and Callen. The daughter, Cloghan. The wife tells me you were standing by the rondal.'

'Indeed. And I am grateful for your welcome, Ma'Mhoran. But I am no stranger. I am Morag Ag'Hugh, grand-daughter of Conor of this town.' For the first time, she refused to name herself by her father. Let her name the one who stood by her, she thought.

Her hostess stared with sudden intensity. 'Then you are Morag Mi'Mhurdogh? No wonder there was something made me stop. I'm Bridie Mi'Tharguid! You must remember me!'

For a confused moment, as realisation dawned, recognition and uncertainty vying with each other, the two women hesitated. Then Morag felt herself wrapped in the warmth of the other's strong arms.

'Och, but look at you! It's all damp you are. Come and get those wet things off you and then warm yourself at the fire. Cloghan!' The girl in the corner looked up. 'Is the soup ready yet? Go and see!'

'Yes, Mother.'

'And you two, you great lumps!' Bridie scolded her sons. 'Go and help your sister and get some firewood in.'

A heavy press stood against the wall. A soft scent of fern arose as Bridie opened the lid and took out a clean shift and leine. She almost pushed Morag through a curtain into her bed-alcove.

These must be the girl's clothes, thought Morag, for they fitted her well. Bridie was plumper than she, if not a little stout. But it felt strange not to be wearing her own gown.

When Bridie saw the knife on Morag's belt, she said, 'It's good the shareg didn't see that under your cloak. He wouldn't like a stranger bearing arms.'

Morag started. She had not let herself consider the knife a weapon.

'We'll hide it, shall we?' Bridie continued. 'In the press!'

When they came back into the room, Finn was whittling at a piece of leather as he sat by the hearth. One of the boys was building the fire. There were noises from the kitchen: the other boy and Cloghan arguing.

Bridie was saying, 'Cloggie and I will wash your things tomorrow. There's peat all up the back of your skirt!'

After the evening meal Callan went to do duty at the gate. Bridie refused to let Morag help with anything. 'Na, na,' she said. 'You rest here.' Morag sat by the fire, glad to be warm and dry and fed.

'Ye'll have met our shareg, then?' said Finn.

'Yes,' she responded, drily.

'And what do ye make of him?'

'A hard man. But fair.'

'Aye. He's a good chief. Shrewd. Did he tell you there's scurvy in the town.'

'I … I'm sorry.' She looked down, embarrassed.

'It's been a hard winter a' right: we've little to eat. But we can still share what we have when there's need, or we don't deserve to have it.'

'I promise to stay no longer than I must,' she said.

'Ye're our guest, and welcome. But what brings you here?'

Before she could answer Bridie clattered in, followed by Cloghan taking off her apron, her forearms red.

Bridie sat and smoothed out her apron, while the girl picked up her distaff. Morag noted the skill with which she twisted the spindle, and thought of Shinane.

'Bridie, tell me.' It was a question she had been waiting to ask. 'Blind Targuid wasn't your father, was he?'

'No. My father was Targuid Ma'Tharguid. Targuid the Blind was my grandfather.'

Long gone, thought Morag, even if he lived to a great age.

Aloud, she said. 'He could recite everybody's ancestry.'

'Aye. He was a wonder. It was as if when he lost his eyes the Sidhe gave him another gift instead. He had the second sight as well, you know.'

Morag leaned forward. 'Who now holds the people's tales?'

'Well, I do for one. But if it's ancestry you want, it's my uncle Finneuchan.'

'That is why I came here.' Slowly she told her story. Bridie remembered Hugh – remembered covering for Morag while the two lovers met, those years ago. Cloghan's eyes opened wide at the tale. Then Morag told of her life since, finishing with the time of Hugh's illness and his passing. 'It was he who told me to find out about my mother,' she said. She did not say that his word had reached her from beyond the grave. 'Hugh has been my staff all these years,' she went on. 'Now he is gone, I must learn to stand alone. To do that, I need to find the knowledge that was denied me. Do you see?'

Bridie nodded. But Morag thought: *No, she doesn't. She's too comfortable here with her man and her family around her. How could she understand?*

'So you'd like to visit Uncle. Tomorrow?'

'As soon as possible.'

'Morning's his best time. He sleeps a lot in the afternoons. Then he complains he doesn't sleep at night. Finn: where shall we make Morag a bed for the night?'

'Moran!' Finn called. The young man looked up from where he had been sewing together two pieces of leather, carefully pulling a narrow strip of hide through the holes he had punched. 'Ye'll give your bed to our guest tonight.'

'But Callan …'

'Callan's at the gate tonight, and we don't want him coming and disturbing a lady's sleep.'

'All right, Da.'

Moran disappeared, Morag supposed, to ensure his bed was presentable.

❧❦

She was pleased to find that they said a short prayer before retiring. It brought a peacefulness into her heart. She lay in the alcove Moran had left to her and looked back on the day past. The waterfall, the rocks she had clambered down, and her leaving of Dhion, already seemed long ago. The shareg's words had disturbed her. So many years she had taken for granted the food the people of Caerpadraig provided. Yes, there had been her own kale and beans and neeps that some years were plentiful and others gave scant cheer. But for flesh and milk, for fish and oil as well as grain, she had depended on the town. Had they sometimes gone hungry to let her eat?

Then she thought of her last night's visitor. The wolf – what did that mean? Why to her? And why had she not been afraid?

Chapter 14

She woke with a sense of excitement. This morning was the goal, the summit of her journey; the moment she had fought for. This day, surely, she would know the answer to her question. Was her mother still alive? Not likely. But not impossible. Would she learn her name at last – today? Her thoughts ran ahead with eager anticipation and she had to hold them back, telling herself firmly: *Let it be enough for today to know her name and her kin*.

Bridie gave her family porridge for first-food. Thin – but plenty of it. Usually, she said, she would have liked to follow this with a piece of rye-bread spread with thick yellow butter. But in this season – well, it was just the porridge. Afterwards Finn disappeared to his workshop behind the house, where he and his sons tooled leather, making buckets and coracles and targets.

Rain had come in earnest, sweeping down off the western hills and turning the lough into a tossing patchwork of white and grey. Peering through the dreich, Bridie pointed Morag towards Finneuchan's house, and while Cloghan reached for the wooden tub that hung from the ceiling, she wrapped herself in her now-dry cloak, pulled her hood well over her head, and splashed through the mud of the town.

'In the name of God, and in peace.' She knocked at the door Bridie had described and waited. After a moment there was a shuffling sound from inside and the creak of a bar being drawn back. The door opened a few inches and an old man's face appeared.

'In peace, and in Ghea,' he responded, questioningly.

'I seek Finneuchan son of Targuid. Have I come to the right door?'

'Ye have,' the man replied. 'Come in.' He stepped back, opening the door wide. He must once have been tall, Morag thought, but was now stooped. He wore a long black robe belted at the waist, his shoulders covered with a creamy white shawl. His chin with its white beard, straggling, and stained around his mouth, was sunk below his shoulders so that his red-rimmed eyes peered at her from under his dark brows, giving him a constantly questioning expression.

'And who might you be?' he asked as he closed the door behind her.

'I am Morag Mi'Mhurdogh,' she replied at once. 'I come to … '

'Morag Mi'Mhurdogh,' the old man muttered. 'Morag Mi'Mhurdogh … Ma'Chonor, Ma'Chormac, MacEuan … Well, well. Ye it was who married the daekin, was it no? Hugh, who was daekin here under Father Callen? Sit ye down, sit ye down.'

He moved slowly, stiffly. She sat on the dusty settle he indicated beside a smouldering peat fire. An old grey-muzzled bitch lay in its warmth and raised her head welcomingly.

Finneuchan disappeared behind a curtain, and there was a clattering of beakers and vessels. He came back with a beaker in each hand, set them down and, in his slow way, took mulling irons from the fire and plunged one, hissing, into each. He thrust a beaker into her hand, and she sipped. Whatever else was in it, there was a fair measure of spirit. She coughed, but the liquor was instantly warming.

He sat, slowly, stiffly, before her. At his side was a plate with a knife and a wizened yellow apple upon it. 'And what is it ye're come about?' he enquired.

She answered him cautiously, thinking he must guess why she was there. 'They tell me it is you who hold the people's lines now. That your father, Targuid the Blind, taught you. And that his spirit is upon you.'

'So they say; so they say ...' His lips went on moving, as if silently repeating his words.

'Ma'Tharguid, I believe you are the only one who can answer my question.'

'And what question would that be?'

She was sure he knew already.

'Ma'Tharguid, can you tell me of my mother, and of her ancestry?'

He took a meditative sip from his tankard. The fire crackled and the bitch lay with her head between her paws, watching. Morag waited.

'They never told you much about your mother, did they?' he said at last.

She shook her head.

'An what they did tell you, they mostly made up for themselves,' he observed in his measured way, 'for she came not from hereabouts. Her line was not known.'

He took another sip.

'I am not going to tell you what I do not know,' he went on, and looked from his rheumy eyes straight into her own.

Morag's heart was beating fast. 'But please! You must know something.'

'Not much,' he said. 'Only a little.'

Why was he leading her on in this way? She waited.

He seemed to decide something. 'Did they tell you what they called her?' he asked. 'For no one knew her true name.'

A chaos of things they had called her mother came to mind. She shook her head.

'They called her Bron.'

Another sip. Morag's own beaker steamed in her hand. Unsteadily, she set it down. Her hand shook.

'Bron ...' she repeated.

'It is a part-name, not a full name,' he told her, 'in a foreign tongue.'

Then, was her mother from another land? But the old man was continuing to speak. She listened, longing for more.

'It means breast,' he went on. 'More than that I do not know. They called her Bron.'

He stopped speaking.

'Do you know how she came here? Where she came from?' she asked, wanting him to say more.

'Drink a little, Morag … Mi'Bhron. It will do you good.'

Morag reached for the cup at her feet and brought it to her lips. The warming liquid set a fire spreading within.

'Bron came here with her mother, running from some trouble or other. They stayed through a summer, working on one of the outcrofts. But at summer's end, when her mother moved on, Bron stayed. It was for your father she stayed. That was how you began. And when you were weaned, your grandparents took you, for it was clear Bron could not care for you, a woman alone with no man. They left her to go her own way.'

Morag saw how it must have been. Her father willing to lie with a stranger-woman who took his eye; not willing to wed that stranger. But why did he not take her, Morag, into his own household when he married, as would have been custom?

She asked this question and the old man shifted his head from side to side, seeming to consider. At last he said, 'I do not know that. So I canna tell you.'

'But do you not – have an idea?'

Finneuchan seemed to draw into himself.

'We all have many ideas, do we not. Some are no doubt good. Many are bad. But I am not here to give you ideas. Only truth. I have told you what I know.'

'Surely at least you know who can tell me more! Which of the outcrofts was it where she stayed? I'll go there.'

The old man waved his hand at her. For many breaths he sat in silence. But his hands in his lap were restless, the fingers and thumbs continually rolling over each other. In the end, all he said was, 'I canna tell you more of your mother. An I do not think you will learn more of sense by askin around here, but only more of the town's gossip. People's … ideas.'

He reached for the apple beside him and started paring it with the knife.

'I know you know more!' She was angry now.

He struggled to his feet. In his haste he overturned the stool beside him and stool, knife and plate clattered to the floor. 'I canna tell you more, because I canna! If you want to know more, you will have to wait for those who can to find you. I canna.' he repeated.

'Who?' Morag began.

But he subsided into his chair again. The old dog got stiffly to her feet and rested her muzzle in his lap. When he spoke again his voice was quiet – so quiet that even in that stillness Morag had to listen carefully. 'It's sorry I am, to be sure. But ye must take that as my answer. Go away, Morag Mi'Bhron. I know the quest you are on. Well, take what I can tell. Even that will feed ye a little. An wait. For maybe in time, they'll tell ye themselves.'

He paused, his eyes fixed on something by their feet. Morag followed his line of sight. He was staring at the knife, its tip bedded in the beaten earth of the floor. She heard him mutter, 'Now would ye look at that!'

He flapped his hands at her, to shoo her away like a trespassing hen, his chin resting sadly on his chest. She rose, turned, and found her way to the door. The old bitch followed, as if sensing that her man had fallen short of his duty. Morag ran a hand over the crown of the dog's head between the grey-tinged ears, and softly closed the door. As she walked away, the sight of the knife with its blade in the floor returned to mind. Why had he bent over it with that intent expression? Another unanswered question.

It was near noon. The rain had eased. Now she could see patches of blue between the grey clouds. There was so much churning in her heart that she needed to be alone to bring all to mind. She walked down to the shore, where fishing boats were drawn up. The town wall came down to the water, and there was a small gate. The guard had clearly been told about her, for he greeted her civilly as she passed. A path clung to the lough-side, sometimes in the trees, sometimes diving below the tide-line to skirt a rocky promontory.

She turned and looked back towards the stockade. All her life in Caerpadraig she had been the foreigner from the north. Now, she knew, she was a foreigner here, too, in the place where she was born. A foreigner, born of a foreigner. You couldn't be more foreign than that.

'What do I do now?' she said to herself.

What can you do?

She looked around. 'Hugh? Are you there?'

Here, as everywhere.

A shiver passed down her spine: she could not help it.

'All I can see to do is go back home. Back to Caerpadraig.'

Yes.

'And there, I'll sit at home. No, I'll sit in Dhion's home,' she corrected herself. 'And nursemaid the child and never know ...'

She took a great gulp of air.

'Hugh, you sent me here. What for?' She stopped, covering her eyes. Tears flowed through her fingers. She let her breath out in a sob.

Silence.

'Hugh? Hugh! What else? What can I do?'

A honking from down towards the open sea drew her attention. A flight of geese was noisily making its way up the lough. She watched them skim the water and come to rest. Long years had passed since she had seen that sight.

It was a dull afternoon. As she returned to Bridie's house she saw her washed clothes drying on the frame outside. She was silent as she entered. Bridie looked at her, but asked no questions. She brought in her clothes to air by the fire while Cloghan energetically ground grain from their diminishing store. The sun, briefly shining between the clouds, was westering when at last Bridie sat beside her and asked:

'Well, Mora? What did he say? You've been like a wet rag ever since you came back from hisself. What did he tell you?'

Morag sighed. A heaviness lay on her heart. She did not want to speak, but still she said, 'He kept back much of what he knew. I know he did. And now I'm not clear of my way.' She felt herself close to tears. She blinked them back and looked up, uncertain, at her friend.

Bridie sat back. 'It's wondering I am at that. Uncle knows everyone's mother – and father, and cousins and grandsires and all. Why wouldn't he?'

A hard note crept into her voice with that last question. A note of suspicion. And in Morag's heart a voice began. A chorus of children's voices in a circle around her, taunting: *Who's your mother? Who's your mother? Who's your mother? Don't you know?*

At that, the tears dried on the steel of Morag's heart. 'I don't know, Bridie. What are you thinking?'

'Well, Mora.' Her voice had recovered almost its usual tone, but the kindness lay over the hardness; not melting, but concealing it. 'I'm thinking it doesn't matter about your mother. You have your father's name: that's enough, isn't it?'

Bridie's voice had never joined in with the taunting. She had always hung back, outside the circle. But neither could she break through and hold her hand, stand with her. 'No Bridie, you know it's not enough! And he did not own me as a father. I cannot bear his name.'

'Why was that, then?' Bridie demanded. 'And him a man of standing, commanding everyone's respect? I don't know who your mother was, I'm sure. But I heard the talk about her. And I do know that if your father kept you from her, it was for a reason.'

Reason? What did reason have to do with motherhood?

Bridie rocked back, thinking. Then she said, 'Don't take this wrong. But I tell you now, all this delving around … You don't know what you'll find, and it might be something you'd rather have left hidden.'

Morag gaped. What would she find? She knew she would find what she needed. But Bridie seemed to be growing more sure of herself.

'It's just that, if Uncle won't say, then it's for a reason. We're a good family an … well, we don't hold with … witches, an … ' She trailed off into an awkward silence.

Morag drew herself up. Bridie had been good to her, but she saw now the limits to her goodness. Here, after a long winter, goodness had, like butter, been eaten up. 'I'll take my clothes now,' she said. 'They'll be dry enough.'

'Mora! Don't take offence. I speak for your good. I didn't mean …'

'Bridie, I thank you for what you've given me. Food and shelter for the night, and clean clothes. But I won't stay where people feel uncomfortable with me. I can sleep in the rondal.'

Her clothes as she changed into them – Bridie protesting that she hadn't meant any harm – were still a little damp. But they would do. Morag left the house, Bridie still flustering behind her. But Morag sensed her former friend's relief as she left. She turned her steps back to the rondal.

Chapter 15

As Morag reached the door of the rondal, the priest was coming out.

'Father,' she said, bowing her head respectfully before him, 'I am a stranger to this town and have no roof over my head. I ask your permission to sleep before the Presence tonight.' It was the accepted form: she had been with Hugh on a few occasions when a passing vagrant had asked him.

He looked at her doubtfully. He was younger than herself by maybe a dozen years. Maybe he still had that certainty of youth unclouded by the mists of experience. Maybe he still thought that a woman on her own was most likely up to no good. Then she saw his face soften. 'Tonight only?'

'Only tonight. I shall be gone in the morning.'

'Very well. Go you in, daughter, and be at peace.'

The stillness, the silence, the half-light; and across the empty space the single point of the sanctuary light glowing. All this was familiar to her, comforting. She knelt in reverence.

She found a corner against the rough wall and put down her pack. She had eaten little that day, and now she felt hunger. Well, she could manage without food for a time: for long enough. Her feet felt the woven rush mats that surrounded the altar where, as she expected, she found incense and a candle and water. She settled herself for prayer. She quieted herself, listened. Her mind was in turmoil.

Finneuchan knew something – saw something about her mother that he was not going to tell. What was it? Surely nothing could be so terrible that its knowledge was worse than not knowing. And Bridie – what was this talk of witches? Well, she had been sent on her way by those she trusted. By Hugh. And by a voice that spoke to her from within. She must trust that voice.

Half-way through the meditation she heard a small noise at the door. She noticed it, and let it go.

She finished her prayer and was settling herself for a hungry night and a hungrier day on the morrow, when she heard the noise again. The door had opened, and against the dim light of dusk she saw the shape of a woman who entered, made a reverence towards the sanctuary light, then came towards her. She was shorter than Morag, and her build reminded her of Aileen, with that supple but strong grace of movement. Her face she could not see in the gloaming.

'I saw you at prayer and told my husband. We can see you're in the Way. Will you break bread with us?'

'Thank you,' Morag replied. 'Who is your husband?'

'He is the priest here. You spoke with him outside. Father Fingoel.'

'Then …' Morag hesitated – she felt the irony – 'I should call you A'Phadr.' The woman inclined her head. 'I am Morag Ag'Hugh A'De, and I thank you. My husband was priest of a town away in Westerland.'

The other looked at her. She knows there's a story there, Morag thought. But the woman simply said, 'I am Kethia. Bring your pack. I will make sure you sleep in more comfort tonight than this.'

A wave of relief came over her, and she let it out with a sigh. 'You are kind,' she said, thankfully.

Father Fingoel looked up as they entered. His earlier slight stiffness had gone and his smile was warm. 'Welcome,' he said.

'Husband, this is Morag Ag'Hugh. She is widow of a priest in the Westerland.'

111

The sky outside was almost dark, and the children of the house were in bed. A sleepy voice called out, 'Mammy, who is it?' and was hushed.

They had finished their evening meal, but Kethia found her some food and sat her down. She ate, gratefully. They made her a pallet beside the fire. It rustled of dry fern, and the sweet scent of it surrounded her as she made ready for sleep, grateful for the fire and the food.

It had been a long day, and she was tired. She turned her mind back. She had made so much effort to come here, countering the will of all nearest to her. What now? It seemed she could only return to Caerpadraig defeated. There was no other course open to her.

Her sleep was restless. When she woke it was deep darkness, except that thin moonlight seeped between the slats of the shutters. For a time she lay, trying not to think. She set herself to prayer. She prayed for Shinane, whose confinement must be soon. Then it came to her to pray for the little thin child she had seen on her first evening. Finally, she repeated to herself the Heart Prayer: *O Lord, Light of the World, Chrisht of my heart, be near me*. But she seemed only to grow more wakeful. At last she threw over any hope of sleep.

She rose carefully, reached for her cloak and wrapped it around her. Silently she felt her way to the door and inched back the bar. Blessed be, it ran smoothly in its wooden stays. The door creaked a little, but now it was open wide enough for her to slip out.

A waning moon was high in the sky, and its light silvered the thatch. The frosty blades of grass lanced her bare feet with a hundred needles at each footprint. At first she gasped, and then each further step was a drawing up of energy. She felt alive.

The gates will be barred, she thought, but there is still the loughside. There was almost no wind, and long smooth rollers sailed majestically towards her across a sea of glass. Their steady, plangent rhythm – break, and swash, and backwash – was like a solemn song. She caught up her skirts and raised one foot, expectant. On the break she slid it forward. Lifted onto her toes. Closed with the other foot. Forward. Lift. Close. A stately dance. This was where she felt most truly herself.

Shining down on her, the moon slowly, slowly paled. Frost on the stones tingled her feet. The line of the eastern hills gradually appeared, a deeper darkness against the dark. The sky greyed into pearl. Then, quite suddenly, she saw a small cloud flush with pink and peach. She stilled her steps, turned, and watched. The stars went out: all but one, that hung like a herald above the world. The eastern sky brightened, brightened; yet no sun appeared. It was as if the world awaited some powerful chieftainess to come forth from her house, and though the door stood open yet they did not see her. Still not, and still …

A line of fire ran along the hills. And an arc of unbearable brilliance burned a dimple in the etched horizon while silent trumpets sounded from the sea-clear sky. Morag stood, bowed, raised her arms and washed herself in the first rays of the sun.

She stood still again. She turned, and almost with surprise looked upon the town above her, clear now in the morning light. Here and there smoke began to appear from the roofs. A baby cried. A woman's voice was suddenly raised, and as suddenly quieted again. Three children burst from a door and ran calling to each other into the jumble of houses. She heard a slow, regular splash, and turned to the lough. A fishing boat was coming in, low in the water, rowed by her silent crew.

She turned again, and slowly walked up to the town. Each step brought her a little further out of the otherness into the world of everyday.

Morag stopped. Against the wall of one of the houses, in a narrow space where two dwellings crowded upon each other, was a small heap of rags. It began to move. Then a tousled head emerged, a shock of dirty brown hair tangled around the thin face. The child sat up, then saw her. She crouched, ready to run. It was the young girl she had seen the evening she arrived; the girl she had remembered in the night.

The waif looked to be maybe ten years old. Then she spoke, and it was clear she was older. 'Please, I dinna mean nae harm. I willnae take naethin.'

Morag drew near and squatted beside her. 'What are you doing here, child?' she asked.

'I … I was waitin for ye, Mither. When I saw ye yestereve, I knew tae wait for ye.'

'Why? What do you mean?'

'I've naeone here nae more, Mither. Not since me mam died mid-winter.'

Morag did not know what to say. She hesitated. 'What's your name?'

'Sorcha, Mither. I willnae take naethin …'

'Peace, Sorcha. I mean you no harm. Have you nowhere to go?'

Morag studied her. The thin grey face, the sunken cheeks: she was trembling with cold. But there was something about the child's eyes that held her; reached through to touch her heart.

'Please, Mither …' the child looked up at her with huge brown eyes. 'Do ye have a wee bite I could have?'

'Sorcha, child … I've nothing. I'm a stranger in this town. It's only because the priest's wife took me in that I had a roof over my head last night. But – I will try to get you something. Why don't you go and shelter in the rondal? I'll find you there when I can.'

'I dinna like to go alone,' the child replied. 'It's a holy place, an I'm only … I'm only Sorcha the beggar-child.'

'It's all right, love,' Morag said. 'Holy places are for such as you, who see that they are holy places. Come – take my hand.'

Such a fragile wrist, she thought, as she stood and led the young girl towards the rondal: skin and bone. She saw her into the same corner that she herself had settled in the night before. Then: 'Here. Take my cloak,' she said. 'I shall need it later, but it can keep you warm for now.'

She knocked quietly on the door of the priest's house and pushed it open. The family was at prayer, and a little girl's wide grey eyes were turned momentarily upon her; then, as she winked back, instantly closed tight again. She padded across to them and knelt into the silent circle.

And now, the final blessing spoken, Kethia introduced her. 'Children, this is Mother Morag. She came after you were all in bed last night, and she's joining us for first-food.'

They rose, and almost at once Kethia was bustling into the kitchen, calling to her offspring. 'Nial, go and fetch some water… Chriosda: oats in the pot with a pinch of salt… Bring some more sticks from the back, Keith. Yes – now!'

She told Kethia about Sorcha.

'Oh, that wee mite! First her grandmother died – she was a widow who had nothing – then her mother followed her. Maeve used to serve, until her master got her with child. Then his wife wanted her out of the house, and no other would take them in. They lived in the old woman's hovel at the edge of the town and did

115

what they could to make ends meet. Never enough. And since Maeve died she's lived on scraps here and there that folk have slipped her. For we all see her and want to do what we can.'

'May I take her a little of my porridge?'

'I have some dry food here to give you for your journey. Perhaps you can give her some of that.'

As they were finishing their first-food, Fingoel turned to Morag. 'So, you are on your way today.'

She paused. 'I am, Father. But … may I ask your advice?'

'I am listening.'

Kethia sent the children away and quietly sat down. Morag told them everything that lay heavy on her heart.

They sat, listening, as she and Hugh might have done in another time and place. Fingoel listened quietly, his chin in his hand. Hugh would have placed the tips of his fingers together.

When she had done, Fingoel was still for some time. He was about to speak when they heard a call at the door. He raised his head. 'Perhaps an answer comes,' he remarked as he rose. He seemed to know who was there.

Morag listened to the half-heard conversation. She had heard that voice before. In a moment Fingoel ushered in the old, stooped man in his black gown: Finneuchan. She stood.

He stepped towards her. He had something in his hand. Suddenly, with surprising energy, he drew a knife from its sheath and dropped it, point down, into the earth before her. She stared at it as it quivered, still vibrating from its fall. Her own knife.

'And don't go without it again!' he cried. 'Ye don't yet realise. This is a tool of your trade.'

At once he softened. 'It's because ye dinna yet ken who ye are. Take it, an don't be separated from it. An learn how to use it!'

Gingerly she bent down and grasped the haft. She could feel it, still shaking – a finer tremor than her own hand. 'It's my knife …' she said, stupidly.

'Aye, it's yours. An I wasted a deal o' time finding it as well.' He folded his gown under him and sat, uninvited.

'How did you find it?' she asked him.

Finneuchan looked at her with his red-rimmed eyes. 'Knife speaks to knife,' he said, with a slow smile. 'Ye saw my knife, yesterday, plunging of itself into the ground. Speaking it was.'

He paused, as if to let his words sink in. Then he continued. 'I asked, *Whose knife?* It answered, *The knife of the Daughter.* Then I asked, *Where is the knife?* and it said, *With your brother's daughter. Is there danger?* I asked. *Not now*, it said. *But the Daughter will have need of it.* So I went, and that silly niece of mine had forgotten all about it until I got angry wi her. Then she found it and I brought it. I knew you must be here.'

'Father,' she began. Fingoel looked up, but her eyes were upon the old man. 'How can a knife speak to you?'

He sighed. 'It jumps up on its hind legs and opens its mouth!' he cried. Then he raised his hand and let a stillness gather around it. 'It speaks in here, girl.' He tapped his chest. 'An those that will listen can hear it. For nothin happens without meaning. An I fancy ye can hear it too, only ye don't know yet what to listen for, do ye?'

'Father,' she said, 'I value your wisdom. I was asking just now whether I should return directly to my home, or if there is something more I need to do.'

'No. For now, nothin more,' returned Finneuchan. 'It's sorry I am for your trouble. Ye came to find what I couldnae tell you, an now it's to home ye must turn agin without gaining what ye wanted. But I think ye'll no return alone. And – go by Kethia's Stone.'

Fingoel spoke. 'Aye. That would be the safer way. To the Crossways, and then the west road onto the muir.'

'It's no for safety's sake that I tell her, priest. No road is safe. There's more to it than that.'

She opened her mouth to speak, but Finneuchan had not finished. There was an energy in the way he addressed himself to her. 'An one thing more. Never call yersel Mi'Mhurdogh again. Ye're no his daughter, for he disowned you, he and his family. When you have need – you will know – call yersel the Daughter. That's a good enough name for anyone.'

He stood to leave, and the energy seemed to drain from him. Again he was just an old man, bent and feeble. Finneuchan, the son of Targuid, the son of Tarshan.

Chapter 16

Fingoel closed the door on Finneuchan. Quiet fell on them. Morag looked down. What did he mean, *the Daughter?* What was he telling her by this? Strangely, even remembering his words that no road was safe, the title brought a new calm to her. And Kethia's stone: it was long since she had heard that name. She raised her eyes and looked from one to the other.

It was the priest who broke the silence. 'You'll have come by way of the Stone, of course.' Before she could deny it, he continued, 'It's from that tale my Kethia is named.'

'Aye,' his wife replied. 'But I hope I never have to match her for courage.'

Morag called to mind the story told by her grandmother: how Kethia – some called her Saint Kethia, but most tellings were from a time before Rortan came – had met the three armies at the crossing of the ways. Their chieftains had refused to talk to each other, for they were sworn enemies. But Kethia had driven her flock between them and struck her staff into the ground in anger against them. Before a sword could be drawn or a spear cast, a thick fog came over all, so that no man could see his enemy to strike at him, and could not tell if each grey shape were friend or foe.

Kethia's staff still stood, a column of stone the height of three men. And her flock: great boulders strewn across the strath, there at the Crossways.

'You know your way back?' inquired Fingoel. 'Follow the road from the main gate of the town southward.'

'I didn't come past Kethia's stone,' said Morag at last. 'I came by the downfall.'

119

Fingoel raised his eyebrows. 'You'll find this an easier path then,' he said. 'Walk up to the Stone, where the ways cross, and take the westward road from there. It climbs up onto the muir.'

The three sat moments more in silence. Then Morag rose, gathered her skirts and said, 'Then, thank you. I must leave you and make the most of the day.'

Kethia rose and returned carrying a neat bundle. 'Look,' she said, 'Here's a little food I've got ready to help you with your journey. Slip it into your pack.' It was dry food, easy to carry: two bannocks.

Morag took her leave of the priest and his wife. Before she left, she blessed their grain jars by way of thanks. 'You do it like a priestess,' Fingoel said. Then she turned towards the rondal to find Sorcha. She hated the thought of taking her cloak away from the starving girl, but knew she needed it herself. She thought the child might be gone; that she might have to waste time finding her. But as she left the priest's house she almost stumbled across her. Sorcha was crouching by the wall, still wrapped in the cloak, waiting for her.

Morag said, gently, 'Child, I hope my cloak warmed you. But I must ask it from you now, for I am leaving this place.'

To her surprise she saw the girl was already taking it off, bundling it in her arms, offering it to her. It might have come easier, she thought, if she had had to pull it from her.

She took it. But now Sorcha grabbed the last corner, holding on with her thin little hand, the sinews standing out from the white skin. 'Take me with you, Mither. Please.'

Morag gasped. 'Child, you know I can't!'

'I willnae be a nuisance. I can make a fire. I can catch conies. Please: there's naethin for me here.'

She saw the desperation in the child's eyes. She recalled the hard, stern look she had seen for herself in the eyes of the shareg when he spoke of the town's want. But this child, denied food, was yet full of life. She saw hope of life in her. And something else. Something in Morag resonated with Sorcha's presence, as if there were threads in them that tangled, entwined.

'Who's your father, child? Why will he not care for you?'

'Me da willnae have naethin to do wi me. He an me mam nither married. An when he married another woman, he turned aside from us.'

It was a repetition of her own story. How did this shareg allow it, she wondered. But what she asked aloud was, 'Who is your da?'

'His name is Eoghan. Eoghan Ma'Mhurdogh Ma'Chonor. He's a big man in the town, an talks wi the shareg.'

Morag's grip on her cloak slackened. Once more she was standing before this shareg, seeing those hard eyes, hearing the curt voice: *No, Shareg. I cannot say I know her.* She hesitated a moment more. She decided, took a deep breath, and opened her hand.

'Come then,' she said. 'Is there anything you need to bring?'

'Ye'll take me wi you? For real? Ye're a good one, Mither: ye willnae regret me.'

'That's all right, love. It seems we're family, you and me. Eoghan Ma'Mhurdogh is my brother, through his father's line. It seems I'm your aunt.'

The child stared at her. 'Me antie? So – I'm no alone wi no family?'

'No,' said Morag, wondering. *And nor am I,* she thought. *I have a blood relation who will own me.* She took Sorcha's hand and together they walked towards the gate. She knew that, for both of them, once outside there would be no more admittance.

They walked in unclouded sunshine, a gentle southerly wafting the first of the spring's warmth in their faces. The two bannocks Kethia had given her would not be enough for both of them over two days' hard walk. Somehow they must manage.

They soon passed the town meadows and the wood that filled the valley floor beyond. She paused to rest a hand on the fallen oak and murmur a word of thanks.

The tumble of rocks Morag had climbed down two days before rose in the distance. She was grateful that today their path was easier. Sometimes they had to cross streams and bigger burns that bubbled down to the river flowing beside their way. Here and there were slab-stone bridges, but mostly they splashed through the water, she holding her skirts and thanking the good boots Hugh had provided her with; the child paddling her bare feet across the stones.

Always as they walked, the hills on both sides rising to brown humps streaked and patched with white, Morag felt their smallness. She pictured them, tiny and vulnerable, walking a narrow track in the vastness that surrounded them. There were eyes in the hills: green and red and grey. Watching, always watching. She wondered: with what intentions?

As the sun reached its height, she saw Kethia's flock scattered across the strath: some no taller than she, some as big as a house: grey rock, and rock that sparkled white with quartz, all patched with grey-green and black and yellow lichen. The stones stood rooted in the valley floor, for ever grazing the wiry mountain grasses that had grown around them for years beyond counting. Their stony heads were down, pointing up the strath, their crutches ragged and fronded with fern. A fox, dark-coated and watchful, turned her head at her footfall and slunk into her earth somewhere beneath one of the flock.

She passed between them. Ahead of her, like a giant shepherd's staff stuck in the ground and drawing the eye, she saw the Stone. They stopped. Kethia's staff rose before them, taller than three men, thicker than a great tree. As they approached, they saw it was marked on all sides with carvings that must be the letters of a lost tongue. Might they be marks of power?

'Is this the Staff?' Sorcha's voice sounded even smaller in that large place. 'They say that if ye put your hands on them marks, ye'll receive wisdom from the saint.'

'We could do with a bit of wisdom just now.' Morag looked down at her companion. The girl nodded solemnly.

Morag looked up at the Stone. A tuft of grass sprouted from a crack near its tip. She unslung her pack, took off her shoes, and slowly approached. As she went forward she felt as if something quickened within the stone itself, a flow of energy catching flame, filling her to the marrow with awe. She raised her hands. Hesitated.

Come, said the Stone.

How? said her heart.

Come.

May I?

You may. But can you? Can you overcome yourself? Come.

She hesitated. Then she took a step forward and spoke aloud: 'In the name of Ghea.' But she felt as if an unseen force was pushing against her hands. She could not advance. She took a deep breath and pushed back. Pushed, and suddenly broke through. Her palms stuck to the deep-chiselled marks. They held there as if to grave the solid stone with the imprint of her hands.

She stood in the embrace of the stone, and slowly her body softened. Moments passed. Then, in an instant, something changed. Joy. It seemed to bubble up from a deep well that lay somewhere in those wild hills. Even if she lost sight of it, she knew it could never be quenched. She clung to the stone and the joy coursed through her. A space, and the vision began to recede. Slowly she withdrew her hands. She stepped back. Pressing her palms together before her breast she bowed in reverence. She straightened. Turned. Walked slowly away to where her pack lay in the grass. She was hungry.

Sorcha looked at her.

'Ye look different, Antie. Like … the saint's spoken with ye.'

She looked at the thin girl. What was it she saw? But all she said was, 'Come. Sit down, and we'll share some food.'

Chapter 17

The path from the crossroads climbed steadily across the face of the braes towards the west. By mid-afternoon they had reached the high moor that stretched before them. They passed the spot where she and Dhion had slept, where the visitor had come in the night. With little in her belly, Morag was beginning to tire. They walked on.

It was Sorcha who found them a place. She spotted a clump of low trees bent by the weather. As they drew closer she pointed towards a stand of trees that stood at the head of a little glen, where there was shelter from the wind that blew steadily, searchingly, around them. Between some rocks they found a pile of last year's fern, dry enough to sit upon.

'Hae ye a knife, Antie?' the girl asked.

Morag started. 'Ye…es,' she replied. She wondered, but unsheathed it and passed it to the child.

Sorcha took it and looked admiringly at the blade. 'Dang,' she said, 'It's a knife like this that I'd like.' She jumped to her feet and, without saying another word, disappeared down the glen.

She returned after a short while with some sticks and a small rotten log. Morag watched, curious and a little in awe, as the child whittled a short, stout stick to a point. Another she bent like a bow and, seeming satisfied, released it again. Neatly she ripped a thin strip of cloth from her dress. It was so torn already it scarce made any difference. She tied it across the two ends of the bowed stick.

'What are you doing, child?' she asked; but she guessed the answer.

'We'll want a fire, won't we?' Sorcha replied. She seemed in her element. Knowing. Sure. First she

125

squatted and prepared her tools. The log she held between her bare feet, with the pointed stick pushing into its pale, dry fibres. Back and forth flew the little bow. The stick whizzed. At last, a thin thread of smoke. It grew thicker, yellowish, acrid-smelling. And then … a tiny glow in the tinder. It winked red, disappeared, came again, crawled snail-like round the edge of a crack. As the tinder began to glow she blew, so gently, upon it. A yellow flame sprang up. She held a thin dry twig in its heat, then carefully plunged it into a small pile of dry fern. So precious – no newborn babe could have received more tenderness.

As the evening darkened around them, they prepared for the night. Morag was glad to rest, to warm herself by the fire the child had provided. As for food – they must do without. To take their minds off their hunger, Morag started to talk.

She praised Sorcha's skill in getting the fire going and said how glad she was for its warmth. Then she thought it would be good to tell her something of where they were going.

Did she have a home of her own, Sorcha wanted to know.

Well, yes – for a little while. One with plenty of room for the two of them. But soon? Morag began to think about how it would be for her to return, not one person, but two. She had not noticed that Caerpadraig was so very short of provisions, like Kimmoil. But was it just that, as the priest's widow, people had been looking after her? As they had always done before.

At length Sorcha damped the fire down, surrounding it with clods of earth. 'That'll stay in for the mornin now,' she said. Morag spread her cloak so that the two of them could share it and she and the child lay down together.

She lay awake a long time, turning over all that had passed. She had come away without the thing she had sought. Yet, how different was the landscape of her mind from that which filled her the last time she laid her head on the moor. Then she had been all eager expectation. And now? Her mind was filled with tantalising fragments. Bron: a name, or a part-name, meaning breast – which was the one thing her mother had certainly given her. And then Finneuchan bursting in: *You are the Daughter.* And a hint of unknown persons who might, one day, choose to tell her more. In all these hints and half-hints there was one very clear change. The last time she had lain on the moor, it had been under the protection of Dhion. Now, instead of her son, it was her new-found niece who lay slumbering beside her.

Morag listened to the deep, even breathing of the child. But how much of a child was she, she wondered? The want the girl had been living in had surely stunted her growth. Did she herself know how many summers she had seen? At least she seemed to be having a good night's sleep now. And who was protecting whom, Morag wondered. Without the girl's skill, they would be cold this night as well as hungry.

She woke in the middle of the night. Sorcha was snuggled against her, her knees drawn up to her chest. Morag drew the cloak more closely around them.

Then she saw the eyes.

A pair of eyes, faint in the night, but looking straight at her, reflecting the fire-glow.

Her mind sprang to the wolf that had visited that other night on the moor. But these were not wolf-eyes. They were the eyes of a man. 'In the name of Ghea,' she whispered.

'You've awakened at last, Mother.' It was a man's voice, rough, a little ironic, very quiet. 'I've been watching you this while.'

Morag sat up, reaching about her. She had left her knife with Sorcha.

The ironic voice spoke again: 'Looking for your knife, is it, Mother? Well, you won't be needing it just now.'

She sat up, placing herself between the man and the still-sleeping child. She was numb with fear. Her mind went to Micheil's words before she left Caerpadraig: *There are men out there who would knife you for a bag of corn.* 'We've eaten the only food we had. Look.' She reached for her empty pack and turned it upside-down. Her knife fell heavily into the fern. The child must have put it in there.

Before she had taken in what had happened, the man uncoiled, and quicker than thinking his hand closed upon the knife's haft.

'So you did,' he said. 'But here's something worth taking care of!' He tossed the knife into the air, spinning it, and caught it again. Suddenly he leaned forward. 'Shouldn't you be looking after it rather better?' She saw in the dim glow of the fire that he had actually caught it by the blade. Now he held it, its haft towards her, offering it to her. 'Take it. You never know when you might need it.'

Her fingers closed around the haft. 'What do you want?' she asked.

'Well. A share in the warmth of your fire for a start, Morag Ag'Hugh.'

Her heart turned cold. *How does he know my name?* She felt the solidity of the knife in her hand. What game was he playing with her?

'Morag Ag'Hugh. You are, aren't you?' Suddenly his voice was dark, rich, warm, with more than a touch of humour. 'You have nothing to fear from me. Will you trust me – who gave you back your knife?'

She stared at him.

He went on, easily, 'We can talk more in the morning,' he said. 'But for now, sleep. May I take the other side of the fire?' And with that he chose his spot, opposite them.

For a long moment she gazed at him across the embers, searching this side and that for any way out. She found none. What could she do but consent? She did so wordlessly. And saw that he saw it. At once he lay full length, wrapping his cloak around him. Before settling down he turned his head, looking at her over his shoulder. In the dull firelight she saw his face – sharp, strong, wolfish, his black beard short and pointed. 'Goodnight, Mother Morag,' he called softly. 'Sleep well!'

She could not get his measure. She would stay awake. At all costs she must not sleep. She felt the knife, still in her hand. Even if he was the stronger, more skilled than she, if need came she would defend them as best she could.

She woke. Sorcha was gone. The morning was cold and grey. She jerked awake and stared across the smouldering fire. There was no sign of the man either. Dread fastened a clammy hand on her belly.

How could she have slept? Could she not watch this short time, even for the sake of a child? She jumped up, knife in hand. She had heard how some could follow tracks through the wild. She lacked the skill, yet still she looked about her for any clue which way they had gone. The girl would slow him down, perhaps … Oh, why did she sleep?

A voice! A young voice: Sorcha's, calling from behind her. She span round. There she was, coming down the glenside, the man behind her.

'Sorcha!'

'Antie! Look what we caught!'

The ragged waif ran up to her, dangling a hare proudly in her hand. Morag grabbed her other arm and gripped her knife tight, holding it before them.

'Antie! What're ye doin? He's no a bad un. This is Wolf.' Sorcha wriggled free of Morag's protecting arm and stood before her. 'We caught the cony taegither, we did!'

The man came nearer, a slow grin spreading across his face. He held his arms up, the hands empty. She glanced at him. There was his own knife, stuck in his belt. He could so easily draw it the moment she dropped her guard. 'Keep away from her!' she commanded. But her voice sounded feeble: wrong, absurd.

'Antie!' The girl's cry was now desperate. 'He's awricht! Look!' She waved the hare frantically before her. 'We've bin huntin conies taegither!'

Slowly, his hands now spread open before her, the man came closer. 'She's right,' he said. 'I'm no a bad un. Really.' He was looking right at her. 'So, your first try at knifework, and before first-food too!'

She dropped her guard, overcome.

'Who are you?' she asked weakly.

'One who wanders in the wild. But – like she said – I'm no a bad un. They call me Wolf. God be with you, Morag Ag'Hugh.'

She felt foolish standing there, her knife pointing weakly at the earth. 'Ghia keep you,' she replied in a subdued voice. She slid her knife into its sheath.

'May we cook you some first-food?'

His words released her. There was Sorcha, blowing up the fire, feeding it with twigs. They both seemed more sure of themselves out here than she. Still feeling foolish, she sat down to watch.

Wolf and Sorcha squatted by the fire, the hare between them. She caught snatches of their talk. Despite herself she almost smiled to hear them, as if the child was teaching the man. 'An ye must haulk it like this – take out the guts – Mind that green bit: it's well bitter.' She suspected he already knew.

She took stock of the man. He wore leather boots and woven woollen trews, strengthened at the knees by leather patches. His body was cased in a leather jerkin. His dark beard accentuated the lines of his angular face, while his hair, long and jet-black, was tied behind the nape of his neck, like her own. When he moved he seemed to flow, as if he had long before considered the best way, and perfected it. A high-crowned brimmed hat lay crouching like a wild beast on the ground where he had slept.

They had found some herbs – she smelled bog myrtle – and an appetising aroma soon arose from where pieces of meat were broiling on hot stones around the fire. She watched the man whom Sorcha called Wolf. Certainly the name suited him. But it disturbed her that he knew her full name, and had not given in return his own. Now he turned towards her. 'Come and eat,' he invited. 'Bring your knife. You'll need it.'

She suddenly hated him, his bearing, so assured. But why hate? When she only hated him for having what she used to have; what, since Hugh's death, she had no more. She took her knife: saw how he was using his, cutting and spearing pieces of meat on its point. She took charge of herself.

Sorcha was sitting close to Wolf, clearly completely at her ease. She was gnawing the meat off the bones hungrily, holding them in both hands. They had left her her portion.

Morag squatted by the fire, beside the girl. The smell on the air! Her own hunger made her bold. She stabbed at a piece. Bit. It tasted delicious! But there were still questions she needed answers to. Between mouthfuls she asked them.

'How did you know my name?'

He paused, licking his fingers. 'I've known of you a long time,' he said. 'And I've been expecting you to make this journey. It was my friends told me when you were on the road.'

'What friends?'

'I cannot be everywhere, but they can. They tell me much that happens.'

'I haven't seen anybody – not out here.'

He smiled. 'I think you have, only you didn't know. Don't you remember, the last night you slept out on the moor?'

She remembered only the wolf. Did wolf talk to Wolf?

'You're a canny man?'

'Some people call me so. Some call me uncanny. Most people don't know. But I think you know; except you don't realise it yet. That's why I'm here.'

'How can I trust you? That you are what you say, and not what you seem?'

'Och, for God's sake, woman! I've given you your knife, in your hand! And there you are, holding it. Besides …' His voice softened. 'Feel inside you. What do you feel me to be?'

She took a breath. She saw Sorcha's big eyes upon her. They were both watching. He watched intensely, not just with his eyes. So had she seen Shean Blacksmith, watching the temper of a billet of iron in the fire; she felt the intensity of mind.

'How did you know I was here now?'

'I saw your smoke. Besides, I knew you must come this way. Shareg Donal of Kimmoil let you stay longer than I thought. And I knew you wouldn't be climbing up the way you slid down into Strath Moil.'

'Have you been watching me all the way?'

'I told you. Not always myself. I hear from my friends. Not many people cross the moor without my knowing of it. But listen: I didn't come here to bandy words with you. I bear a message.'

She stared at him.

'You crossed the moor to Kimmoil to find yourself, through knowing your mother. Isn't that so?'

She nodded, slowly. She had gone beyond surprise.

'You will know your mother in time. But not just yet. Finneuchan knew the time is not ripe. You must wait for it to ripen. We will call you when it is time. Only wait.'

He speared a last piece of broiled hare, and chewed slowly on it.

She did not know what to say. She sat in silence, looking at her hands, holding the knife uselessly in her lap. At last she found words.

'Who are you? What is your real name? Who sent this message by you?'

His grey eyes stared at her. He went on chewing.

At length he swallowed.

'I know it's hard for you not to have answers. But I've said all I have been charged to say for now. If I say more, well … It will be better for you to wait until the time when you can be told in the right way, and can understand fully. For now –' He wiped his fingers on the grass and rose in one smooth movement. 'We must all be on our way. You know your road from here? Tell it me.'

Morag looked at him. Another wave of mistrust made her waver.

'We will be continuing along the path we trod yesterday,' she said, seeking to fend him off.

'And then?' She felt the keen eyes boring into her, Sorcha watching them both. She hoped she knew the way. Dhion had schooled her in it. But that was four days ago. Much had happened since. And everything was now seen from the other side.

So he told her, in minute detail, what to look out for, and bade her repeat it after him. Morag felt he told them true. But it was Sorcha who did the repeating.

He nodded at the child approvingly. 'The girl has it,' he said.

He looked back at Morag, looked her in the eye. She held herself aloof.

'Well,' he said. 'You go that way, and I, this.' He nodded across the dull dun moor. There was no path

Morag could see. He stooped, picked up his hat, and turned, his eyes once again looking deeply into her. 'Look after this little one.' He put his hand on Sorcha's shoulder. The girl turned her brown eyes lovingly back to him. 'There's more to her than you yet know.'

He smiled.

'We will meet again, we three. Until then, wait – and thank you for your hospitality this night.'

He turned his back and walked off. She watched him stride into the wilderness. It was time to turn to their own path.

Chapter 18

Shinane moaned. It was the dark of the night. She felt a tightening of her belly, stronger than the ones that had come before. She eased herself out of bed and walked around. The cramp would not let her go.

Dhion was snoring lightly. She prodded him.

'It's getting worse.'

He turned, drowsily. 'It's only the weather.'

'The pains, love. They're worse. I think it's starting.'

He sat up, suddenly awake. 'You're sure?'

'They're worse,' she repeated, 'and they're coming more often. I feel it's time.'

She knew she was right. Tight and cramping and inexorable, one spasm would grow and peak and subside again. A short while, and another would come: one after another, like the waves of the sea. Not bad – not yet – but ominous.

He swung his legs off the bed and wrapped a cloak around him. She caught his man-scent as the bed-covers stirred. She sat back on the bed, took his place, feeling the warmth where he had lain, listening impatiently as he blew up the embers of the fire. At last, a tiny point of light, and a flame caught on the spill in his hand. He lit a rush-light and looked into her face.

'Should we send for Rhona?'

Another spasm came, harder. She heard herself moan.

He turned from her and balanced the light on a stone that jutted from the wall. By its faint glow she watched him pull on his clothes. Fumbling in the dimness of the house, he found the lamp, lit it and set it on its stand. He reached over her for the rush-light.

'Tell Mother first, will you? She could come straight away.'

'I'll be back very soon.' He bent and kissed her.
'Be quick, won't you. I'm scared.'

She heard the door close and a few moments later a muffled knocking at the smithy. There would not be long. Not long before her mother came and there would be no more silence. This was her time. Frightening as it was to be alone, still it gave her the space she needed.

Her thoughts came in between, in the troughs between the waves. When a pain was on her it took her over completely. But this was also urgent. She waited for the troughs.

Almost as pressing as the pains that were insisting on her energies, more pressing than the fear that was creeping into her, was this other question. Could she let herself be carried and held? Could she descend into this unknowing between death and life, and emerge whole: not as before, but as she must become? Or would it conquer her, lessen her, take her prisoner, overcome her entirely?

She rested her hands on her stretched belly. It felt hard: rock-hard, harder even than the hardness of her man's thigh-muscles. Solid. Purposeful. It was gathering its strength for its purpose. She thought: this was where she and Dhion were joined. Here, in this being – these two beings – who this day would make their way into the light. This was where she must feel into. Deep. Deep. Here they were one. She breathed, and it was as if each breath went deeper, until her belly was filled with fire, a deep red glow that filled her, melted her. Now.

The door grated open. There was her mother, still drawing a shawl over her round shoulders. She came near. *Hold. Hold deep.*

'There you are, pet. Are you warm enough?'
She nodded.

'See, this one was first. We've tied this wool round her wrist. This is your eldest.'

A noise at the door. Someone coming or going. The doorway briefly giving onto a larger world. And beyond, the twilight.

Chapter 19

'Why did ye doubt him, Antie?'

They had broken camp as soon as Wolf left them. Morag's mind was in a whirl. Not only was she still turning over what their visitor had meant, by his coming as much as by his words. But also, again and again, she was amazed by Sorcha's assurance. Was it that the child was too innocent – Morag could scarce believe it – to think ill of people? Or that she was so much better than herself in reading them? Very definitely the girl was older than she looked. She knew what to do, here in the wild. And the man she called Wolf was also a man of the wild. He had made that clear.

Now they were following the well-worn track that crossed the moor from north to south, from the Northland to Westerland. At the girl's question she paused her thoughts without breaking her step.

Why did she mistrust him, really? Of course, it was not surprising she should be alarmed by his sudden appearance among them at night. But after that, she had to allow, his actions had shown him true. Still it rankled with her. His assurance, like the girl's, was what she lacked. Sorcha had at first been vulnerable, in need, crying out for help. Now, she had to acknowledge, they were each helping the other. Wolf? In him she saw an utter lack of need. She coveted his needlessness.

'He really is a good un, ye ken, Antie,' Sorcha was insisting. 'Do ye no feel it too?'

Yes, if she was honest, she did feel it. But something else stood in the way. What was it? Something she was not yet prepared to admit. Something she had just made a great effort to try to resolve. It was all tied up with not knowing any more who she was, where she stood.

⮞⮜

They reached Caerpadraig in the light of a luminous green evening. Niall the cowman was bringing Micheil's cattle in from the loughside, and they followed the swaying black backs as the kine patiently plodded the path from meadow to byre.

A figure hailed him. She looked up and saw in the distance the unmistakable rolling gait of the shareg. He had seen her at once.

'Morag,' he called. 'It's glad I am indeed to see you home again so soon!'

The cowman looked over his shoulder, unaware he had been followed. 'A'Phadr!' he exclaimed. Even the cattle stopped, and swung their slow heads round, jostling their mottled horns as their big brown eyes rolled.

Micheil let his herd pass, and they followed on together. The scent of the cattle filled the air.

'It's good to see you home again,' he repeated. 'Safe, and well.' Then he turned his gaze to her companion. 'And who is this?' he inquired.

He looked down with his searching eyes at Sorcha, who looked back at him, as candid as an open flower.

'This is Sorcha,' Morag explained. 'My niece. And an orphan since mid-winter.'

She watched her shareg's face. She knew he appraised, not just the child, but the whole situation. She remembered the shareg of Kimmoil. She waited while he paused a good while, considering.

Then he said, slowly: 'Well, Sorcha. Your aunt is a woman of standing, much respected in this town. As we welcome her home, you are welcome with her.'

Relief spread through Morag – though what had she been expecting? As she turned to Sorcha, she saw a huge smile light up the girl's whole being, shining through her tatters. And she was saying, 'Thank ye, sir. Ye'll no regret it. I'll make mysel useful for sure.'

Micheil's eyes twinkled. 'Will you now, young Sorcha,' he said. 'That's good. There's plenty for a useful person to do here.'

He turned back to Morag.

'And there's news for you as well – I'm no the one to bring it. Let it be that son of yours. But I'll say this much: it's good news!'

'Shinane?'

'Oh aye,' he replied. 'I've never known Shean so free with his beer. But hurry ahead and see for yourself. Don't wait for me. I'll plod along behind my girls here.' He slapped the nearest cow's rump. 'Come to us when you're ready.' he added. 'When you're quite rested!'

Morag turned to the big-eyed girl who stood, waiting beside her, taking everything in. 'Come, Sorcha,' she said. 'This can't wait. It's family. It's a birth.'

Taking the skirt of her gown in one hand and her new-found niece in the other, she forced her way between the black hides and flicking tails and pushed to the front. 'God be with you, Niall,' she called out as she passed. She scarcely heard his answering, 'Ghea keep you, A'Phadr,' as she almost ran, Sorcha following, up the path towards the town and the little house behind the smithy.

Before she was through the door there was a voice from within. 'Who is it, Mother?' Then, 'Morag! Is that you?'

Before anything else, as she entered the dark little house, she noticed the smell. A warm, milky smell. A comfortable, motherly sort of smell. As her eyes accustomed to the gloom she saw Shinane, lit by the only light in the place. She was sitting up in the bed-space, a cloak over her shoulders, her smock unlaced and her breasts bare. In the crook of each arm lay a tiny shape.

'Shinane,' she whispered. 'Micheil hinted, but – you're glowing. And twins! A two-fold blessing!'

The new mother leaned a little towards her and the child in her left arm mewled and made little sucking noises. Morag bent to look at the tiny, puckered face.

'When?'

'Only last night. They're not a day old yet.'

Dhion brought more lights and more stools. Sorcha stood near the doorway, looking in, waiting her turn. Now Morag told the story of their meeting.

'So my family is bigger by three!' she ended. She said nothing of Wolf.

Fineenh went to bring food for the travellers and returned with Shean, bearing mugs of hot beer. Huddling into a space not built for so many, they sat down together, Morag with the unaccustomed feeling of a tiny child in her arms.

Aileen had gone at once to the priest's house to make up the fire. Fineenh was giving Sorcha a clean-up, as she put it. From somewhere she had found some fresh clothes that would do. Sorcha walked to the priest's house a different-looking girl from the one who had arrived in Caerpadraig. Once inside, she looked around, big-eyed, taking in the coloured needlework on its frame, the book-stand, the big Book of Caerpadraig that rested upon it, bound in its wooden boards and covered in tooled leather. And Morag's teaching chair. 'Ye live here, Antie?'

'Just for now,' Morag replied, leaving Sorcha's question, and her own, largely unanswered.

Morag settled Sorcha in the bed-alcove Dhion had once used, and the girl fell almost instantly asleep. She took her cloak and quietly went out, a few steps beyond the houses, until the sounds of the town faded behind her. It was dark, but still a green-gold glow silhouetted the ridge of Beh' Mora. Before her, the water of the burn chattered quietly.

She stood still and listened. From up towards the pass an owl called, long and low. Another answered. A dog barked from somewhere in the town.

She breathed in the stillness and let it out again with a sigh. Again she turned over all that had passed on her journey. Backwards she trod in time, each face coming before her, tasting again their meaning. Wolf. Kethia's Stone. Father Fingoel and his family. Finneuchan. Bridie. The hard faces of her brother, Eoghan, and his shareg. The eager face of Coll Ma'Lennish as he lent forward, asking, *And the marvellous coat?* And before that, the long grey muzzle, those eyes: the wolf of the first night she had slept out in the wild.

Someone new and important had come back with her in the shape of Sorcha. Something had shifted inside her with the new life that had come from Shinane. For now, she did not need to find answers. The changing shape of the new world she was entering – that she entered each day – was enough.

She stretched out her arms to the fading sunset. Brought her hands round in an arc to her chest. Bowed her head. And for a long moment was still with the stillness of night.

Chapter 20

The new day dawned. Morag rose. And at once, there was Sorcha in her new clothes – rather too big for her: 'I've blown up the fire, Antie.'

Morag took a breath. The crackle of the new-kindled hearth had worked its way into the close of her sleep. 'Thank you, dear.' She hesitated, then added, 'I greet the day with prayer. Will you join me?'

'I will, Antie,' Sorcha replied at once. 'Show me.'

So Morag showed her where they knelt at the house altar, and bade her sit and just be for this first time as she chanted the prayers of access and protection, the blessing of the beings of earth and air and sea, and then the slipping into the wordless silence. Finally came the prayer of dedication to enter the day.

'That was beautiful, Antie. Ye're the priestess!' said Sorcha when they were done.

Morag smiled. 'No,' she said. 'There have been no priestesses here for a long time. But I was a priest's wife, until just before Samhain last year. That is why I live in this big house with a book and a stand.' The girl listened, wide-eyed.

'But soon there will come a new priest. And then I must leave,' she finished.

After first-food, Morag wished to return to her son and his new family. Indeed, she was expected for the choosing of names.

'You go, Antie. I'll tidy here and follow after.'

When she arrived, Fineenh had gone to busy herself with the washing and Shean had started work at the forge. Morag took in the new little family. Saw how the new mother's eyes were hollow and there was a greyness in her cheeks. She had had a wakeful night, Dhion said – first one twin had mewled, then the other.

No matter. Shinane was as intent as Dhion on hearing her news.

She told them of her lone journey on the moor; of the memories seeing her first homeland had evoked; of the hardness of Shareg Donal and her own half-brother.

'Your own brother!' exclaimed Shinane. 'How can that be?'

'I can understand the shareg, though,' said Dhion. 'It's the lean time of the year. And it may be they've had it harder than us, on the north of the Island.'

She told them of Bridie's welcome on the first night.

'A blessing on her! That is what we hoped for you,' cried Shinane. Morag said nothing of the exchange that led to her leaving.

She told them of her meeting with Finneuchan, and what he had told her. They listened in silence.

'So it seems, on my mother's side, I am a foreigner, like you,' she said, looking at Dhion.

He was silent a while. Then he said, 'That doesn't surprise me, somehow. It fits with your wisdom, and how you can see things from different standpoints.'

She did not tell them of her second meeting with Finneuchan and what he had said then; something held her back. Just as she felt reluctance at the thought of mentioning either of the wolves who had visited her at night.

'But you have returned with a niece! How did that happen?' demanded Shinane.

Morag told the tale.

'Well, she has been wronged!' she declared, 'As have you, by your father's people.'

'Not by my grandparents,' Morag corrected.

'Then what has come upon them since?' Shinane demanded. 'Their injustice goes beyond the common law and I do not know how their shareg upholds it.' Then, 'I wonder – could it be something to do with your mother?'

Morag made no answer. She was realising how much of her story she did not feel ready to disclose, even to these dearest ones. Finally she said, 'It may be that one day I will find out more.'

Fineenh came in, her hands and forearms red from her task. She settled herself down as her husband came behind her, and looked expectantly towards him. He took his place on the only chair in the room.

'Well,' began the new grandfather, 'We have a job to do.' Morag saw how he was relishing his new role of *shareg na teigh*, the head of the house: bringing the family together to choose the names the children would bear. Names that were no mere whim of the parents, but which would bear their ties of kinship in the town, in the world. He sat up, solid as a shareg, his hands on his knees. Shinane and her mother perched on the edge of the bed, each with a babe in one arm. Morag sat on a low bench.

Dhion was standing. He took a step forward. This was new to him, but he seemed to know what was expected. 'We have thought to have names from our mothers. So, Fineenh and Morag – but also Lois. That is the name of my birth-mother,' he told them.

Shean stared, and tried the unfamiliar sound on his tongue. '*Loesh* … I don't know. What kind of a name is that? What does it mean?'

'To me,' said Dhion, 'it means the one who helped me take my first steps.'

'Dhion tells me that in his native land it was custom to have two names,' Shinane put in swiftly. 'We thought of Lois Fineenh. The names sound pretty together. And then Morag. And now we know Morag's mother's name, perhaps … Morag Bron?'

There was a silence while Shean considered this. Then he said,'This *Loesh* sounds very unIslandlike to me. We have to think to the time to come, when the girl will be married. And who will marry her? And what questions will he ask?'

He looked defiantly from one face to another.

'Well, with mother's name as well … '

Shinane's words were cut short by a high, clear voice from the door. 'Ye have tae call the firstborn Regan!' The child's voice in the rough Northern accent – the stress on *gan* was unmistakable. Sorcha had come in unnoticed. The words seemed to burst out of her.

Shean scowled. 'Be quiet girl. It's no your place to speak.'

Sorcha did not move. She stood, her chin lifted a little. 'I meant nae harm, sir. I jus needed to tell ye. For it came to me clear last night when I saw her. Her name's Regan.'

Morag saw the intended cuff coming and, before Shean could rise, placed herself in front of her niece. She bent, holding Sorcha's eyes on a level with her own. 'Sorcha, why do you say that? We are choosing names we know; names that are in the family.'

Sorcha hung her head. 'It came to me strong, Antie,' she said.

'What do you mean? How do you know?'

'I dinna ken that.' The child was looking about her wildly now. 'I jus sometimes know things.'

Morag was not sure what to say. For Sorcha to over-step the mark so strongly on her first day at Caerpadraig did not bode well. She looked to Fineenh, seeking a clue. But before the other could shake her head, Shinane spoke slowly. 'Regan means Queen in the old tales,' she murmured. 'Great Queen.' She looked down into her firstborn's face with a seeing gaze that drew the eye. 'I like it,' she said, softly. 'It feels right.'

Morag felt a wave of relief.

Now Dhion looked to where Shinane sat rocking the child. He tried the new name. The baby made a little lip-smacking sound. 'Look,' said Shinane. 'She's smiling!'

Fineenh leaned across to see. She turned to her husband. 'Did you see that? The babe agrees as well. You'll have to let her.'

But Shean's face looked black. He slapped his knee. 'I'll no have a child of my house named at random without a name from the family!' He glared at Sorcha. The child sat cross-legged on the floor, her new skirt stretched over her knees.

'It is in the family,' insisted Sorcha. 'Ma antie's in the line of Regan.'

'Hush child,' said Morag, anxiously.

Shean's scowl swept them all. It was Fineenh who broke the silence. 'Well, I'd like my granddaughter named for a queen. And aren't we all descended from the Great Queen? Isn't she in all our lines? All say aye but you.'

Shean stood. For a moment Morag feared his anger. But then he seemed to sense he was outnumbered, and the one other man in the house against him. She could see him seeking a way out.

'We agree on Lois Fineenh,' she suggested.

Shean turned to her. 'It seems you're all set on Regan,' he complained. 'Well, don't blame me.'

'Regan Elizabeth.' It was Dhion. 'That was my birth-mother's second name.'

'Elisaith,' Morag quickly threw in. 'That's our name most like your mother's, son.'

'Oh, that's lovely!' Shinane said. Morag could see Fineenh smiling.

'Well, there we are.' The smith took charge again.'Mother, bring some beer and some bannocks. We must drink the wee ones' health.'

Morag watched Fineenh flustering, caught between her desire to serve them and her reluctance to let go of the child who would soon be named for her, Lois Fineenh. 'Let me,' she said, and gently took the babe.

Dhion turned to her. 'Mother, about the naming … the ceremony, in the rondal … We don't know when the new priest will come. I've long felt you and Hugh as priest together. Would you bless them?'

She did not answer him at first. She sat, the tiny child a tender burden in her arms. Into her heart crept something she felt with surprising force. The memory of that last day with Hugh. His stole, that she had kept from the depute, from Hugh's grave; that she still kept. A slow smile came over her. 'Let's see what I can do,' she said. 'I'll mention it when I go to see Micheil.'

Chapter 21

Micheil and Aileen invited her to tell about her travels. 'Come and join us after the Tollach, for the midday meal,' Aileen said. Sorcha came too. Morag spent a while combing out Sorcha's hair, then took her hand, and together they walked the few steps to the house next door.

'Am I to meet the shareg in his own house then, Antie? It's feared I am of people like he.'

Hardly surprising, Morag thought, after her experience of Kimmoil.

'Micheil and Aileen are friends,' she told her. 'You remember how Shareg Micheil welcomed you?' But when she called the greeting at the door she noticed how Sorcha held back.

She told them her story over the meal, repeating what she had said to Dhion and Shinane; leaving the same things out. Sorcha sat silent, looking on with her big eyes.

When she had finished, Aileen said slowly: 'So now you know your mother's name. But still – not her lineage.'

'Part name,' Morag corrected.

'Does what you've learned satisfy you?'

'No,' said Morag, simply. 'It gives me a scrap, but nothing like enough. But it seems there's nothing more I can do to find the answers.'

Had they been alone Morag knew that Aileen would have questioned her more closely. Held back for now, a silence fell between them.

It was broken by Micheil. 'Still, you've found some family, it seems. And brought a new young life among us. It is time to turn to you, young girl.'

Sorcha stood, no doubt feeling the weight of the occasion. In answer to the shareg's questions she spoke in a small voice that still kept its strength. She was the daughter of Eoghan Ma'Mhurdogh Ma'Chonor, and of Maeve, not his wife. And this same Murdogh, Sorcha's grandfather, was father to Morag.

'Indeed, that is so, Micheil,' Morag agreed.

'Then why,' the shareg asked, 'has your father not taken you in?'

'He never noticed me,' said Sorcha. 'I only knew him for my mither pointed him out. He didnae care for either of us. I dinna ken why.'

'Is there any guilt upon you, child? You must be truthful. Do they seek you for any cry against you?'

'No sir. Only I had to take a morsel or two sometimes when no one was lookin. If I hadnae done that, I wouldnae be here today.'

Micheil sat back quietly; looked at her a good while. Then he said, 'And there is nothing else?'

'No, sir. Nothing.'

Sorcha stood, a little cowed. Morag longed to say she knew the girl was honest. She also knew she must give the shareg time to come to his own view.

At last he seemed to decide. 'All right,' he said, slowly, in his resonant voice. 'Now let's move on to practical matters.' He turned to Morag. 'You are content to give a home to this girl?'

'Yes, Shareg. But I have no home to give.'

He looked at her shrewdly. 'Indeed,' he said. 'It is now almost eight weeks since Bride's Day and more than five months since Hugh left us. I expect the archpriest to announce the one to take his place soon. And the hut Dhion has prepared for you will not be enough for two.'

He paused. Morag looked questioningly into his eyes. At length he continued. 'There's a strong possibility of old Rhiseart's place. I spoke with his two daughtersmen this morning. It's been empty since he died, and a worry to them. It seems they may be willing to release it for you for as long as you need. You know it?'

imagine writing about Hugh's passing and all the events that followed. If only someone else could do it! It was then that the thought came to her: Shinane could write, too. She had developed a fair hand, now no doubt out of practice. But it would soon come back. The thought came strongly. She felt Hugh smile. She drifted back into slumber. But the thought stayed with her.

'You were talking in your sleep last night, Morag.' Fineenh addressed her, her back turned as she saw to the pot on the fire for their first-food. 'You said, *She can write, too*. More than once. There's meaning in that.'

'It was Hugh,' Morag said, simply. 'I dreamed of him last night.'

Fineenh half-turned, a dripping spoon poised over the pot. 'And what did he say?'

Morag hesitated. Could she tell her? Yes, she thought, she could.

'He wondered who would keep his book, with all the events of the town. I don't feel … I can write about the most recent events myself, you see.'

Fineenh stirred the porridge.

'I do see that would be hard for you,' she said. 'But won't the new priest keep it, when he comes?'

'He doesn't know us yet. I don't … I don't want to leave it for him. It wouldn't be right. Not before we know him, anyway. And then I thought about Shinane.'

'To be sure,' Fineenh, said, slowly, keeping an eye on the porridge, her face now fully turned away. 'The girl can write. But she's a new mother and all. She'd no have time. Whereas you – you'll have all the time in the world.'

Morag knew this would not be true. At Teigh Riseart she must plant beans and kale. There was an orchard to tend, which would give them something to exchange. And Micheil had promised her a small milch cow who would come with a sheep for company.

'Well, perhaps we can do it between us,' said Morag. 'For now. I can only tell you what came to me in my dream.' She took a step forward. 'Fineenh, Shinane's a wife and a mother, and she's good at both, but she's something more as well, isn't she? Don't you see it?'

She heard a sharp, indrawn breath. The other woman paused, stock still. To Morag's surprise, a tear was forcing its way out of the corner of Fineenh's eye. It paused a moment, caught on a crow's-foot, then rolled down her cheek. A single sob burst from her.

'What is it? What have I said?' Morag asked in consternation.

'Oh, nothing. Nothing … '

In an instant, Morag guessed at the limits that had hemmed her in through life; the longing she, Morag, had just unlocked, for her daughter to go beyond them.

It lasted no more than a breath. Then Shean came stamping in from the forge, his hands red and dripping.

Fineenh turned back to the pot and gave it a brisk stir. 'Your porridge is ready.'

Shean wiped his mouth with the back of his hand. 'I'm at Leighan's this morning. An I'm taking Dhion with me.' He rose and went out into the late spring sunshine. She heard the men's voices growing fainter down the path.

'Good,' said Morag.

Fineenh looked at her, questioning.

'My two chests are in the forge. I didn't want to go to them while they're working in there. I'm going to get Hugh's book out. I want to take it to Shinane.'

Fineenh glanced towards the door, standing ajar as her man had left it, letting in the flower-scented sunshine, the warm breeze, the buzz of bees. Her voice came faintly, as if from some far-off place. 'Are you sure?'

'Yes,' Morag answered. She was on her way out, but she turned and looked straight at her. 'Oh, yes.'

She clasped the precious book to her. Hugh's ink-horn could wait for later. There were also a couple of quills, small pots of ink powders sealed with wax, his sharp little pen-knife; all these could wait.

It was only a few steps from the smithy to the tiny house.

'In the name of God and in peace.'

Shinane opened, looking tired, but with a radiance shining through her. When she saw her visitor she put a finger to her lips before giving the response.

Then, 'Come in! They're asleep.'

It was clear how motherhood suited the girl. Morag felt the book hard against her breast and a qualm passed through her. Was it right to bring this, now? But she must hold true to what she felt had been given her. She remembered the Shinane of two years before, who had dared displeasure to learn to read. This mothering was good, and she was good at it: but there was more.

'I've brought you something.'

As she revealed her burden she watched the young wife's eyes grow round.

'You remember reading from it, when you were learning?'

'To be sure.'

'I am keeping it, for now. But when Sorcha and I leave – perhaps the book would like to stay here. I thought you might like to write in it. To take over, where Hugh left off.'

Shinane did not reply at first. Her eyes looked far away. 'It could have its own house in the lean-to. It will stay dry there, and out of the way of the forge. Everything would be kept tidy.'

She looked up at Morag. 'I'm out of practice, you know. You would have to help me. Not only with the writing, but also to know what to put down.'

Morag nodded. 'Gladly, my dear. We will start it together. And then, we'll see.'

Shinane sat. Morag saw the basketwork crib, the two little forms lying snuggly within. One wriggled and opened her mouth in a tiny yawn. Morag gathered her gown and sat with them, laying the book carefully across her lap.

The young woman give a little gasp, and raised her hand over her mouth, her forefinger resting along her upper lip.

'What is it?' she asked.

'I... Mora – I haven't told this to anyone. Not even Dhion. It was the day before they put him to trial. I went up the mountain and the clouds parted so that Atain shone down in a great shaft of sunlight. And I saw, I felt ... ' She related how, as the fog cleared, it had seemed as if a voice spoke to her. How she had descended the mountain, as if clothed in power.

'I have held that vision in my heart ever since, Mora. I do forget it. But I come back to it when the world pushes me down. I don't know what it means: what the power is for. I feel ... could this be part of it?'

'I've seen it in you, love. And I'm glad you feel like that about Hugh's book. So, what do you say?'

Shinane looked down, and Morag saw again the shadows round her eyes. She sighed. 'If only I could!' She turned to stare out of the open door. 'The girls need me, and there's always so much to be done.'

Then it was as if something broke through, like a dragonfly in its splendour bursting out of the drab body that had served it beneath the water. The young woman rose, and Morag almost believed she saw the shimmering wings spread out to either side. She reached for the book in Morag's hands and opened the clasps, turning the pages carefully.

'Writing is not like everything else,' she murmured, 'needing to be done straight away. And I'm sure there's not so very much happens here in Caerpadraig that has to be set down. If we can think together what must go in, I can set it down in my own time.'

She stood up. 'If you will help me ... I will try,' she said, fiercely. 'We'll hold the balance between us.'

Chapter 23

After the business at Leighan's, Dhion climbed the steep path that took him up towards the Pass of the Sea. Beside him ran the burn. Splashing from one pool to another, sometimes bright and open over a shingle bed, sometimes rushing deep in a narrow cleft, it was this he had now come to listen to. He brought with him his idea of building a water wheel, and the intention of consulting the burn. That other man of three years ago, John Finlay as he had been, would have been bemused, embarrassed by the notion. Now, tutored by his new mother it seemed a natural thing to ask: what will the water allow, and remain their friend?

He sat beside a pool and dipped his toes in the water. These days, he often walked barefoot, like many others. Ice-cold, the burn sent shocks up his body. Awakening. Enlivening. Both feet in: he stood. He willed himself to bear it, and slowly the water became more kindly. He squatted, brought his face close to the surface, gazed at the stones on the bottom, shifting, changing shape as the sinuous water moulded them. He cupped water in his hands and drank, poured water onto his head and watched it craze the surface as it fell into a hundred ripples that turned the stones into a kaleidoscope of greys and browns, yellows and smoky red.

He stood again, and listened.

A sudden outburst of song. High, sharp, staccato. He looked round. At last he found him. A robin perched on an overhanging branch, his beak open in shrill song. Closer than he had imagined. The song stopped. The bird pulled himself upright, straightened his tail, leaned forward again with intensity of purpose. 'Keep away,' he felt the bird saying. 'This is my territory. Keep off, off, off!'

This was not the place. He felt it. This was not what the burn would gladly allow. He waded out of the pool, back to the path. Lower down there was another pool. Deeper. He would need no weir. If he was not greedy he could still take off enough water for his purpose. The burn was generous: it would give freely to one who came with respect.

And a sluice-gate. He must be able to close off the lete in time of drought, so that the other creatures who needed the burn might still find water.

He stood listening, within and without. He would have said that what he now called the One in him was speaking with the One all around.

Slowly he walked downstream. A small cascade had scoured the pool, deep and brown. He came to its edge, saw its floor sloping steeply before him. It must be a metre deep – more. Its sill made a natural weir, and on the far side the land was folded in a shallow groove that offered an obvious course for the lete.

He splashed across the sill. The water felt good. He followed that wrinkle of the land as it tracked across the brae. It petered out, but the land continued good until he looked down upon a green corran at the foot of the short, steep slope. It was, perhaps, a dozen or more paces from the lower course of the burn. From a blackthorn, covered in its small green leaves, the robin fixed him with his beady eye. The bird hopped down, pecked at something, cocked his head on one side, flitted back into the bush.

Dhion took the day to help Morag and Sorcha take their things to Teigh Riseart. There were the two chests Morag had brought, but also some bits of furniture from townsfolk, gifting her what would be needed to start a new home. Shean had made her a fine cauldron, strong and firm. And Micheil had his elder son, Tamhas, drive two sturdy ponies with a cart up the hill.

It took the women some time to get everything ready from the smithy, and Tamhas was taking charge of loading the cart, so Dhion took the opportunity to go back up the brae. The corran where he hoped to build his mill lay barely two stones' throw from the shareg's house. It would be essential to have him on his side before his idea was put to the town.

Micheil puffed up the slope behind him and they stood at the top, catching their breath.

'I'm getting old, young man. I remember when I brought you first over that pass to roof you to Hugh. You looked as if you could barely struggle up from Fisherhame, and I thought to myself, ill or not, this man is a sickly specimen. Now look at you – you have better wind than I, by far.'

Dhion outlined his plan, but the shareg was still asking questions when Tamhas called to them from halfway down the slope. The cart was loaded, ready to go.

The little procession set off. Tamhas at the head, leading the ponies; Dhion with Morag and Sorcha walking behind. The path was overgrown, rarely used for such a purpose, and the going was slow. More than once, Dhion had to help Tamhas free a wheel. The sun was beginning her descent when they arrived. But slow as the journey had been, the unloading went fast. All hands together made quick work of it, and mid-way through the afternoon they sat down on two benches left over from Rhiseart's time. Some of Shean's good beer had come with them and, once they had discovered the beakers they'd brought, they were all glad of it.

Tamhas soon left with the cart, while Dhion stayed to help them settle in. Fineenh had filled the cauldron with the makings of a meal, but it needed a fire. Siocan and Odhran had left one laid ready, and a good supply of wood outside. To Dhion's surprise, Sorcha set to work with determination, and it was soon clear she knew the business of lighting a fire from cold far better than he.

He left Morag making up the two beds and walked outside, looking around him. How would it be for her to live away from the town, up among the hill farmers? He felt uneasy. But what else could be done? If Sorcha had not come she could have stayed in the town with them. And yet – after the space and quiet of the priest's house, he knew that would have been hard for her, too.

Such a pity, he felt, that she could not have been their priest. In the world he had left, he knew it could be possible. It was out of the question here.

At last it was time for Morag to bid him goodbye and watch him lope with his long stride down the brae. She turned back to the house, where their dinner was now bubbling over the fire Sorcha had made.

'Well,' she said to her niece. 'This is home now.'

'Ain't it grand, Antie? All this space! Outside, and all around.' The girl's face glowed. Morag could see she was in her element.

But as she lay down in her new bed that night, her own heart felt heavy. Instead of feeling that she was setting out on a new path, she felt as if her life was over. No longer the priest's wife, she was now a hill farmer. And without a man to help with the heavy work. It was not what she had been raised for, and not what she desired. She had never for a moment imagined she would come to this.

She thought of Hugh's stole, now laid in the clothes press, deep down where it would not be disturbed. She would have no need of it. What would be handy, though, was the good knife Shean had made her. She could imagine that would come in useful in so many of the tasks that lay ahead.

↾↽

The First-day after the move, Morag and Sorcha descended the brae to go to the Tollach, the last to be held by Mungo. Morag did not know what she felt, her feelings such a jumble. Beyond the rondal lay the priest's house, her house no more. As they drew near, it seemed to reach out to her. To be so close but not to enter felt like a betrayal.

Afterwards they went to the smithy for their meal and found Shelagh and Fengoelan there. Something about the presence of this pair always settled her: the dependable fisherman with a twinkle in his blue eyes, and his forthright, sensible wife. Somehow they all found somewhere to sit, even if, for those who could, it was the floor.

After the meal, Dhion laced on the tattered running shoes he had brought from another world, and went with Sorcha up Talor Gan. He wanted to show her the paths, and the soft ground where it was not safe to go. Shean went out, to *see what's going on*. Fengoelan had a call to make, and Fineenh sat down with Shelagh. The two sisters would mind the twins while sharing the gossip. At last came Morag's chance. She motioned with her head for Shinane to follow her to the forge. There on the work bench she laid out Hugh's pens and inks, the little pot for mixing them, the pen-knife. She showed Shinane how to sharpen a quill to a nib. The bench, clean and tidy and ready for the next week's work, stood under a window that gave light for close work once the shutters were removed. Dhion had fashioned one or two of the clay tablets he used to make for Shinane when she was learning to write, and she had practised forming the letters again.

Hugh's last entry in his book told of the sun-darkening. It ended, *People ask what this may mean*. Had it fulfilled its meaning in his passing, Shinane wondered.

Morag shook her head. 'I am sure it was seen far and wide, in places where Hugh was scarcely known. His passing may be part of it. But surely it means more than this.'

They agreed the words together. Shinane took a breath and reached for the quill. Carefully she made her own first entry. It read: *In the sumer that folowd the Seeborns retern the wite sicnes fel on Father Hew. He did not linger but dide before Sahwain and was graytly mornd.*

Shinane stood back to look at her own hand on the page beneath Hugh's. She had written slowly and carefully, and the letters were well-formed, if less practised than Hugh's.

'Then we must say about your visit, Mora. To Kimmoil,' she added.

'Oh, no!' Morag protested. 'For what did that amount to?'

'Yes!' insisted Shinane. 'I know what to put.'

And Morag stood back, quietly rejoicing that the young mother was so quickly bold to write as she saw fit. Yet still anxious what she might say.

Shinane wrote: *In hir greef his widow Morag reternd to the town Kimoil in the Northland whair she had been a gerl seeking news of hir mother whose liyne she new not. There she was towld by the Keeper of the Liyns that hir mothers name was Bron but he told not her ansestree.*

Morag knew that spelling was done as the writer saw fit, but she was pleased when Shinane asked her for her view on one or two words. She finished:

When she reternd the too days travel home Morag caym with Sorcha a young gerl and hir kinswoman desendit throo hir fathers liyne so that Morag is hir ahnt.

The next time Morag saw the Book, the entry ran: *Then caym Father Aydn.*

THE SECOND PART:
THE GUARDIANS

Chapter 24

Father Aidan woke, and for a moment wondered where he was. The darkness of the house confused him: he was unsure which way he faced. And the smells were strange. Then his aching limbs reminded him of yesterday's journey. He remembered the ride to Three Bridges. *An easy ride, Father*, one of his men-at-arms had called it. Hard enough for him, who was not in the habit of riding.

For a while he lay and listened. The house was quiet. He had become used at the monastery at Kilrivain to rising before dawn for the first office, and he'd forgotten how lax things had become here in his homeland. The township priest, his host, must still be asleep.

He reached for the small book beside his sleeping-place. *On the Epistle of Saul the Apostle to the Hebrites*, written by Denys of Reims. A precious volume bound in leather. He read a page of the Latin text. It had been Father Denys himself who had taught him his Latin: a tall, ascetic figure with olive skin, come from the Frankish lands far to the South. He himself had given the book to him, with his own hands. Aidan remembered his hands.

There was still no movement in the house. He rose, slipped his feet into his sandals and buckled the thongs. He would say the office anyway, alone if necessary. A horse gave a soft whinny as he opened the door of the priest's house. In the blue light the sleeping forms of his escort were darker shapes on the ground.

Later as he left the rondal the sky was hardly lighter. Again, he'd forgotten: these long, slow mornings in the north, when in summer the sky never grows completely black. The soldiers were still asleep. *Could ye not watch with me one hour?* he thought.

Father Tarvas was stirring as he entered, and a woman slipped in silently and saw to the fire. Over first-food the older man turned their talking to where he was bound.

'Caerpadraig? I've no had call to go there. Though there was quite a gathering when the wise-woman, Coghlane, died thereabouts, and many priests did attend. But why are ye no going by boat? It's a hard journey through the passes. Ye'll be tired afore ye get there.'

Boat – he inwardly shuddered at the thought. Two days he'd spent on the ship coming to the Island: two days of foul smells and foul language, a hard bed and hard rations. But when the ship rode the waves, the sickness had been the worst. He blenched at the memory. He'd been relieved when the archpriest sent him overland by way of Midland. *You'll be able to see the country*, he'd said. *Visit your own town again.* That was why he'd been chosen, he supposed, because he came originally from the Island. The archpriest didn't know that Aidan's parents had both died, and there was little now to draw him back to his homeland.

Now here he was in Three Bridges, the chief town of Midland, the place his father had journeyed to once a month with his fleeces, and he as a boy had sometimes gone with him. But Tarvas had used the town's name in the Island tongue. Tridrochad, he'd called it. Aidan preferred the Common Speech, and was more fluent in Latin than in the Island dialect now.

Could Tarvas tell him anything about the place? The archpriest had said little except that Hugh, their priest, had died the previous year. *A good man, but too easy-going,* he'd said. *The old religion – it was still strong among the people.* He thought even the priest had been infected by it. *It will be your task to mend their thoughts. The best way may be to make light of the old stories, until they learn to treat them with proper contempt,* he had counselled.

'I met Hugh once,' Father Tarvas replied. 'He was a Tridrochad man, too. Brother to our shareg here. He was married, ye wit.' He must have noticed Aidan's raised eyebrows. 'They often are still, away in Westerland and the Northland.'

The horses were saddled and the men waiting by the time he emerged from the priest's house.

'We must be away, Father,' the serjeant said. 'We've a hard ride today.'

Aidan glanced to the north-west, the way they must go. He could discern three peaks on the skyline, rising into the morning air, and then the long shoulder disappearing into the north. Beh' Bhica, they called it. There was some pagan tale connected with it. He had never liked mountains since a boy, and as soon as he could he had travelled south, to the towns and the peopled worlds. Now it was his mission to go back into the wilds, and he saw this as a mortification that would bring his soul benefit. Inwardly he sighed, then turned to the sturdy cob they'd found for him, and, ignoring his protesting body, mounted.

Three Bridges lived up to its name, for the river circled the hillock on which the town was built. They clattered over the north bridge, the serjeant and a man-at-arms before him, the two pack-horses and the third man behind. The wind was soft from the south-west and a warm sun peered at intervals between the white clouds.

Slowly the gentle grazings and the hedged arable lands rose to a moor where only the occasional shepherd leaning on his stick watched them pass. Aidan blessed each one with the sign of the cross.

By mid-morning they had rejoined the river, now not much more than a tumbling stream, and their road ran upon its banks while on each side the braes rose higher. Aidan saw the serjeant's head turning frequently from side to side, and the realisation grew on him that here would be a good place for an ambush. Would not his cloth protect him? Perhaps not, here in the heathen wild.

Now the mountains loomed above and they were climbing steeply, while the stream leaped beside them in rapids and low falls. His whole body ached appallingly; this was part of the mortification he must endure. They came out eventually on a high moor, dotted with lichen-covered boulders. Desolate, he thought. The moor swelled towards the north-west, and there he could see a gap between two bare summits. Beyond, a third great mass of rock rose before them.

'Serjeant,' he called. 'What is that mountain?'

The soldier turned in his saddle. 'An Innean,' he replied. The man was a Westerman and spoke the Island tongue naturally and easily, but remembered Aidan's more limited grasp of the language. 'The Anvil,' he translated.

He remembered from his boyhood: the Anvil, the cold iron heart of the Island. He remembered seeing the miners, small, wiry, quarrelsome men with a wild gleam in their eyes, coming down the north road with their heavy little carts laden with ore.

'Do we go over that?' he asked, controlling his tone.

'Nae, nae. The road goes round it.'

That, at least, was some relief.

Now they were among the peaks, and each man rode, one hand on the reins and the other on his sword-hilt. On either side were great piles of stones, and between them opened the black mouths of tunnels and passages and shafts. Here and there smoke rose from shacks and bivouacs and camp-fires, and sullen women and dirty children watched them pass with a cold stare.

His spirits rose when at last the land opened before them onto a long strath winding between the hills. A snake of water gleamed in its floor, fed by streams that they crossed again and again on crude slab bridges.

They had not stopped since leaving Three Bridges except briefly to relieve themselves, one man at a time while the others kept watch. But now – it must have been well after midday – the serjeant called a halt and they dismounted and took from their saddle-bags wallets of dried meat and small travelling skins of beer. Still one man was posted as sentry, taking turn and turn about.

The men talked together in their Westerland dialect. Aidan listened, and made out the gist of what they said.

'Ye'll have to get used to it, Father,' said the serjeant. 'They don't much use the Common Speech where ye're bound.'

He tried, and spoke in dialect. Aidan caught a smirk on the face of the other soldier, while their sentry turned away.

He had asked the archpriest's chaplain, at the time he was given his charge: would not language be a problem? The man had made light of it; but now they had crossed into Westerland and the heart of the Island was between him and the strong castles of Caerster, he sensed it would be more difficult than his superiors had anticipated. How would he convince the people of error and instil in them the true faith, if every time he spoke they laughed behind their hands?

Cuckoos called as they continued down the strath. Their road was now little more than a narrow track winding beside the river. Aidan guessed that only pack-horse trains came this way.

The sun in their eyes was well down as they turned a long bend. Far away he could make out a smudge of smoke on the wind. The serjeant called over his shoulder as he pointed towards it.

'That's where you're headed, Father.'

A bar of rough, tumbled land lay across their path, and while the river cut through in a torrent of white foam between black, gleaming stones, they were forced wearily to climb the hillocks. On a spur above them he saw the grey steading of a hill-farm and heard in the distance the farmer calling in his herd. Then from the summit of the road, at last he saw it: a lake curving away from them lit by the evening sun and, at its head, four or five long bow-shots distant, the town.

'Caerpadraig,' said the serjeant.

Aidan was prepared for less comfortable surroundings than those he had been used to in Sharilland and beyond. Kilrivain had been cold, but its buildings were substantial. His home-town in Midland, primitive by comparison, may have had its poorer end, but most of its dwellings had been of stone. This – could he call it a town? It seemed to have grown out of the ground, itself earth-coloured, earth-mottled, wattle-brown and mud-grey.

And this was his charge. These people were placed in his cure.

The sun dipped behind the high ground to the west of the town as they passed its outer dwellings. People watched them from their doorways as they passed. Little children ran to the protection of their parents at the sight of the soldiers, while older boys formed a ragged procession behind. Again, his hand was busy making the sign of the cross, but no one he saw responded.

The serjeant stopped a man and asked where they could find the shareg. The man pointed to the left, away from the most part of the town. They turned by the rondal – Aidan noted that it stood beside a sawyer's pit – and drew up outside one of the few stone-built houses.

He eased himself out of the saddle with difficulty. His aching limbs seemed to have set in a rigor around his horse's sides. Relieved to have his feet once more on the ground, he brushed down his cassock, creased from having been kilted round the saddle.

A man came out of the house, broad, stocky, black-browed and black-bearded, his hair laced with grey. He wore leine and trews, a cloak pulled roughly over his shoulders. He looked the soldiers up and down, then turned to Aidan.

'In the name of God, and in peace. You are Father Aidan?' He spoke in dialect.

'In the name of God,' he replied. 'I am.'

The man's eyebrows flickered up, and down again. A momentary thing, but Aidan wondered what he meant by it.

'We have been expecting you,' the man said. 'I am Shareg Micheil.' He spoke to the serjeant, too quickly for Aidan to follow closely, but he caught some words: horses … food … sleep.

He slept that night on a pallet made up in the shareg's house after the shareg's wife, slim and quick, had served them supper. Plain food, but good, and a hard bed that rustled of fern, with covers that looked old but kept him warm. Again he woke early, but by the time he had said the office by his bedside his first-food was ready. The shareg questioned him in the common speech. He was direct in his questioning and blunt in his own answers. 'But it will be best if you get used to speaking in Westeraig,' he told him. 'You'll seem too distant else.'

He watched the men unload his things and install them in the priest's house. Then they rode away, turning out of sight around the rondal. He listened to the sound of their hooves fading into the distance. The sounds of the town took over: a dog barking and the cackle of geese; two women calling to each other; the see-saw song of the saw from the carpenter's shop – too close for comfort. The town sloped gently away from him. Beyond, the lake glittered into the distance in a pale morning light.

So this – this – was to be his home, till death or the archpriest saw fit to move him. The shareg ushered him through the doorway into the priest's house. He looked about him. It would do.

Chapter 25

The new priest's first Tollagh was not auspicious. A single man: but if the girls of the town had hopes for a husband of higher rank, they would soon be disappointed.

Not that he wasn't handsome in his way, Morag thought, as she toiled back up the brae to her new home. Tall, though not as tall as Hugh; and still young, though approaching the middle age. And dark-haired, though it was strange that he'd shaved his beard. It made him look – well, *unIslandlike*.

His eyes seemed to stare at you, with an intensity she found disconcerting. Where Hugh would have drawn up a chair at the edge of the sanctuary and sat to tell a story, finally drawing out its meaning to their own lives, this man had stood behind the lectern and grasped it, for all the world as if he were confronting an enemy from the breastworks of some besieged town.

But what most took her notice was his way of speaking. Certainly he had a good voice. Deeper than many, yet he knew how to use its full range of pitch and power. Though he spoke in Westeraig, it was haltingly, and much of the time he used the Common Speech which made him sound even more formal and distant. She should have enjoyed listening to him; yet somehow she afterwards had a vague feeling of discomfort; of guilt, even.

There was something about him she couldn't put her finger on. He reminded her of Gormagh.

Teigh Riseart was a good house, well-built, with the thick thatch that Siocan and Odhran had generously patched and repaired. But it was smaller, simpler – she caught herself thinking *meaner* – than the priest's house in town. The door was of sawn planks, heavy and solid: a crofter's door. When first they came, she had needed all her strength to move it on its old hinge-pins, and it had caught shards of stones on the floor as it grated open. A house without windows, the only daylight shafted in when you opened the door. There were three bed-alcoves, recessed into the thick walls that would keep them warm in winter and cool in summer; one, where she slept, was covered by a faded curtain.

Up above the town, few came, though Dhion visited when he could to help them with the practical tasks of settling in. It was he who greased the door-hinges and raised its sagging boards so that it swung more freely.

But for Sorcha, it seemed the crofthouse was a palace. Whenever they found they were short of this or that, which was quite often, Sorcha made it her business to find a way around the difficulty or go down to the town to fetch what was needed. But if they were to till the soil in the hope of planting kale for the winter, they must have proper tools. Morag put the problem to Dhion, and in a day or two he climbed up to them with her old fork and spade. 'Father Aidan doesn't expect to be doing anything with these. I asked him,' he said. He added, 'You haven't been down to see us yet, except on First-day. You don't have to stay here all the time, you know.' But day after day passed when Morag did not find it in herself to take the path down into the town.

More and more, it felt as if Sorcha was leading and she following. For Sorcha, it seemed, the life was better than anything she had known. For herself, the long hours without human contact stretched out endlessly. Yet she could not bring herself to seek company. She had been glad to be gone from the smithy, where the round of common tasks and light chit-chat seemed endless and wore her down. But here she did not belong either. Since Hugh had gone she belonged in some place that no longer existed.

First-day again. It was one of those mornings when you start to know that the year has turned: that her growing and swelling to life and power has reached its height, and is now beginning the slow shrinking again, the darkness of winter still far away but now as unstoppable as the flooding tide. In this seventh moon Atain was already well up behind the house. Her light touched the hills fringing the north-western coast with the pure light that only sunrise brings.

She could not see Sorcha anywhere.

She took a few steps out onto the dewy grass. Chaffinches called from among the branches of the apple trees, where green fruit were beginning to swell. The house was half-sunk into the hill, and she walked a little way up the slope. A small stand of birches grew here, silver and purple stems half-hidden among a green shimmer. She took a leaf between her fingers. *A little torn heart*, she whispered to herself. Suddenly, the tears came.

She wandered back to the door. Sorcha was within, cooking the first-food: how had she missed her? She sank down on the chair while the girl lifted the black pot. The song that had filled her heart at the time of the twins' naming … where was that now? She thought of the Tollach to come that morning. She could not face it.

The next day, Fineenh toiled up the hill. Sorcha was busy in the vegetable garden.

'Ye're no well, Morag.' It was not a question. 'What's up?'

Morag gazed through the open door at the grey sky that wept a grey drizzle. She could find no words.

She wandered round the corner of the house. Up the slope. The effort. She sat in the grass among the birch-trees, looking at nothing, but feeling the sunlight's warmth touch her skin pleasantly. She sat, and nothing was happening, within or without. Nothing at all.

A movement caught her eye, her ear. A rustle in the long grass. Without thinking, she let her eye follow the disturbance. Whatever it was had vanished, but she went on looking after it.

A shape. Red and white. A ball, half-hidden among the grass-blades. Not red: orange. And chalky-white. And not a ball. A half-cup, tipped over, empty. Like her.

She raised her eyes. Looked around. Another – over there. A small cluster of toadstools, standing, like an invitation.

She had been told since childhood about these. They were poisonous; not to be eaten. But perhaps that would be good for her now. What did they taste like, she wondered. Would it be quick? Was it sure? These questions came to her without urgency. They floated through her mind and a feeling broke through the fog of her melancholy: curiosity.

She made herself take the few steps. She reached out a hand and touched the toadstool. Then her other hand came to her mouth, as if to cover it. A Yes and a No. She looked away, down the strath where the town smoked in the late afternoon. Where Sorcha had gone. Where her friends were, her family. She hoped they could forgive.

She gazed at the toadstool. Surely it had been sent to her. The Sidhe. They knew; they understood. They were giving them to her. Her hand closed around the cap.

It came away so easily. It gave itself.

It smelled earthy, dark. Earthiness seemed welcome to her. She paused. She bit.

It tasted foul. She retched, and almost threw up. Determined now, she forced it down. She crammed the rest into her mouth and willed to swallow. She rose, paused, then turned and crossed the few paces to where the other cluster stood, welcoming. Three – four caps she plucked, and sat with them. After the first, the remainder tasted not so bad.

A thought came to her: not here. She didn't want them to find her here, outside. She stood again and walked to the door. Bed. She would lie on her bed. She would bar the door, and lie on her bed.

Inside, she lay down and waited. She sang to herself, songs from her childhood, chants she had sung with Hugh.

She stopped singing. Now she began to feel sick. It came in waves, like breakers on the shore, rising, rising, then spilling themselves. A warm feeling creeping up within her. She closed her eyes. This, then, was it: this was the long journey.

Her hand touched the fleece she was lying on. It felt – pink. She began to hear the sound of the touch, like a tinkle of finger-cymbals; like sweet music. She lost herself in the sweet music …

There were sounds. Brittle, brown rattling sounds. Black bangs. And words. Words were coming from beyond the door – cries, far away and faint. Red, jagged words, with coloured fringes round them. Slowly they faded. Now someone was beside her, shaking her. More words. Orange, green, swirling into mauve. She tasted the shaking, like nettles, sharp, bitter. The shaking faded, the words faded. Dark. Not black, not anything.

It was dark. No, not dark: it was as if light did not exist.

Fear spread over her. Not fear of something, but Fear itself. She could not move, nor hide, nor fly. Not even tremble at the terror.

She floated in space, weightless. Her limbs were not. Her body was not. There was no time: no sense of before or after. The not-darkness did not go on; the terror did not last. It only was. The present moment. An eternity.

Now there were forms in the darkness. Not seen – there was no sight – but felt. Close beside her. Hungry. She could not push them away.

A whirling confusion. Unseen shapes swirling around her: evil, malign, predatory. They were going to consume her. There was nothing she could do.

Red. Sight, returning. A reddish light, dim, vanishingly dim, and all around. And purple – deepest purple and mauve, shot with dark green. A whirlpool of dim light, slowly turning around her, its centre and hub. The forms, fading with the growing light; the terror slowly seeping away.

Then the voices began. Mutterings, ripples of orange, and sibilant whispers of glowing sky-blue. Words formed, in languages and colours she could not comprehend.

Morag.

Morag.

Morag.

Where are you, Morag? Where are you, priest's wife? Where are you, witch's daughter? Where? Where?

Priest's wife?

Aye, and witch's daughter. Priest's wife and witch's daughter. She doesn't know who she is. Not know, not know, not know …

A screech in her face: *Do ye not know who you are?*

Agony swept through her, a searing heat. She wanted to flee; she wanted to scream. And she could not make a sound nor move a finger. It burned, her skin charring. It broiled her flesh. Her very bones glowed with its intensity.

And then at last it faded. Passed. She lay, still, silent, not being.

She opened her eyes. There was a point of flickering orange. A light. She stared at it. A very ordinary light. Their own lamp, lit with its steady flame.

Was she … No, this was too familiar. She was not dead. She had failed to do even this.

She felt an urgent need to relieve herself. Slowly, she tried to move. She swung her legs off the bed-shelf. They felt like lead.

As her feet reached the ground, they touched something. A something that was both solid and yielding; warm. It shuddered a little as her toes pushed against it. It was alive. It moved away from her, rolled over, groaned. A young girl's mutter.

Then a face, rising out of the darkness of the floor.

'Antie! Ye're awake! We kept the lamp alight for ye.'

The sounds knocked into her, sending shocks through her head. She clutched her temples, her sudden embodiedness pressing in upon her. The floor beneath her, the sounds around her, the air filling her chest.

Who was this – other? Then she remembered: the child … Sorcha.

'Antie! Are ye all right?'

'Yes, child. I feel – queer.'

'We've been so worried for ye! What did ye do to yersel?'

'I …' She paused. What had she done? 'I ate some … mushrooms … some …'

'Scrying-caps.' It was a deeper voice: a man's.

Dimly she became aware of another presence. The light hurt her head. She saw a sharp face, a black pointed beard. Piercing eyes. She struggled to pull a name out of her memory. It came: Wolf.

She swayed. 'Excuse me,' she blurted, and stumbled towards the door.

The cold air outside swept over her like the splash of a wave. She crouched behind the house, and found herself retching, bringing up bitter bile. She wiped her mouth on a handful of grass. Her head ached bitterly, like a bell rung by a devil.

After a little, Sorcha followed her outside, helped her back into the house. Wolf was waiting for them, sitting on a stool.

'I've come,' he said.

She stared at him blankly.

'I told you to wait, remember. That we would meet again. And here I am. For it's time. But you need sleep now – proper sleep. Will you lie down on the bed.' A strong arm under her ankles lifted her legs and swung them onto the couch. He pulled the cloaks over her, felt her brow. His hand felt firm and warm and strong.

For a moment the touch of his hand brought back memories of Hugh. Then he was gone.

A smaller shape wriggled under the bedclothes and snuggled against her.

'I'll be beside ye t'night, Antie. I'll look after ye.'

They brought her back to the house and she lay down again on her bed. Sorcha cooked. Wolf stayed outside. She could not eat. They let her doze.

The wind rose through the evening and the rain began. It was dark in the house, lit as it was only by the friendly glow from the hearth, the smoke finding its way through the thatch. Wolf had her sit by the fire.

'We must clear you of the ill,' he told her. 'When you journey unprepared, evils can enter and take up lodging in you. Never do anything like this on your own again, without someone with you who knows the way.'

With the tongs he took coals from the fire and dropped them into the fire-pot. He had picked some more of what he called the scrying-caps and dropped pieces of them onto the glowing charcoal.

'Breathe the smoke,' he told her. 'Like will banish like.'

He began a chant. She was aware of Sorcha beside him, listening, intent.

It was not so bad this time. She was no longer terrified; rather, she felt stronger, that she could hold her own against the unseen presences. Resist. They retreated. Shrank. Went out, like spent flames.

Once more she felt her gorge rising and hurried out into the rain. She retched and puked, threw up over and over.

At last it was finished. She felt empty, drained, like limp washing wrung between the hands, hung on a bush, scoured by wind and sun; but she knew that it was done. She entered the house, made for the stoop and drank. She dipped a finger in the water and traced the sign of the encircled cross on her brow. 'In the name of Chrisht.'

That night there were no dreams.

❧ ❧

They walked, all three, to the burying-ground. There, on the western fringe where the sharegs and priests of Caerpadraig were laid, was Hugh's long mound. She stopped and said a silent prayer while Sorcha and Wolf stood quietly, a few steps distant.

Then a little west again, away from the common lairs of the town, to the place where Coghlane's body lay. She remembered the day they had put her to rest, the town filled with visitors come from far; the townsfolk a little bemused. Her grave stood, unlike any other, marked with a standing stone as tall as she had been. Unhewn, just as it had been prised away from the mountainside by some mighty force of Earth.

She stood. Then she turned and looked questioningly at Wolf.

'My… mother? In truth?'

He nodded. She knelt in the wet grass. She laid her hands on the green turf and leaned forward and kissed the ground.

She rose. Her mother was a woman held in high renown by Hugh and Dhion and all those many people who had come to Caerpadraig for her funeral rites. Others condemned her, calling her a witch – but these others did not know her. This, then, was what was flowing through her veins: these two faces. Two natures, both a part of her, and the power that went with both. But for what? She could not see clear.

He called her early the next morning. The wind was still blowing briskly from the west and the clouds were unbroken, but the rain was over and the air had a brightness to it. Her head was clear. She felt strong.

'Come, eat,' he said. 'Then we have work to do.'

As soon as she had taken her first-food he said, 'Where's your knife?'

'Which one?'

He looked at her and she blushed. Of course! The one Shean had made for her.

'I'm not sure,' she admitted.

'I'm not surprised,' he allowed. 'But not a state of affairs you should repeat.'

She remembered Finneuchan's words. *Take it, an don't be separated from it agin. An learn how to use it!*

'Here it is, Antie!'

Sorcha held out the black leather sheath, the haft of the knife towards her.

'Put it on.'

Morag fastened the sheath to her belt.

'Let's go outside,' he said.

They went into the orchard and stood among the apple trees in the scented air.

'What is the first use of the knife?' asked Wolf.

'To cut,' she returned. Then, speaking with feeling, 'To kill.'

'That is your very last recourse. But you are right: its first use is to cut. We cut with our minds also when we exercise discernment. But for that, we must master fear. Sit down.'

She did as she was told, though now she felt a little self-conscious. Sorcha squatted apart, watching. He sat beside her. She could smell the leather of his jerkin.

After a moment Wolf spoke. He began quietly, slowly. 'Yesterday, you found your mother. Do you remember how people thought of her? They were divided, weren't they. I heard what some said at her funeral games.'

'You were there?'

He nodded, and went on, 'If you're going to be her daughter in truth and follow in the path she has made, you must know how to face fear, as she did. When we met on the moor there was fear in you and it robbed you of clear thinking. When you meet danger, don't you want to meet it as Coghlane's daughter? Ready to

200

look Fear in the face until it stands aside. This knife is now your tool, to teach you. If you learn its lesson, you may never have to draw blood with it; except, perhaps, to eat.'

Morag looked into his deep-sunk eyes. 'Have you ever … killed a man?'

He returned her gaze candidly. 'Yes, I have. Twice. The first time I was young and rash. I hadn't fully learned. The other time – I don't like to talk of it.' He turned his face away, gazing out across the strath. 'He was stupid and left me no choice.'

He shook himself like a dog. 'Come on, Mother Morag. On your feet.'

They stood facing each other.

'Draw,' he commanded.

She pulled at the haft. Held up the knife. Sparkling, it pointed to the sky an armslength before her face. She fixed her eyes on it.

'When a man threatens you, he doesn't look at his knife.' Wolf paused. 'He looks at your eyes, to see if there's fear with you. And to see if you know how to use yours. Where were you looking just then?'

Morag blustered. And fell silent.

Wolf continued. 'Look at me. Only me. Right in my eyes.' With the forefinger of his free hand he jabbed at his forehead. 'Don't drop your gaze. Then you can begin to read me. Know what I'm thinking of doing. The one who comes against you will see that. Now … watch.'

He bent and picked up a stone. 'Look at me … into my eyes.' She did so. Suddenly, he flung the stone high into the air. A breath's space later it thudded onto the grass somewhere.

'Where did the stone land?'

'I don't know. I was looking at you.'

'But you still had the use of your hearing. You must learn to watch a man closely, yet still know what is moving to your side. He may not be alone. Learn to watch.

201

Then learn to sense with more than your eyes. You will find, when you do this with full attention, there will be no place left for fear. Fear comes when you do not attend.'

No one had spoken to her like this before. She watched him, carefully.

'There are two ways of seeing,' he went on. 'With a soft gaze, you see the whole round of where you are. Everything has your attention, and nothing is singled out. It is good to walk in prayer like this. I think you know this way of walking.'

She nodded.

'There is another way too. The warrior way of the hunter and fighter. And you need to practise this, too. To look sharply at one thing, yet know what is going on around you. See with the edges of your sight. See with your ears. Hear with your eyes. Know what is.'

He paused.

'Tell me,' he went on. 'Without moving your eyes, what do you know of what is going on around us now?'

She stood still. Listened. In the distance over to her right, she heard the faint creak of a hinge, carried on the air. Someone must be going in or out in the neighbouring croft, three bow-shots away. Silence. Then the soft sigh of a breeze stroking the grasses, sieved through the leaves of the apple trees. The buzz of wild bees; of wasps moving between rotting apples, fallen to the ground. Behind her, a rustling – was it a mouse? A vole? And, at last, the minute sounds of tiny insects carrying out their inscrutable work ...

He drilled her, as much as she had strength for, all through that morning. And she found she was learning; she felt in herself a steeliness she had forgotten. She forgot how, only two days before, she had scarce strength enough to walk.

They paused for a meal at noon. Sorcha laid it for them. Then they trained again. This time, he had her hitch up her skirt for ease of movement. She no longer cared. She practised holding the knife, holding her opponent's eye, while still being aware of all around her. He said nothing of how to attack: of the lunge, the stab, the slash. 'Another day,' he said, 'I will show you how you can parry a blow. Turn it from you. May that be the most you will ever need.'

'You have done well,' he said at last. I would not have taught you this if I hadn't seen it in you.'

They were resting, talking over their supper while the light, still seen through the open door, faded from the sky and the shadows deepened.

Wolf continued. 'I foresee you may need this skill one day. My brothers and sisters asked me to teach you. They also foresee.'

She looked at him questioningly, but he went on, 'Tomorrow, we will repeat what you have learned. Then we will prepare. For, the next day, we must leave by dawn.'

'Where are we going?'

'I told you. I've come to take you to your mother's house.'

'To Coghlane's house in the hills? Where Hugh used to go?' She looked her question. 'Why there? Will it not be empty? Or taken by someone new?'

'It has been taken by no one. But it has been cared for. Coghlane chose her home well. It is a special place. The Guardians will meet you there.'

'Guardians?'

'The Guardians of the Isle. Coghlane was one. I am another. Now since her passing we are twelve in number. But we should be three-and-ten.'

He paused, then said, 'The sharegs hold the land in the common world. We hold it in Otherworld. You now know that place better than most. But you do not yet have mastery there. You will meet us all at your mother's house.'

He turned and looked keenly at Sorcha. 'They want to meet you, too, little sister. So tomorrow, take that cow that grazes among the trees back where she came from. And tell your shareg where we are bound. He will understand. The sharegs know of the Guardians. It is part of their preparation to meet at least one of us, before they are charged. But they do not speak of us among the people.

'The next day, we will leave at dawn.'

Chapter 28

The three travellers breasted a ridge and Morag saw for the first time, there below her in the evening light, Coire na Cailleach, the Corrie of the Wisewoman. The tarn gleamed dully, and here and there on the close-cropped grass were the small brown shapes of tents. Above some, banners flapped and drooped in the fitful breeze, bearing symbols she did not recognise. A blue wraith of smoke leaned away from the thatch of the bothy.

'See,' said Wolf, 'the Guardians are gathered.'

She glanced at Sorcha. The girl was brighter-eyed, more alert, than Morag had ever seen her.

'Oh Antie – can ye feel it?'

'What?' she questioned.

'The air – the brightness in the air! It's like I can fly in it!'

The thin path curved down the flank of the ridge into the corrie. As they threaded it, single file, a reedy horn sounded a long note from above. Morag looked up, but saw no one.

They passed a high, dry-stone wall, in need of repair. Glancing through the gaps she saw a wilderness of bugloss, comfrey and fennel overrun with nettles and brambles, suggesting that the soil was good but untended.

'Your mother's garden,' Wolf told her. 'This was where she grew her herbs.'

Her mother. It still seemed strange.

Now people came out from some of the tents and stood to watch them pass. Each raised their hands in gestures of silent greeting. There were maybe half-a-dozen, some men, some women: all different. You couldn't find a more varied group, Morag thought. Yet each had something akin to the rest; something she could not quite place, that distinguished them all. Was it in the way they carried themselves? Or a certain look in their faces? One woman had a much darker skin than Morag had seen before – like the deep, shining brown of the kelp on the seashore.

And their clothes. All, men and women alike, wore a long gown, some belted, others hanging loose to the ground. But the colours! Only one was clad in the habitual earth-colours most people wore. Here were deep green and rich red and orange and indigo blue. One wore a broad purple sash. Morag had once begged a visiting trader for a length of purple thread for her tapestry.

The door of the bothy opened, and a woman stood before them, clothed in black. This was no ordinary flat black. It had a glossiness Morag had seen only once before, in Tridrochad long ago with Hugh, when some lord from Caerster had ridden through on a beautiful, high-stepping black mare. The woman's face was long and angular, the mouth wide and thin, drawn in a straight line with the slightest upcurve at the corners. Her long grey hair hung straight down her back and over her breast. She held her hands towards them, palms open in welcome; then, as they stood before her, raised her left hand to show a ring. Morag remembered at once the ring on the finger of the depute – a borrowed ring, commanding a borrowed authority. This ring was smaller, lighter; it flashed fire. Without knowing why, Morag took the woman's hand, dropped to one knee and kissed it.

She looked up into a smiling face. The woman stooped and raised her, holding out both hands.

'You do well, sister. Welcome. And you, little sister,' she said, seeing Sorcha behind.

The child's face shone. 'It's Sorcha I am,' she began.

'I know who you are, little sister. You are most welcome. And you, brother' – this to Wolf – 'Welcome, welcome.'

She led them into the bothy. A modest fire twinkled on the hearth-stones beneath a blackened pot. Steam filled the hut with the aroma of herbs.

'Sit. Rest from your journey. I will serve you all.'

'My lady,' A sense of awe was upon Morag. 'I thank you for your welcome. I think you do also know me.'

'Yes, indeed, Morag Ag'Hugh Mi'Choghlane.'

The woman smiled her wide, thin smile. 'We are the Guardians of the Island, as the Lord Wolf will have told you. I am Feáránn.'

The Lord Wolf? Morag did not know what to think.

Within were no chairs, but a couple of rough stools and many plump pillows and palliasses ranged against the walls. Two men with signs of age in their hair and skin sat on the stools. But they rose as the travellers turned towards them. One was quick and nimble as he sprang to his feet. His face was almost insect-like, narrowed to a sharp-pointed little chin, his mouth a short thin line while his ears spread wide, making the wedge of his face more marked.

The other could hardly have been more different. Tall and stooping, his heavy body unfolded slowly as he raised himself to his commanding height. His face was a brown oval, dominated by a great hooked nose. On either side of his bald crown long white hair hung down, streaked with a few strands of what had once been black. He wore a simple deep blue gown, but at collar and cuffs was embroidery of what must surely be gold thread.

Feáránn motioned to him, saying, 'The Lord Guirman.'

Sorcha was looking deep into his eyes as if drinking him in. He returned her gaze, studying her, the hint of a smile on his lips, in his eyes. Then he turned to Morag and bowed.

She curtsied deeply.

Now the angular man was being introduced. 'The Lord Tearlach,' Feáránn was saying. He bowed, a sudden, quick bending of his body that kept his face peering towards them.

'Now please, sit,' Feárann repeated.

Morag sank gratefully onto the proffered pillow. She felt as if a dream had woken into life. What would unfold next she could not imagine.

'You are safe here, Mother Morag.' Guirman's deep voice cut into her muddled thoughts. 'No power can come against the Guardians while we hold together. And you have nothing to fear from us.'

Feárann offered them bowls of broth and hunks of gritty bread. When all were served, she blessed the food and they ate. Throughout the meal Morag felt her presence beside her, erect and potent.

There was no sound but the chink of horn spoon on wooden bowl, the creak of dry bracken beneath them, and the spit and crackle of the hearth. Then Feárann took their bowls and brought soft cloths for their mouths and hands.

When all was done, she took her seat and turned to Morag and Sorcha. 'We know you are tired from your journey, Mother Morag,' she said. 'Not just your climb to come here today, but all your journey since Hugh fell ill. And you, little one – you too have been on a difficult journey to reach this place. But know that you have both been safely on your way ever since your two paths crossed.'

Morag looked from one to the other of the Guardians. She had rescued a child. And this had set in motion an avalanche of events that had brought them to this place.

She spoke. 'I set out looking for my mother. I did not guess my quest would end here.'

'End?'

She started at Guirman's sudden rumble. He had said nothing, his head sunk to his chest, as if he had been sleeping. But now, in his deep voice, and without looking up, he almost mumbled through his beard. 'Every ending is a new beginning. You followed the path offered. Now it has led to the place where you can set forth on a new turning of the wheel.'

Morag wondered.

Tearlach glanced towards the speaker. 'My brother speaks truth. Every ending is a new beginning. We know you have lost, not only your husband, but also your place in the world. But there is a new role coming towards you, which is much-needed to stay what is growing into being on the Isle Fincara. We have brought you here now to prepare for it. Already it has taken hold in the south and the east, but not yet in the north and the west. A tide is washing over the Isle, sweeping away the old things and replacing them with a way that does not respect the balance.

'Know, too, that it is time to give thought to finding who will follow your mother, the Lady Coghlane. For the number of the Guardians must hold. We are gathered to take counsel for the Island.'

Morag hesitated. Then, 'Forgive me, sir. Do not the sharegs take counsel for the Island, under the High Shareg?'

'Indeed, they do. They take counsel. And we take counsel. And so the things of Earth and Heaven are held in balance.'

Morag tightened her grip on her hands, clasped in her lap. She raised her eyes. 'And … the archpriest?'

Tearlach smiled. 'The archpriest serves the new religion. But does he serve Spirit within it?' He said no more.

'Come,' said Feáránn. 'It is enough. My brothers will leave you in peace, and I will make up your beds.'

Morag glanced at Wolf as he rose. 'I lodge with my sisters and brothers tonight,' he said.

ॐॐ

She lay a long time waiting for sleep. A draught stole from under a curtain at the back of the bothy, and she wondered with lazy curiosity what lay behind. She wrapped herself tighter in her cloak.

'Antie?'

Sorcha was beside her, curled into her back. She turned over.

'What is it, child?'

'Ye're no sleepin, then?'

'Not yet,' she answered. 'Aren't you sleepy?'

'Sleepy? I couldnae be sleepy in a place like this. The air! An all these … lords and ladies. Do ye no feel something… like … coming from them?'

The girl stirred, drew her knees under her, wrapped her cloak around her thin shoulders and stood.

'Where are you going, child?'

'I'm jus going outside. I've got to feel this air. I'll be awricht, Antie. I won't go far.'

She lay in the darkness, alone. She missed the warmth of Sorcha's body beside her. What did she mean, about the air?

Then other thoughts crowded in. She called to mind the last weeks, destitute of hope. She had sought her mother, and at last knew her name – and more than her name. But why could they not have met in life? Her mother must have known of her. She must have.

Then Morag remembered how, whenever Hugh returned from climbing up to consult Mother Coghlane, he would say, *She asked after you very particularly*. She did know. So why …

A thought struck her. The Guardians were meeting to appoint Coghlane's successor. And she was the Daughter. Did they think it was she?

Her whole body shuddered. It had been hard enough, living in Teigh Riseart. But here? She would go mad. She used to feel she had some wisdom and understanding. But wisdom had deserted her since Hugh's passing. Almost everything she had done had been in response to pressing need. And the wisdom she used to have was not enough for here. She knew it. Surely they must, too? Surely, they would not try to make her?

Her quest was at the last nothing but a glamour, a delusion, a false road. It had led here, and here was not where she wished to be. She longed for the ordinariness of Caerpadraig. She was not one of these. Could not be one of them. She had failed them. Failed her mother; failed Hugh; failed everyone …

She lapsed into an unhappy, restless sleep. She did not feel Sorcha's return.

Chapter 29

It was dark in the bothy when Fearánn woke them, framed in the open doorway by a vision of grey clouds and soft drizzle that veiled the sweep of land down from the corrie. 'Your first-food is ready,' she said. 'Then we have work to do. Come.'

Sorcha stirred at once, sat up, rubbed her eyes, sprang to her feet. Morag followed more slowly. What kind of work was expected of her? Her thoughts, her feelings of the night hung round her heart like weeds, sucking her substance, denying her light.

Fearánn lit a lamp, then softly closed the door behind her. Morag shook out her crumpled skirts.

After a little, Fearánn returned with bowls of porridge.

'Lady,' Morag began. 'The council this morning. Is it to choose the one to take my mother's place?'

Fearánn's grey eyes smiled down at her. 'It is.'

'And – who has offered?'

'It is not our custom to choose from those who might offer. Rather, we wait until one of us meets with a soul ready to begin. Then we gather with that one to discern the rightness of their calling. Finally, if the council agrees, we ask if they are willing. Know that a name has been put forward by one of our number. Now we sit in council to discern if that name be true.'

'Lady,' Morag's words came slowly. 'I must tell you that it cannot be me, for I am not able. I know it. My place is with my townspeople, and my family. I want to see my grandchildren and watch them grow.'

Morag heard her own words. They were telling her something she had not known she felt so strongly.

Fearánn laid a hand on Morag's shoulder and looked into her eyes. Her own were still smiling, and there was a light laughter in her words. 'Do not judge the counsel of the Guardians even before we have sat, Mother Morag. You will see. All will be well.'

The door opened again. A woman of middle height entered, her brown hair bound back to hang behind her. Her eyes were blue – a sapphire blue. Morag noticed their brightness at once.

'The lady Freia is our weather-watcher,' announced Fearánn. 'She tells us the rain will stop and it will be fair for our council.'

'And indeed, the rain is easing now,' Freia declared. 'The circle is ready.'

Fearánn rose. 'Come,' she said. 'The Guardians have fasted this morning and we are ready for you to join us now. Do not be afraid, Morag Mi'Choghlane. It is your good as well as that of the Island we have at heart. But we may sit long in council before we choose, so be patient. And be free to move as you have need. You are not a prisoner among us. Come.'

'What of the child?' Morag asked, as Sorcha also slid from the board and followed them.

'She too has a place among us. Come.'

The rain was indeed stopping as they stepped outside. A glistening pearliness in the sky cast its sheen over the land. The tents of the previous day were dull with dampness; the small, hardy ponies that had carried them grazed nearby. But Morag looked to a place where, gently sloping towards the tarn, was a lawn of close-cropped, springy grass. There in a circle were the Guardians. Some stood; others sat or knelt. More than half were grey-headed. The dark-skinned woman whom Morag remembered from the previous evening sat cross-legged, her knees on the ground, her hands resting in her lap. Wolf was kneeling, supported by a low seat, his face set straight forward, his eyes half closed. And there stood Guirman, his arms folded, imperturbable as a mountain.

Nearest her, a space had been left where rounds of cut tree-trunks formed simple seats. Fearánn ushered them into the circle and, with a hand on the shoulder of each, whispered. 'Stay here. And take whatever posture you like. We are going to enter a time of prayer.'

Morag dropped onto the offered seat. Then, feeling the solemnity of the occasion, she lowered herself to her knees. Sorcha sat stolidly on the ground beside her, her arms clutched around her legs, looking about with candid curiosity.

Fearánn took the place that had been left for her at the eastern point of the circle. Beside it on a low stand stood a small brass bell, its handle a supple leather strap. Now Morag watched her raise the bell and strike it … once … twice … three times.

'In the name of the One, the Intention within all being … '

Morag knew the invocation. Had she not repeated it with Hugh day after day, year after year, until it was part of her?

Then came a prayer of protection. A prayer of direction. A prayer of calling forth. And at last Fearánn led the gathered voices in a chant. It was not one Morag knew. She recognised the words as from a very old language. She rested on the ebb and flow of its sounds, carried like a seabird, resting upon the waves.

Silence fell over the hollow in the mountain. Morag fell easily into the stillness. From somewhere in the distance, she heard the deep cough of a raven. She found herself dropping deeper, deeper down.

After a good while came the beginnings of a cramp in her calves. 'The time will soon be done,' she told herself. 'The day grows, and surely they have need of speaking.' She could tolerate the growing tension for a while.

But no bell sounded to bring their contemplation to a close. A shower passed over – soft, chill. It moved on. Now Morag's legs longed for respite. She must move. She allowed her eyelids to flicker open. The shadow of the mountain was touching the western rim of the tarn. She saw that Guirman no longer stood where he had been, but was pacing a little distance away, so slowly that he seemed to glide. Freia too had moved. She was lying full-length, prostrate on the damp grass. Slowly Morag uncurled her screaming calves and, with difficulty, stood. She glanced at Sorcha. The girl sat still, motionless, her face so deeply peaceful she could scarcely recognise the waif of Kimmoil.

Little by little the pain eased. She felt the blood return to her feet, her toes. She too would walk, like Guirman – as much like Guirman as she knew how. She began, very slowly.

She walked. Now the peace of the mountain began to sink into her. Her concerns began to seem small, far away. She was just a woman walking on a mountain, step by careful step, feeling the springy grass beneath her bare feet. Somewhere high above the peak an eagle screamed. She could see the mountain's shadow on the water. She stopped. Now she felt the first pangs of hunger. But these others had fasted all day. Slowly, she turned. Slowly, she walked back to her place in the silent circle. Sorcha had not moved. She closed her eyes and settled herself anew, dropping back into the bottomless well that had opened in the space among them.

At last, the sound of the bell. She opened her eyes. Still no one was moving. She watched. Then the bell sounded again, slowly, three times. This time, there was a stirring around the circle, and all knelt forward, Guirman lowering himself slowly, leaning on a staff. They bent and kissed the ground. Now the mountain's shadow covered all but the further rim of the tarn.

The Guardians stood. Fearánn began to chant. All joined in except Freia, who walked slowly round the circle, holding out a small wooden bowl before each of the Guardians in turn. Each placed a small object within.

She came to the end of her circuit, stood before Fearánn, and emptied the bowl onto the ground. Morag saw a small pile of white pebbles.

Slowly Fearánn spread the stones with a bare foot. She spoke. 'Twelve white. No black. ' She looked up. 'The council has agreed,' she announced.

Morag remembered Hugh telling her that this was how they elected a new member of a monastery. At this thought, the same fear that had gripped her before reared up, breaking the still surface of the calm that had fallen on her. Was she indeed to be chosen without speaking, without herself being offered a choice?

Fearánn turned, was now walking towards her. She gathered herself. She must tell her: *No*. They must find another. They must choose again.

But it was not to herself that Fearánn was coming. She took a pace beyond Morag, to stand before Sorcha. She stooped, took the girl's hands in her own and raised her to standing.

Then she spoke in her clear, strong voice. 'Sorcha Mi'Mhaeve, Mi'Bhriged. The Council of the Guardians looks to you to follow in the steps of the Blessed Coghlane. It is a calling none can bear unless they be called truly. Yet, if you accept, you will ever have the aid of your brothers and sisters within this circle.

'Know that this day you are free, to take or to leave; to walk towards our circle, or to turn away. If you say *Yes*, we will train and prepare you. At each step, you may continue to walk towards the circle, or no. If you endure, at the end of your preparation we will ask you again. Only then will you make your final vow. Are you ready to take your first step now?'

Morag wanted to speak, to raise her hand, to protect this waif whom, she now recognised, she loved with a fierce love. Surely the girl was too young to make such a choice. It was not fair. She opened her mouth to protest.

But Sorcha was all eyes. 'Aye,' she said, simply, before Morag could find a word.

Her radiant face was reflected in Fearánn's shining eyes.

'Will you now declare your choice before these, the Guardians of Fincara? If you will, step forward into the circle, and we will bless you.'

Morag stood dumb. Her belly churned. Her heart thudded in her chest..

Sorcha stepped forward with all simplicity. Fearánn took her hand and guided her to the centre of the circle.

'Sorcha, receive the blessing of the Guardians.'

On all sides the Guardians were raising their hands in blessing; each one wearing a smile of welcome. Sorcha turned in a circle, her face beaming at them, radiant as sunlight, receiving their gift.

'Sorcha Mi'Mhaeve, the Circle of the Guardians of Fincara welcomes you among them.'

Sorcha's face broke into a broad grin.

'Among the Guardians, we place you this day in the care of the Lord Wolf. But you will not be always with him: each of us will have something for you. And if she is willing, your home for now will remain with Mother Morag. Are you content?'

'Aye,' the girl answered, as if graciousness and ceremony were a language she had grown up in. 'I am.'

Now Fearánn came to stand before Morag. Her eyes danced. 'Mother Morag,' she said, 'you are not over-looked.'

She spoke in a clear voice, which yet held warmth. 'As we have said, there is work awaiting you. But it remains yet to come. So, for now, are you content to give shelter to your kinswoman, giving her leave to come and go as her preparation requires?'

Morag thought of her recent collapse and felt shame. Rather than giving shelter, she felt she had been a burden.

Feáránn was still speaking. 'And there is more,' she declared in her clear voice.

'Morag Mi'Choghlane, we foresee a time of trouble coming upon the Isle Fincara, which will reach even to your door. You have seen the first sign in the heavens.'

For a moment Morag was not sure what she meant. Then it came clear to her mind – the day of the sun-darkening.

Feáránn continued, 'Since the day Atain veiled herself from our sight we, the Guardians, have watched and seen signs, in this world and in Otherworld. We do not know when the storm will break. Not this year perhaps, nor the following. But the time is coming. We foresee that you have work to do for your people, and your people's children. Are you willing to prepare for this work?'

Morag lifted her head. She was conscious of Wolf's eyes upon her, Freia's, Guirman's. She spoke. 'Lady, I do not know what this work is.'

'Your work will be to hold true to who you are and what you know within,' replied Feáránn. 'Beyond that, what will be asked of you will come clear only when it is needed. But, if you are willing, we can help complete in you the knowledge you have sought, for your own sake, and so that your life may be a service to the people. Are you so willing?'

A hot sensation came behind Morag's eyes. She swallowed. She thought of Dhion, of Shinane, of little

the hills she saw each morning; these were the fields she tended, this was where she grazed her sheep. My mother.

She began to feel a great weariness. She returned to the house and sat. The fire was low. She tried to pray. She reached her prayer beads from around her neck and began to tell them, reciting a prayer with each: *Ghea, strengthen my wisdom; O God, still my fear*. But her head nodded and she could not keep her eyes from closing. Wearily she lay down.

She was in a dark cave, and everywhere she turned, darker passages led away, who knew where? She was walking down one of them, on, on, into darkness and more darkness and still, on… She turned a corner. The passage was lit by a glow as of a small fire just around the next corner. There it was: a gentle light, a fragrant scent, a sense of deep joy. In the centre of the light – she knew at once – her mother; not clearly seen, but known. Her mother, saying, *Come. Come further in. I am waiting for you*. And standing beside her, Hugh.

She woke, and found she was wiping quiet tears from her face. Rain was dripping through the thatched roof. Wolf was stewing herbs over the fire while Sorcha tore shreds of flesh from the carcass of the ptarmigan and dropped them into the pot.

Their meal was a sober one. Even Sorcha seemed almost solemn, and Wolf was unusually quiet. Fearánn taught Morag her mother-line: the daughter of Coghlane, the daughter of Catrean, the daughter of Regán, back, back to Lornha the Old. She had her repeat it until she was satisfied.

Wolf looked towards Morag. 'You were dreaming, sister, when we came in from the hunt. Do you recall your dream? Can you tell us?'

It was not a dream she could forget.

She looked towards Guirman. His silence reassured her.

Even as Morag re-told her dream, it gave her peace. She saw Hugh's eyes shining at her, as they used to do. When she had finished they were quiet for a while. Then Fearánn said, 'How does this dream speak to your heart?'

Morag shook her head. But her answer was direct. 'I will go into the cavern, into the Womb of the Mountain. I know there is love there, waiting for me.'

There was silence. The three Guardians seemed each to have turned within. Then they looked to one another, a searching gaze.

'I must go,' said Morag. 'I know it.'

A spider scuttled out from beneath her stool. Passing between her feet, it ran straight towards the edge of the curtain and disappeared.

'Well, nothing could be clearer than that,' said Wolf.

Chapter 31

The mid-autumn sun rose through a mist that shrouded the lands below.

Fearánn wrapped herself in her travelling cloak, hiding her rich black robe beneath a patched and weather-stained plaid. Of her fineness only the ring showed, fiery on her thin finger. She embraced Wolf, and then Guirman. For a moment she held the old man's shoulders, looking into his eyes. 'Farewell, brother.'

'Sister,' he replied, gently taking her hands down from their perch and responding with a slow bow, 'farewell.'

'Little sister.' She stooped to Sorcha. 'We shall meet again.'

'And you, sister.' She turned to Morag, holding her hands in hers. She stood in the doorway, silhouetted against the grey sky. 'Farewell.' She turned, and was gone.

'I would talk with you, daughter. Alone.' Guirman's words were quiet as always, and solemn.

Morag rose. He took a burning stick from the fire and led her to the back of the hut. Pulling aside the old hide curtain that hung there, almost black with age, he revealed another: also old, but woven, patched and threadbare. Beyond, he revealed a passage that led deep into the rock of the mountain itself, the floor in the flickering torchlight worn to a shine. A short descent, and the tunnel opened into a broader chamber. She could not see its walls. Even when Guirman lit a lamp from his guttering stick she could see no more than a gleam here and there where the light was reflected off wetness.

'Sit.' He nodded towards a low platform of wooden boards, covered with a pile of skins.

When they were settled, she on the skins, and he on a low seat, he began. 'Daughter,' he said, and paused. In the weight of the single word she heard her heart-beat; waited for what he would say.

His eyes looked on her where she sat on the fleeces. The lamplight threw shadows across his long face. 'Do you see that passage yonder?' She turned her head. Another mouth could dimly be made out, black in the blackness. 'That leads deep into the mountain. Men made these tunnels, a long time ago. They searched for lead – and other things. The passages branch out from there in all directions – left and right, up and down. I know them all now.

'Since your mother died, only I know the way to the Great Chamber. It is vast. And it opens in the very heart of the mountain. To be left alone in that chamber is always, in its nature, a test. It cannot be otherwise. If you are to follow the prompting of your dream, I will leave you there, without food and without light. The cavern is warm enough for comfort, and there is water. There you will meet what you will meet. I will wait for you three days. Then I shall return to guide you out again. Do you agree to this?'

Did she? Could she? Darkness she did not fear, nor fasting. But to be left alone in that labyrinth …

Finding the steel inside her, she stilled her doubt. She turned to Guirman.

'Father…' She saw the old man in a new light. She understood the significance of the title she now gave him. 'I will submit to this. I will take the test.'

She looked up at him. Through the white hair covering his lip he was smiling. He reached down for her shoulder. 'Well done, daughter. It was not an easy choice. Had it been, you had not been ready for what lies before you. But know that I will remain in the first cavern. I will be here. We will work together.'

'When?' She sat, her hands in her lap. A stone in the floor held her gaze.

'Tomorrow. Use this day well. Tonight sleep, and look to how you sleep. When day breaks, your first-food will be something I will give you. It will help you open to the Womb of the Mountain. Then I will lead you again to this place, and we will go on.'

The afternoon faded. Rain came again and held her within while she looked out through the half-open door at the surface of the tarn, picked into myriad points, rising and vanishing again, rising and vanishing. She could not escape – not from the bothy, not from her own thoughts and imaginings.

Wolf sat quietly, whittling a stick of willow with his knife. Sorcha watched at his side, asking occasional questions.

Morag turned restlessly from the open door.

Wolf looked up, his hands ceasing their work.

'He is good at what he does, Guirman. Very good. He will take you through.' He paused. 'Now, listen.' He cleaned a few small fibres of wood with his blade, and put the knife down; raised the piece to his pursed lips and blew. A single soft note sounded in the still air of the bothy. His voice picked up the note as he lowered the pipe. 'You may know this.'

It was a song she knew from a girl. Later, she had sung it with Hugh, sitting outside the priest's house on a First-day after Tollagh; she singing while he played his pipe. She blinked, and reached a finger to the corner of her eye. Then she took a deep breath, opened her mouth and sang.

The next verse, Wolf lowered his voice to a drone. They reached the refrain and sang together, their voices a fourth apart. Sorcha looked on, smiling, clapping the rhythm.

ॐ ॐ

In the afternoon, while Wolf and Sorcha went out, Guirman came to her. They went again to the first cavern, and he invited her to tell all that had passed to bring her to this place, starting from her childhood in Kimmoil. It was long in the narration. Sometimes he asked a question, often about prayer. He seemed satisfied with her answers. When they climbed back up the passage to the bothy, their supper was waiting for them. Night fell, a tenderness filling the space among them. Wolf went out. Guirman retreated back down the passageway behind the curtain.

Morag blew out the lamp and felt the darkness all around. She lay on her pallet thinking of what Guirman had described. Sorcha was curled up in her cloak on the floor beside her. As her eyes accustomed to the darkness, she saw the faint red glimmer of the embers. Little by little, she felt the whole of the inside of the bothy lit in the faint glow. She lay on her back and stared up into the roof-beams.

'Antie… Are ye no sleepin?'

She answered wearily. 'Not yet, child.'

'What was it Hisself was sayin to ye? When he took ye yonder?'

She could imagine the girl, gesturing with her unseen head towards the back of the hut, where the curtain lay, where Guirman had taken her. 'He said … He told me how he is going to take me into the Womb of the Mountain. And leave me there, alone.' There. She had said it.

'Are ye feared, Antie?'

She rolled onto her side. She faced the girl, a small black mound in the red glimmer. 'Yes, dear. I am feared. I don't think I've ever been so afraid in my life.'

'Me mam used to say, fear's like a big noisy sheep. It keeps on bleatin an buttin an gettin in yere way. An you just have tae ignore it. Know what ye're really goin

228

for, an go for it. An don't give in to it. That's what she said. I wit that.'

Morag lay back. The picture was vivid. How many sheep were jostling in her mind, demanding her attention? And only one thing was needed. For a while she was quiet.

'Antie?'

'Yes, child. Yes, I'm here.'

'I love ye, Antie. Ye're a well brave un, aren't ye?'

'No, my love. I don't feel so. I don't feel very brave at the moment.'

'Nae. It's only the brave knows their fear.'

Suddenly tears came, shaking her. At once she felt two thin arms working their way around her and a child's firm dry kiss on her cheek. She hugged the girl back, fiercely, strongly, feeling her little hard body against her own.

'Antie! It's squashin me ye are!'

She let her go. She rolled onto her back. In the darkness she held a hand out on the floor between them. A smaller, bonier hand found it and held it firm.

Guirman led them in their morning prayer round the fire. When they had completed the time of silence, he took a dish covered with a cloth. Removing the cloth, he offered it to Morag. Mushrooms. Not like those she had crammed into her before, hoping they would give her rest. These were smaller, more delicate, a blueish tinge where the stems had been broken.

'Do not be afraid,' he told her. 'These are much kindlier than those you took before, and the path they open leads to a better place.'

She hesitated, but only for a moment. She had to steel herself to eat, but sure enough, they did not taste foul like the scrying caps. She felt nothing untoward.

When she had done, Guirman dipped his finger in water and anointed her feet: 'Where your feet lead you …' Her hands: 'What your hands do for you …' Her mouth: 'What your lips say of you …' Her brow: 'What your mind thinks in you … Go, in the name and the power of Chrisht.'

Once more he led her through the curtains, along the passage, to the cavern where they had talked together the previous day. Without stopping, he led her on to the mouth of the tunnel he had indicated, the one that descended to the heart of the mountain. Before they entered, he said, 'Hold on to my arm here, just above the elbow and I will guide you, step by step.' Now he carried no torch. The light soon faded behind them, and she only sensed the widening of the tunnel by the change of air and the soft echo of their bare feet. Guirman set a steady pace, quite slow. At first she felt tense, uncertain. Little by little, she relaxed. When the passage narrowed, he brought his arm further round behind him, and she fell into single file. If he ducked, she felt it, and she ducked, too. She began to relax, to feel secure in his guiding. She felt her trust in him grow.

The sound of dripping rang in the silence, mingled with the splash of their feet in shallow puddles on the rough floor. She felt the cold and ooze of mud beneath her. Faint red globs floated dimly before her eyes.

His feet padding in the darkness. The vast weight of the mountain, all around her. It could crush her in a moment and be quite unmoved. And something else: something unknown, just beyond awareness, undis-tracted by the busyness of sight. She thought of Sorcha, and Sorcha's mam, and of sheep. She noticed her fear, accepted it, owned it, and knew it was not her. She followed.

danced slowly, in this Womb of the Mountain? Slowly, stately, to the music of the exquisite dripping water, she raised her arms and began to dance, reaching into the void, bending, flowing in celebration of the Holy.

Slowly her body began to speak to her. She was tired. She did not hunger, nor thirst. But she began to long for some relief from the constant hardness. To stop. To sit. To lie on something soft. Not here, not on this endless hard ground. Then she asked herself – why not? She bent, meeting the rock with both hands, with her knees. Feeling her way with her fingers, stretching out. Now she was lying prostrate, like Freia in the circle of the Guardians. She extended her fingers, her toes. She kissed the hard rock. She turned her face to one side.

How long she lay there, she could not tell. She roused to find that a stone was pressing painfully into her thigh. She shifted herself. She reached down, found the stone, threw it away from her. Echoes, one following another, fading, dying. Silence. Drip, drip, drip. No longer as extraordinary, scintillating music. Just drips.

Slowly she began to know herself again. She sat up. Sat still on the hard stone. Sensed the void. Then in the silence she heard – yes – voices uplifted in song. Faintly, but quite clearly. She held her breath in a silent gasp. The voices were womens' voices, yet higher than women sing. And surpassingly lovely. Even as she heard them, the sound stopped. Silence. She listened, with all her heart. Then deep, unbelievably deep, as if they came from the rocks beneath her, the voices of men. But not men. Too deep for men. And gone, even as they began.

'Oh, beautiful!' she cried. Her voice echoed back to her: *Beautiful ... tiful ... ful ...* Deep within her, she sensed a warmth. Not from the mushrooms: their influence, she sensed, was past. It came from within her own heart.

She sang a chant:

> *Listen!*
> *Listen to the voice*
> *Listen to the voice of the heart.*

Is that what the voices were? The voices of her heart? Or were they the voices of the Womb of the Mountain? She rose from the hard floor, still chanting. She took a step. Another. A third. Her foot met a soft edge. She bent, feeling before her. She had been lying right by one of the wool-sacks, and she never knew. She eased herself onto it. This would be her bed.

She said the night prayers, and heard her little voice shimmer round the huge walls of the cavern. She opened her arms and spread her hands wide, and felt the tingle of her prayer going out from her into the round world.

She lay down, and in the peace of her quiet mind slept.

Chapter 33

She woke, and listened. There they were again, fleetingly: the voices she had heard before. The beauty overwhelmed her. She strained to hear them better, but now they were not. Only the dripping of water; near, far, distant.

She stood. There was hunger. Her belly longed for food, but there was nothing to be done about it now.

However high the sun had climbed, or however low she had sunk in the world beyond the cavern, here, for Morag, it was morning. She began the morning prayer: 'In the name of the One …'

Her voice rose in the chant, small and delicate in the darkness, yet filling the cavern with its sound.

I will roam in the name of Chrisht,
through the world, narrow and wide …

Her song faded away, its faint echoes running round the walls of the chamber. She sank into the silence of prayer. For a long span she rested there. Slowly she drew her hands together, placing them, one over the other, across her heart. *As it was, as it is, as it shall be for evermore…* She bowed and kissed the stone before her. She pictured herself in a pool of light, warm, yellow, shining from within, as from a single candle. She rested in the glow, opened her arms and breathed out, releasing her little radiance into the round world.

That was when she heard it. Behind her left shoulder there was a faint whispering. Fear jumped up. How lightning-swift it moved! In the part of her that was steel, she saw this. Slowly, deliberately, she took a breath. Placed her attention on her raised shoulders. They relaxed. Her heart was still racing. She watched it slow, settle. Now in her mind's eye she laid a hand on Fear's shoulder to calm it, as if it were a bewildered child. The whispering ceased. There was silence.

Then, away to her right, came an indistinct muttering. A low murmur. A sigh. It might have frightened her before. But now, she was ready for it. She found she was only curious. She stood.

For the space of just a few moments, still at a distance, there were distinct words. A low woman's voice. Not words she knew, but with the clear cadence of speech. She turned in their direction. They were gone.

She waited. Silence. Then, from far away and quietly echoing in the vault of the cavern, more words. A man's voice this time, very deep, but smooth, like beer long brewed.

She called. She surprised herself at her own voice – firm, strong, clear. Not raised. No trace of panic. 'Who are you?'

Her words echoed round the cavern. *Are you … Are you … you … you … you …*

As the reverberations died away, she called again: 'I, Morag, ask you, for the love of Chrisht and in the service of the Mother: show yourselves.'

As the echo of her voice died, she heard a flurry of sounds: voices, some like birds twittering or the calling of bats, on the edge of hearing. Some like the tinkling of a little bell, or the creaking of branches in a wood when a gale blows. They came from all around her; above, behind. Then silence again. She sensed she was watched: as if a hundred pairs of eyes were peering at her without need for light.

'I am Morag Mi'Choghlane, Mi'Chatrean. I am under the cloak of the Guardians. I ask you to show yourselves.' The words were in a level voice, but in that void they carried, as clear as the rondal bell.

Again the sudden flutter of sounds and voices, now with scraps of meaning. The voices were rising in power. They were all around her. Then one rose above all, and the others stilled themselves into silence. This time she heard the words plainly.

'The Guardians we know. Coghlane we know. But who are you? Why are you here?' A woman's voice, clear, sharp, as resonant as a harp-string.

'I am called here,' she declared, her own voice ringing out. 'By my mother. My mother, Coghlane.'

A twittering. Then she remembered.

'I am the Daughter,' she called.

A long silence. A single drop of water fell and splashed by her foot.

'The Daughter …' It was as if the voice assayed her for her worth. Then, 'Is the Daughter ready to see us?'

'I am not afraid.'

From before her, behind her, a whisper ran around the cavern. *The Daughter, the Daughter, the Daughter … not afraid. Not afraid of us, of us, of usss.* It died into a long hiss.

'Stand then, Daughter Morag, and you shall see us. Then we shall know if you be not afraid.'

She stood quite still. She steadied her breathing: not too shallow, in … and out. The beating of her heart in her chest; her blood, surging through her veins.

Then, in the corner of her eye, she saw a spot of light. A pin-prick, but bright, intensely bright; blue-white, with a cold fire. She turned to face it.

The light was growing. It seemed to be approaching, slowly at first, then quicker, gliding over the ground. She saw a shape within: a figure. A tall figure, impossibly slender, unbearably bright.

Morag stood. The brightness assailed her. Beat upon her gaze. She bore the unbearable light. A woman's form towered over her, half as tall again as she herself. If she was clothed, it was in dress that could not hide her shape nor dull the light that burned within her; if she was naked, then her form seemed to flow like folds of incandescent cloth into the radiance around her. If it was a spear that she held, there was no distinction between its long shaft and the long arm that held it high.

The light, the figure, stopped before her. She felt its cold brilliance. It rose like a pinnacle of ice.

Look at me: Wolf's words, as she stood, holding out her knife. *You look at me. Only me. Right in my eyes.* And Kethia's Stone; the power flowing from it into her.

But here was a power bearing down on her, seeming to force her sight away. *I shall look. I shall not be cowed.*

A strength rose in her. She raised her eyes. Where the eyes would be, she met a whirling pool of light. Deep. Intense. Burning. A vortex, like consuming fire. Before that glare she stood naked. Her pitiful gown, her very flesh, had no power of covering.

For a moment that was eternity she held that terrible gaze. Held it, while her breath seemed to stop. Held it, until she doubted she would ever see again.

Do you know who we are? She no longer heard words. The ideas formed themselves in her heart.

And in her heart she answered. *Tell me. Tell me your name.*

You know our name, and do not know. You call us Fincara, and the Island, and other names beside. But these are only names from the world of men. Would you know our true name?

'Lady, would you tell it me?'

Can you hear it?

'I do not know, until you say it.'

The pool of light burned brighter, colder. It burned into her.

Daughter of Coghlane mish Catrean, is it? Coghlane we know, and Catrean. You we do not know yet. Are you ready to know us?

'I pray I may become so.'

The cold incandescence dimmed, then flared out again. *You answer well, Morag. Daughter. Listen well, and we shall see.*

For a moment more Morag saw the figure before her. Then the form seemed to melt, as snow melts before fire, and at the same time, grew. Waxed, until it filled the entire cave. It seemed to sweep through her, filling her. Did it fill the whole mountain?

There was no sound. No voiced name. But a kind of knowing grew within her, as if, could she frame her mind like *that* again, then the Presence, the Sidh of the Island, would attend.

The brilliance contracted. Once more she saw a figure before her. But now the Sidh-woman was only a little taller than herself. A sense of beauty, of power, of elegance even. And beside her, another: smaller, more definite, and open like a flower. Small and bent, with the signs of age, yet beautiful to behold, with a beauty that came, not from form, but from within.

'Morag …' The Sidh-woman was speaking again with a different tone, a tone of tenderness. 'Behold your mother.'

She looked at the bright being before her. And saw behind, a host receding into an impossible distance, fading into darkness. Instinctively, she knew. Before her was her mother-line, her ancestresses, receding to the dawn of time. Right back to Lornha the Old, her many-times greatmother, and still behind her …

The small, bright, bird-like figure at the front, shone.

'Mother! Is it you?' She longed to dart forward, to hold on, to embrace. And she knew she must not try to touch her.

For a breath's space they stood and she saw her mother's face and looked into her eyes and tasted once more that sweetness, remembered as a whisper from a time before thought; the sweetness she had held on to all her days, the source here before her. A communion without words. A long breath in, and out. Then, as the glow on the wick of a candle fades and is no more – only a thin swirl of smoke rising into the roof-beams – so the vision faded and was gone. There was no Sidh-woman. And the ancestors, as if they had never been. Yet in her heart it came to her as knowledge: there was a sense in which her mother had been always with her, through all her long years, and ever would be to the end of her days. She stood, swaying slightly. Her breathing level, even, steady.

Only the unceasing drip of water; near, far, away off in the distance.

A glimpse. A glimpse was all that had been vouch-safed her. It was enough.

Chapter 34

The pattern of her day supported her: the prayer, the rhythmic repetition of chants, the beads. A walking meditation through the vastness of the lightless cavern; and the evening office again, the night prayer. She rested a great deal, sleeping much. She did not hear any more voices.

She dreamed. It was early morning. There was dew on the grass, its coolness on her bare feet. She was standing on the summit of a high mountain. Not a pinnacle of bare rock, but a broad green shoulder, a spacious field in the sky. All around, the land fell away: mountain and foothill and folded valley. And now here was her mother, coming towards her. A small, robin-like woman, filled with life, as vivid as if she was right there. A sense of joy and lightness; of laughter and deep seriousness; of knowing the warp and weft of the world.

They were in a great hall, full of people. Many were strangers, and many, she realised, she knew. There was her brother Eoghan, passing with Shareg Donal of Kimmoil. Bridie, her one-time friend, held down, held back by ties that hemmed her in. Yet now, as she looked upon them, they had no power to sway her from her sense of joy. Her mother was beside her.

Then she saw Aidan. Like a fallen tree he lay across her path. She could not move him; she could not climb over him. He brought her to a stop.

But here was her mother, still standing beside her, the life flowing between them, stronger than any of these. She knew she would not always see her, but now there flowed between them an understanding, wordless: we two will meet again, when the long day is done.

She slept.

Morag woke. The same emptiness, darker than darkness itself. The same sounds, of water, dripping and echoing.

But – she had met her mother! As she sat up, she felt she really had met her. The dream had been so vivid it was scarce different in memory from a meeting in the flesh. Her mother had come to her in a dream. She knew there would be no more. Her mother's love was woven into her now, and her mother's wisdom, and always her sweetness, remembered down the years. It was well.

She finished her morning prayer. In the quietness that followed she heard a sound: heard it, she was sure, not with her heart but with her ears, mingling with the ever-present dripping of water. Faint, but regular. A footfall.

She stood, and turned towards the sound. She saw, with the eyes of her body, not her mind, a faint light, a circle of light showing forth the darkness of the cavern. It wavered, a little lamp held in the hand of someone walking a passage towards the chamber. Guirman. Had it been three days?

The light grew. Now it began to shine on the floor of the cave, gleaming off puddles and pools of water. Suddenly, as the walker emerged from the passage into the spaciousness of the cavern, it lit the walls. And there was the figure. Tall, robed in his dark gown, his white hair making a halo around him in the lamp-light.

'Sister!' he called.

'I am here.'

'Come.'

She walked. She felt a sorrow that she was leaving. Yet she was glad. She knew that the cavern and all she had found in it would be inside her now for ever.

'Welcome, sister.' His brown eyes shone in the lamp-light. 'Take the lamp. See where you have dwelt these three days.'

She took the little clay lamp and walked slowly around the walls of the chamber. Its roof soared into darkness, and from the rocks glints of shining stones gleamed. Here what looked like a curtain of stone clung to the wall, flushed with red and orange. There, a fluted column of blue-green faded into pure white. She moved within a sphere of light that in every direction dimmed into nothingness, except where it struck stone or gleamed on water. Glory, revealed. Mystery driven back.

She returned to where Guirman stood. 'It is very beautiful,' she said. 'But I will look no more. I would keep the mystery.'

He guided her back. Returning with the light, she did not need to hold his arm. They came to the first chamber, and Guirman stopped.

'Outside it is night. Daylight would be too bright for you, but it will be good for you to greet the twilight of dawn. We have time to sit and talk.'

'I would be glad to. There is so much to say.'

He laid a long, hard finger on his lips. 'Say nothing of what you met in the Chamber. We do not speak of what we find there, even to one another. It is for you alone to hold that in your heart.'

He beckoned to the platform where skins and cushions were laid. She sat, grateful for their softness. Guirman sat near her.

'What shall we talk of, Father?'

'Do not call me that. Call me Brother, for you have passed into a new place. Let us talk of how you will go forward from here. Tell me, what do you see?'

Morag looked down. She had forgotten how to think beyond the present moment.

Slowly she said, 'I feel my mother in me now. As Hugh is in me, too. How can I not be whole with two such presences?'

'How indeed?' said Guirman. He smiled a satisfied smile. Then he said, 'What will this whole woman do?'

A shadow crossed her heart. She hesitated.

'Say what you see, without judging it,' he said.

'Without judgement? Then – oh!'

She paused, picturing what came to her inner eye. She spoke slowly. 'I see myself standing with Hugh's stole on my shoulders. And blessing … blessing the crops … blessing the people … '

She tailed away. Shook her head. 'But it cannot be.'

'Why so?'

She stared at him. 'Have you ever known a woman who was a priest?'

He made no Yes or No, but looked at her, his head slightly to one side.

'If you mean my mother – she wasn't a priest, was she.'

'Not as you think of one,' he agreed. 'But Coghlane was priestess to the priests, was she not?'

Morag thought about this. Then she said, 'But I can't be that. And – she didn't work among the people. As I long to.'

There! She had said it. The knowledge of the truth of what she had just said followed the words.

Guirman nodded. 'Let us consider what cannot be, and why,' he said. 'The different kinds of impossibility.'

He paused. 'There is that which you cannot do because you were never made to do it. There is that which cannot be because of what surrounds you. And there is that which your heart cannot conceive. But what surrounds you may be overcome. And your heart can change.'

He looked straight into her eyes. Now she felt his will, bidding her to answer.

She said, 'In my dream Father Aidan stood like a fallen tree in my way. Nothing I could do, but wait.'

'What might your waiting look like?'

'I shall return to Teigh Riseart,' she said. 'With Sorcha?' It was a question. The old man nodded.

'And I shall do – whatever I can. The work is hard.'

A pause. Then she said, 'I will go to the Tollagh, and hear only what is needful. For the rest, I will turn within. And when I can, I will start to visit in the town again. Not as the priest's wife. Just as – Morag.'

She looked up, and found the old man, his chin in his hand, smiling at her. 'As Mother Morag,' he suggested, gently.

He looked straight into her eyes. 'That is good.'

Morag knew that she would remember that conversation all her life. She would look back on it, if she was spared, even when she was an old, old woman and her grandchildren were tall young women and men. That strange half-world, between the chamber of rebirth and the outside world where the dawn was creeping up. Guirman and herself, beside his low fire, seated on the piled skins and fleeces that her mother had laid there, while his deep voice rolled out from under his white beard.

At last he rose. 'Come, sister. Come and see daybreak once more. And we shall greet your brother and your little sister.'

He took her hand and raised her, and led her down the passage and through the old, patched curtain and into the twilight of dawn. And the first-food savour of broiling cony and simmering porridge had never smelled so good.

THE THIRD PART:
THE PRIEST

Chapter 35

In the darkness of the priest's house after sunset, Aidan watched the fire slowly die. He weighed what he must do. The archpriest had instructed him to write regular reports. It was his clear duty, and indeed the lamentable state of the people's faith should, he felt, be heard by loftier ears than his own. Yet, did it not feel like – like what? Like spying? Just a little betrayal of the trust – it was plain – that they wanted to put in him? But there again, did he want to spend however many years God might spare him here? For that would be his fate if he displeased his master.

He opened his writing box.

> Aidan Cairpatrick, Priest, to Feirgas, by the grace of God Archpriest of Fincara at Mhreuhan, greeting.

Why on earth did he have to spell it *Mhreuhan*? All those additional letters getting in the way of the simple pronunciation. He preferred the straightforwardness of the Common Speech.

> Your Grace, consequent to my former letter, in which I reported on this the Living to which you have graciously appointed me; its people; the way of their life and their faith; I beg now to enlarge to your Grace further upon their beliefs as I now begin to uncover them, and to set before your Grace a quite extraordinary matter into which I have made some inquiry.

Aidan rested his pen and adjusted the smoky lamp which shone flickeringly onto the parchment. He squinted at his careful, rounded letters, then continued. He wrote about the great stone in the rondal which the

252

people venerated, which was bedrock and could not be removed. He told how, when he asked about their yearly feasts, they would answer, not of saints' days and Corpus Christi, but the pagan festivals of Imbolg, Beltain, Samhain and Iulgh. While they spoke of celebrating Easter, it seemed they did so more as a feast of Rebirth than of Resurrection. And Chrisht's Mass seemed secondary to the celebration of the Return of the Sun.

He picked up the pen. Held its nib to his eye. He was pressing too hard again: the fine quill was splitting. He gave it a couple of strokes with his knife and dipped it in the ink.

And, your Grace, about this other matter. There is a man here who, a year or more before your Grace's Preferment to this Isle, was plucked from the sea barely alive and brought to this shore. And no person, not even he himself, can say whence he has come.

He has in his possession, and indeed I have seen it with my own eyes, a Coat which the people say has magical powers, such that whosoever wear it, no waters can drown him. This same Coat was sent around the Island, and no man, not even your Grace's Foreholder, had seen the like.

Now this Man is causing to be made a Wheel like unto the water wheels which are not uncommon upon the mainland and in the Saison lands of the South; but this Man is not content for his Wheel only to grind corn. He tells me it will make articles of wood of as fine quality as any that are made there. Indeed, the pride of this Man is so great that he declares his *maseen* will turn iron. I do not know what he means by this, but I wonder whether he believes that no sword nor axe will prevail against it. How this may be so I know not; but when he was but a prentice to the smith of this town, I am told he made and shewed to the people a *maseen* that moved stones of itself. I fear where his power may come from and whether it be set against the Pure and Acceptable Gospel of Our Lord and of Holy Mother Church.

I seek your Grace's wisdom in this matter, and whether your Grace would place this man under the discipline of the Church, that at least his Soul may be saved as a brand plucked from the very fire.

I am your Grace's most humble Brother in the service of Holy Mother Church.

He paused. His eyes were sore.

Aidan.

He sanded the glistening wet ink, blew upon it and shook out the parchment. Then, carefully folding it, he slid it into its linen pouch, then into the sealskin bag that would keep it dry through its journey, relayed from one fishing boat to another until, finally, it would be carried by runner across Caerster to the archpriest's high house.

Good. That was done. An irksome task, but necessary if he was to stay in favour and, perhaps one day, be invited to a better township in a less backward land. He would find someone tomorrow to take it across to Fisherhame: that boy from the steading he'd visited above the town.

Dhion stood, watching Shinane sitting with Lois at her breast, while Regan, lying on her back on the floor, was playing with her toes. It was he who had insisted the twins not be swaddled the whole time.

'How long since Morag and Sorcha went away?' she asked.

'Near a week.'

The first time Morag was not seen at the Tollach, he had run up the brae to Teigh Riseart thinking she must be ill. That had been the start of his serious concern for her.

'If it wasn't for Micheil saying this man they went off with is to be trusted, I would not have let them go. I hope Micheil knows what he's doing.'

'I'm sure he does,' said Shinane thoughtfully. 'He said he was one of a Couvent of the wise that the sharegs know of. That gave me, well, one of those feelings I get when something in me senses something important.'

'Whatever the man is, what can he do?' asked Dhion. 'If he cannot alter Morag's situation, he cannot help her, it seems to me. She's been turned out of her house and found a place away from everybody, with nothing but farm work to be done from morning to night. That's not what she's used to. And now she has to sit through these Father Aidan Tollach meetings. I'm sure she could hold them herself in a way that would be much more to everyone's liking. It must be an agony for her. It would be like asking me to forego building the wheel.'

'That would be so bad for you? An agony?'

'Well, I would feel thwarted. I hope I now understand the mistake of trying to use too much knowledge. Knowledge that is too far different from what people here know and can use. But this wheel will be of use, certainly to Olan. Maybe in time to others, as they grow used to using the wheel's power. And now we're actually going to make a start tomorrow morning. We're going to begin digging the lete.'

'Aunt Shelagh is in favour of your wheel,' Shinane said.

'Fengoelan told me. She's full of surprises, your aunt.'

The day before, Dhion had walked up the brae with Fengoelan, the fisherman in whose boat he had once been rescued: solid as rock, wrinkled as tree-bark, sure as sunrise. They had stood together, looking over the burn at the place where Dhion thought to raise the wheel.

'Shelagh can see this wheel of yours rising here,' he said.

'Does she, indeed!' exclaimed Dhion.

'That she does,' said the fisherman. 'She sees that it will give much more than it takes away.' He paused, then added, 'I could wish sometimes that women were allowed to our councils. Men are good at fire and air. But water and earth are more women's business. They have a wisdom that needs to be mixed in the pot. We lose much through denying them their place.'

'And Morag's another,' Dhion said to Shinane. 'She's one who managed to make her voice heard to good effect, when Hugh backed her. Now he's gone, I fear her voice will not be given the space among us it deserves.'

The next morning early, and the ground was ice-starred: the first frost of the autumn. Not cold enough to freeze the ground, but Dhion and Olan wrapped cloths around their hands as they took their tools.

Leighan, long-shanked, stooping, joined them as they broke for their first rest.

'An it's water ye want to bring downaway through this, is it?' He levelled his eyes, unsmiling, at Dhion. 'Water will always find its way, ye wit. It's puddled clay ye need, to line your course wi.' He turned to Olan. 'Go down an talk wi Padragh, son. He'll help ye wi this. Tell him I sent you.'

'An Murdogh. For why have ye no got Murdogh here? Tell him to bring a mattock or two, an anyone who's strong enough to wield them he can find.'

'An picks,' he shouted at Olan's vanishing back. 'Ye'll need picks!'

'Ye'll need lead.' Shean himself brought Dhion his midday meal. Dhion was not very surprised to see his stocky

'And now, may I ask where you are going?' Robert continued, still in his player's voice. 'And if we may escort you thither. For six travel more safely than two.'

Morag thought quickly. It was impossible to continue their journey without disclosing its direction.

'We are returning to Caerpadraig in Westerland, where my home is,' she replied. 'But that is not the way you were headed.'

'Lady, one way is as good as another when you wander the wilds as we do. And maybe the good people of Cairpatrick can give us lodging and let us play for them. What do you say, lads?'

The others gave a variety of nods and smiles by way of agreement. One of the outhouses at Teigh Riseart had a few sheaves of straw in it, and Morag guessed they would prefer to spend the night there than in the wild. She wondered what kind of greeting they would receive from Shareg Micheil. But, seeing no alternative, she said, 'All right then. We must keep going if we're to get there tonight.'

Morag took the lead, with Robert beside her. She could hear Sorcha behind, chattering ceaselessly with the others. She turned to her new companion.

'Now tell me exactly why you're here, Ma'Dhuirmid. You said it was too hot for you in Caerster. What did you mean?'

'First,' the other replied, 'if you go on calling me Ma'Dhuirmid, I shall have to call you Antie Morag. Are we agreed?'

She smiled. 'All right.'

'But I'll answer your question all the same. Time was, we all lived happily together. A little harmless knifing over a woman, fisticuffs over a strangely moving boundary stone, but no more than that. We plied

261

our trades and did quite well. I sold horses and ran a few pack-horse trains into Midland. And at the quarter days, we got together and played. We told the old tales of Aengas and Brede and the Dagda.' She nodded. 'And at Chrishtmas we acted out the stories from the Book about Mother Mair and her babby.' Morag nodded again. Hugh had told her how, in Caerster, Chrisht's Mass was taking the place of the mid-winter rite of Iulgh which they celebrated in Caerpadraig. 'Always, of course, we turned everything upside down and inside out and poked fun at whoever deserved it,' he continued.

'But then things began to change. The new arch-priest came from across the water, and brought in priests like himself: un-Islanders. Or men who'd spent so much time on the other side they'd lost their Island ways. And they began to tell us we mustn't play the stories of the old gods any more, because the One God would be angry.

'Then our new priest began to demand that we tell him what we were going to play. And sometimes he would say Yes, and sometimes No. And sometimes … Well, you just couldn't tell if you were going to be in trouble or not.

'We used to play in front of the rondal,' he contin- ued. 'Then they made it a church. Well, that still fitted in all right at Chrishtmas, but not so well for some of our other stuff. So it was Malcolm had the idea. He said: *We don't have to play just in front of the church, do we? What about the market square?* So we moved there. We thought it would be all right for the folk tales, and maybe we got a bit carried away with poking fun at the powerful. It was like the old days, and people loved it.

'God! Was there trouble!' He put out a hand to stop her. Turning to him, Morag saw his long face puckered in pain. 'The priest went to the shareg, and the shareg refused to do anything, so the priest went squealing back to the archpriest.' He stepped back. 'Before we knew what was happening, there were men-at-arms turning over our shops. Turned me out on the streets, and my wife went running with the children back to her mother.

'Now I ask you, since when did an archpriest have an army? That came as a surprise, I can tell you. A nasty surprise.'

She stared at him, open-mouthed. 'How can this be? Do you speak truth?' she cried.

'Indeed I do, Ma'am.'

A chill swept through her. In a moment, she thought back to the time of the sun-darkening. Was this what Atain had meant?

'Have you seen your family since?'

Robert shook his head. He bowed into the wind and strode on. 'Her wealthy brother will take care of them, Ghea be praised. I fear there's no going back for me.'

'But your shareg?' She hurried to catch up with him. 'Could he do nothing?'

He turned as they walked, to look straight into her eyes. 'I don't know what he could have done. Everything's changed from how things used to be only a few years ago. All I know is, none came forth to help us. So … here we are.'

'You've been outlaws ever since?'

'Oh please!' Robert raised his hands in protest. 'Wandering craftsmen, general hands – and players! Our aim is to make ourselves useful – and to delight! Out of our trouble, may we bring joy.'

But Morag had seen behind the mask.

❧

At length, they descended through pine-woods and could see the waters of Lough Padraig glinting before them. The rain had fallen all day. The lough and the air alike were grey; the walkers, cold and wet.

Morag broke a long silence. 'How long do you want to stay?'

'Winter's coming, lady. If we can find lodging and if your town will have us, until the bad weather's done.'

'Before he gives you leave to stay so long, Shareg Micheil will demand you swear fealty to him.'

Robert looked candidly back at her. 'If your shareg is willing to have us – *outlaws* – then we can promise to be good. We only ask one thing.'

'Food? And a dry bed?' Morag suggested.

'Well – maybe three things.' He stopped, and turned fully towards her. His surprised companions ceased their talk as they all but ran into him. 'Freedom!' he proclaimed. 'All we ask is licence to play what we want and say what needs to be said.' Now it was he who looked her in the eye.

They forded the river and climbed to the loughside path.

As they drew near the town, Morag pointed to a track that branched away from the main path and climbed the brae to eastward at the head of the lough. It seemed long since she had walked this way, though it was barely a week. And there, over a gentle lip of the land, it sat. For the first time, Teigh Riseart looked like home to her. She took down the bar and pushed the heavy door open.

Sorcha found her fire-bow and tinder while Morag took the players to the steading. On her return a whisp of smoke was rising from the kindling.

There was little in the house but oatmeal and some wizened apples, but the men produced a pipe and a small tabor, and what they lacked in plenty they made up in good cheer while the rain beat down until it dripped through the thatch. When they parted for sleep, the moon rising through the cloud-wrack and lighting the players as they went, an understanding was growing between them.

Chapter 37

'What do you think of them?' Morag asked Sorcha, when at last they were alone in the croft-house. The girl returned her question with a frank look. 'They're no good uns, but they're no bad uns neither,' she said in her blunt way. 'They're awricht.

'Anyways,' Sorcha went on. 'Ye dinna have anyone to hew wood an draw water, do ye? Let alone all else that could be done to tidy the place. There's good ground here for growin food for us all, but it needs workin. They can go to the shareg in the mornin to do their swearin. Then it'll be up to him.'

Micheil gave them two weeks to show they really meant to be useful, and he'd inspect what they had done. Sorcha, more than Morag, pointed out what needed doing in the vegetable garden, clearing and digging over more ground ready for planting in the spring; and young Iain got on with it while the men put their heads together to consider how best to start repairing the steadings. The roof was clearly the most urgent job and they could do the work, but would need support from Siocan and Odhran and the town. It took a day or two to organise, then work began.

Morag trimmed the light. Sorcha had disappeared.

She rose from her evening devotion, the long stillness enfolding her, and straightened her weary limbs. The scrape of the door made her start as it scratched a bit of gravel across the stone threshold, but she knew it was only the child returning.

Sorcha was not alone. Behind her, not needing to stoop beneath the low lintel, came another. A small, fine-featured face circled by a grey woollen hood, the skin peat-brown in the yellow light. As soon as the stranger had passed through the door she stopped and bowed, raising her hands, palms together, in salute. She gave her greeting in words Morag did not know, but the meaning was clear: 'Peace be to this house.' With wonder Morag recognised the dark-skinned woman whom she had noticed at her mother's house.

'Mother Morag. Please forgive my untimely arrival. I am Amirah.' The woman's voice in the Island speech had not forgotten the cadence of another tongue.

She threw back her hood and straightened her black hair, bound in long plaits over each shoulder: a lustrous black, rare on the Island. She reached with both hands to take Morag's in hers.

Morag gestured to a bench. 'Lady, you're welcome – by night or by day. Come. What can I bring you?'

Amirah waved her hands, bowing her head in gratitude. 'It is late. Do not trouble yourself for me. If I may have a little water, and the welcome of your fire for the night, I will be content. And in the morning, may we talk? Please … you were on your way to bed. Let me not break in upon you.'

Sorcha was already arranging the third bed-alcove for their unexpected guest.

'It's all right, Antie. You gae to bed. Amirah'n I'll be fine.'

She woke early to the sound of rain, and another sound. A soft murmur. She let it wash over her as she dozed. It was a kind of singing, but in a style she had not heard. Amirah's voice, crystal-clear, sliding up and down intervals she would never have imagined, or quavering on an eerily high note. Then Sorcha would follow. Amirah was clearly teaching the child, and by the sound she had an apt pupil.

The singing came to a close and there was a brief silence. Morag raised her head.

'Good morning,' said Amirah. Her voice rang like a bell. 'I trust we did not wake you?'

'It was restful, listening to you.'

'That was the music of my forebears. We call it a *raag*.' Amirah paused. 'We have your first-food ready.'

The men came in to break their fast, and were surprised to see the visitor. But when Sorcha got up to wash the bowls, they went out to get on with their tasks, promising an evening of music to come. Amirah settled on the floor in the cross-legged posture she used.

'I wonder how you sit like that,' Morag began.

Amirah smiled. The deep creases around her mouth looked dark in the lamp-light. 'This is our tradition. We sit like a mountain. When we can be still as a mountain, then we can begin to think like a mountain. Have big thoughts, high and deep. The young one here is learning.'

She paused. 'I asked you last night if we could talk together this morning. Indeed, that is why I have come. May we, now?'

Morag looked back at her visitor. 'What about?'

'When I tell you, we will have begun. So may we start properly?'

Three still points in a triangle, they sat or knelt in silence. The rain on the thatch put Morag in mind of another house, high in the arms of a mountain, and another silence where rain and sun swept over the circle of the Guardians. Gently she let the memory go, gazed upon the blue sky of her mind, unclouded, for a short space, by thoughts. The memory returned. Inwardly, she repeated a word she used to still herself; waited, while what drew her mind dissolved into mist.

A single chime. Slowly, she opened her eyes. Amirah held a wooden striker and the bell, a single folded sheet of brass.

A pause.

'Now, Mother Morag,' Amirah began. 'The Lord Guirman has asked me to tell you of my tradition.'

Morag was at once drawn in. 'Please.'

Amirah smiled. 'It is different from yours, of course, yet our traditions touch at many points. Learning something of mine may help to broaden your heart, which is already wide. We mind that you may need a very great heart for what is to come.'

What did Amirah – or anyone – know of what was to come?

'In the land where my longcestors came from, the people honour many gods. Some are honoured across the land; some known only in one town. As people grew in their understanding of Spirit, some came to see that all these gods were pointers to the One Spirit.'

'Lady,' Morag replied. 'this I know too. And when I see a bird in the sky, a bush in flower, a wave breaking on the shore, I see in these as well a reflection of the One.'

'That is good.' Amirah looked at her. 'And you know that, while we may open in our hearts to the One, when it comes to our thoughts the Holy is in the end quite unknowable, quite unreachable.' She paused, and glanced at Sorcha. The girl was sitting very still. Sitting, Morag thought, like a mountain.

'If that was all we could say, then our tradition would be quiet indeed.' Amirah allowed herself a soft chuckle. 'But there is more, and I think you know it. For inside each of us … ' She struck her palm with the tip of the other forefinger to accent each word. '… each one of us, there is something of Spirit. Yes?'

'We have a word for this in our tradition.' Morag leaned forward. 'We talk of soul. If we tend our souls, they grow bigger in God. If we neglect them, they shrink. Perhaps in some, they peter out altogether. May it be for good.'

'For some, this could be a mercy,' Amirah said softly. 'But let us return to what I want to tell. I want to say to you that, beyond the appearances of gods and goddesses, or of your sidhe, the One Spirit is neither manly nor womanly. The One holds both, but is neither.'

She paused; the expression in her face more serious.

'Hear me when I say this to you, Morag' she said, quietly. 'It follows that the Spirit in you is neither womanly nor manly. It is both, and it is neither.'

She sat back, waiting, it seemed, for some response.

'What are you saying, Lady?' Morag's words came slowly.

She felt Amirah's eyes pierce her, stabbing into her like the sharpest of blades; yet the wound was healing.

'You tell yourself, do you not: *I am a woman, so certain things are not allowed me.*'

At first Morag sat, unthinking. Then a picture came to her mind of another day. Rain, blown in on a gale from the sea. Hugh, pale, drawn, wasted, lying before her. *Pick up the stole. Put it on. Not on me. Put it on you.* And her reply: *I'm a woman. I can't ...*

'I want to tell a story.'

The dark eyes withdrew their blade. Warmth and gentleness flowed from them again. Morag relaxed.

'My father was a trader. We lived far to the south, where the sun rises high and we whitewash our houses to ward off her heat. He would sail with bolts of fine white cloth and dark goat-hair to the north: sometimes to Armorica, sometimes Kernow; now and then as far as Eirinn. There he would hire pack-animals and travel far inland, trading for wool and fleeces and hides. He would take my eldest brother; and, since a child, I begged him to take me too on one of his journeys. After our mother died he agreed. I will never forget leaving the bright sunlight behind and coming into grey seas under a grey sky, where never does Atain show her full glory.

'Up the eastern shore of Eirinn my father traded, as far as the kingdom of Ulastr, where we stayed a good while. And there I met a man from across the northern sea. Then I kissed my father and my brother, and we wept together. I sailed with my man, with joy and sorrow in my heart, to his land, the Isle Fincara. But he died of fever before we had been wed a twelvemonth, and no child had come to us. I had known grief before, but never had I felt so alone, and I considered how to find a way to return to my father's land. Yet even in the darkest hour of my grief, still I felt the Island calling. Then Tearlach and Guirman found me, and it was they who brought me into the Circle of the Guardians.'

Amirah fell silent. The fire crackled and spat. Sorcha added a log. Morag was deep in thought. People in Caerpadraig had looked upon herself as a foreigner from the Northland. But this woman … She felt a kinship with her, the northern Islander with the southern foreigner.

Amirah leaned forward. 'I want to tell you of something from that time with my father and brother among the people of Eirinn. It is a wide land, with few towns. What towns there are were built by the Northmen. The people live in farmsteads, with maybe as much as a morning's walk between.

'My father and brother travelled from one steading to another, trading. He would always deal with the man of the house; but when it came to the end of the day it was the woman who called them all together. She it was who would lead them into silence, and break bread for them all and speak of the things of Spirit.'

She paused. 'So tell me, who there was being priest to those people?'

Morag sat, her head bowed. She was still thinking of that last day with Hugh. In her mind, she heard

271

Shinane's voice: *It was as if something inside you was set free ... I saw you change. You grew.* Had she not spent this past year denying that growth?

'That may be,' she said slowly. 'But still, it is not how we do things here. And yet,' she reflected, 'my husband did anoint me.'

'Perhaps your husband was more ready for the change that is seeking entrance than you are.' Amirah's voice was like a spear thrown. It hit its mark. Her eyes were blazing.

'And what about your mother?' she asked.

Structures began crashing down in Morag's mind. They had seemed so strongly built, their foundations laid long years before. But now they could no longer hold. Words deserted her.

She bowed her head. When she looked up, dark eyes were there that beamed light, ready, gazing upon her.

'I am beginning to understand,' she said humbly.

In the evening, the men came in again and Amirah sang a merry little song for them while they sat, intrigued. She passed another night in the house, then slipped out early the next morning while it was still dark. They kissed and embraced on the threshold, then she was gone into the paling blackness, walking to the east, away from the town.

Morag turned back to the house. She took the fire-pot and blew up the embers, catching the glow on a wisp of kindling. She lit the lamp.

Deep in the little chest where she kept her most precious things, she reached down for the linen wallet she had made. She took it out and loosed its strings. There it was: Hugh's stole. She lifted it out.

Fine white woven wool, on a linen back. She traced the lines of dyed thread that embroidered its symbols: the circled cross, the entwined fishes, the bird taking wing, as lovely as anything the Guardians wore. Hugh's stole, that she had sewn. Now hers. Passed from one to the other.

Sorcha watched. Morag lifted it, gazed at it, felt it in her hands. She bowed her head and slipped it over her shoulders. She remembered that feeling, when Hugh had commanded her: the sudden coming upon her of power – a gentle power. And authority.

'It sits well on ye,' said Sorcha. 'Looks right. Ye're the priestess, Antie. That's what ye are.'

'Perhaps I am,' said Morag. She paused, motionless. Then she lifted the stole from her neck. 'But right now there's water to fetch and wood to bring in. Come on.'

Chapter 38

It was just after Samhain when they raised the timbers
to hold the wheel.

No, Leighan didn't have a suitable baulk of timber for the axle-tree: they'd have to go and find one.
Where? In the forest, of course. Look for a tree that was
sound enough, straight enough, strong enough. When
could they go? Well, they'd have to wait for the waning
moon. No good cutting living timber before.

They went in single file along the narrow path.
Olan and Dillon, the apprentice, carried short hand-
axes; Dhion's knife hung from his belt. The forest was
silent. Dhion remembered when he and Shareg Micheil
had walked this same path on their way to the High
Shareg. But that had been spring, when the trees were
alive with sap rising and the busyness of birds building and insects feeding and being fed on. The whole
turmoil of life, turning and wherning into the business of living. Now there was a stillness that belied
the breeze. The birches on the forest-edge shook down
showers of yellow leaves, but deeper into the woodland
little moved. An occasional ochre-coloured leaf floated,
spinning in the air, to settle upon a drab dun-coloured
toadstool.

Olan knew his way. He had walked these woods
since a child; had let go his mother's hand to follow
his father's long, bent back into the forest searching for
timber. He knew what he was looking for.

Towards the top of a low hill, where the Padraig
River flowed down from the lough on one side and the
big river followed its twisting valley on another, the
trees grew less thickly. Still sheltered from the wind, the
thinner soil made them grow slow and strong; stunted
but straight. Olan had them stop by an oak that rose,

maybe the height of two men, into its thinning canopy. Two or three smaller branches were bare and white.

'What do you think?'

Dhion looked up its height. 'I doubt if we'll find one straighter. I think it's fine.'

Dillon drew his axe to mark on the trunk a nick to help them know it when they returned to fell it.

Olan put out his hand. 'Stay. We must speak to the tree first. We're taking a life.' And with that he reached forward and touched the wrinkled bark. They stood quite still, waiting, listening. They could yet turn back from this one. A crow cawed, once, twice, three times.

'Well?'

Dhion answered. 'Yes.'

'I agree.' Olan looked across to where Dillon was standing. 'All right. You may.'

The lad swung his hatchet and cut a white notch in the bark. Did Dhion imagine that the branches gave a sudden quiver? Three brown, crumpled leaves floated down.

Father Aidan crossed himself and jumped up from his knees. What a rich time of prayer that had been! He hadn't yet heard back from the archpriest, but at least for now he knew how to move forward. He had a plan. He turned from the altar and crossed the sanctuary, looking about him. *Rondal! No more rondal,* he thought. *Upon this rock, Our Lord has said, shall I build my church.* Here was a rock. If he could not ignore it nor move it, then he must give it a new meaning in the hearts of the people. Now, at last, he saw his way clear.

A stiff wind, almost a gale, was blowing down from the pass, driving the grey clouds before it. The wind blew the door against him as he unlatched it, and drops of rain smote his face. He felt an exhilaration, almost a wildness. He would not be deterred any more.

The widow-woman was there in the house, cooking his porridge. He ate with relish. She took his bowl and the crock while he sat, turning over his thoughts. After a while there was a clattering at the back of the house, and she reappeared, besom and polishing cloth in hand.

'A'De, you can leave the housework for today. I need …' He paused. 'I would like to think through some ideas. Some quiet. Some stillness today.'

'As you say, Father.' She turned, went through the curtain and came back empty-handed. She picked up her shawl where she had laid it neatly over the bench.

'God's blessing, A'De.'

'Ghea keep you, Father.' And she was gone. A swirl of wind as she opened the door made the lamps gutter.

Ghea keep him. That was the trouble – it was so deep in the people, this earth-worship. Still, as they said, the City of God is not built in a day.

The more he thought about it, the more straightforward it was becoming. The rock was not so much an obstacle as a gift: upon this *rock* will I build my church, he repeated. Here was his teaching text.

And the time was right. In just a couple of weeks it would be the beginning of Advent: four weeks of penitence before Chrisht's Mass. Four homilies, each building on the one before. It would take time, but slowly, he was sure, he could move the people to see in the rock the faith of Saint Peter, whose very name meant *Rock*. The true mother, he would explain, was Holy Mother Church, founded upon that rock. He would show them how their former ideas of the Mother had ever been pointing in the right way, only awaiting one who could disclose to them the full and glorious truth.

Pride. The sin of pride. He must watch himself not to fall into that. He repeated the psalm: *Not unto us, O Lord, not unto us, but unto Thy Name give glory, for Thy mercy's sake…* Yes indeed. He must mortify himself, that his small self not seek the glory for his own sake. Every

time he caught himself admiring himself – every time –
he must fall upon his knees and beg forgiveness. Had not
Saint James written, *Cleanse your hands, ye sinners, and
purify your hearts, ye double-minded. Be afflicted and
mourn and weep: let your laughter be turned to mourning, and your joy to heaviness. Humble yourselves in the
sight of the Lord, and He shall lift you up.*

He would write to the archpriest at once. Feirgas
would surely see the merit of his plan, and mark him as
one to take note of and consider for higher things. He
reached for his writing materials and soon the scratch
of the quill was the only sound in the house.

When he had finished, he sat back. The house was
quiet. Perhaps he did rather miss the woman's busyness
around the place. He shrugged.

He signed the letter, carefully. Sat long, looking at
it. Then in a rush he sanded it, folded it and thrust it
into its linen wallet.

Chapter 39

Autumn greyed into winter. The snow-line worked its way down the mountains; sometimes a little retreat, and then an even greater advance. One morning, Morag woke to find the whole strath below her white, the lough grey with ice, the trees of the orchard bowed under their weight of snow. She shivered.

Malcolm burst in, a huge creel of firewood in his arms. Robert followed. 'We've come early to break our fast with you ladies this morning,' he announced. 'And to share with you our wit and merriment on this glorious day.

'Besides,' he added, 'it's well perishing in that steading.'

Sorcha glanced from under her brows as she blew up the embers. Morag caught the brief grin on the girl's face.

As they sat warming themselves, Duncan announced that, come the spring and the better weather, he would take Iain back south-away and see if he could place him as prentice to a tailor somewhere in Caerster. The youth coloured and gave his weak smile in reply. The other two were minded to stay, if present company and the shareg allowed.

They all listed their tasks. The work on the roof was done, Ghea be thanked. But there was fodder to take out to the sheep and more firewood to bring down. Malcolm had found an old plough in an out-building and had plans to fettle it for when he could break a patch of land. 'And what beast will you use to draw it?' Robert had questioned. 'Me,' replied Malcolm, slapping his chest. 'And you shall be plough-boy.'

Then they had tumbled out. Sorcha followed them, and came back with the cauldron filled with snow. Morag helped her heave it onto its hook above the fire. While the snow melted, they sorted the washing.

Morag looked at her niece. She was scarcely recognisable as the waif of Kimmoil. Her cheeks had filled out and now, as she rolled up her sleeves, there was flesh on her arms. She would make a strong, stocky young woman.

Morag felt at ease in herself, but for a vague sense of bad things stirring in the world beyond. Winter brought hard times, scraping for food as much as the sheep had to. Yet between the ceaseless toil of autumn harvests and the back-breaking work of spring sowing, it also brought rest. The snow was a cold white blanket pulled up to the chin of the world, kissing it goodnight and sound sleep. There was time to rest. Time, she thought, to turn over all that had happened through the months of light and warmth.

Hugh. It had been not much more than a year since he had left her. She would never have started her quest while she could hold his hand. What would he have made of the woman she was becoming? She remembered the ready give-and-take of their lives together, an ease far distant from her present world. And yet … for all she had lost, she knew she had also gained something; and Guirman said she was being prepared for something. *Must it be so?* she questioned. Inwardly, she shrugged. This was how it was.

But what was it for, all this preparation? Priestess, against priest? She couldn't see it.

The day before, down in the rondal, Father Aidan had filled their minds with mothers. His words joined with what had driven her all year: her quest to find her own mother. She thought, too, of Shinane, now fully entered into motherhood. But it seemed he was seeking to take away from them *the* Mother. The one

279

who brought forth all things, upon whose breast they walked, whose flesh they ploughed to sow new life, to whose bosom they returned when they were laid in the earth. He wanted to replace Her with a new mother: *Mother Church* – a foreign word standing for a foreign idea that remained dark to her. What did this Mother Church have to give that they at Caerpadraig actually wanted? What need was there for this seeming-shadowy body arching over all? No one but Aidan felt this need. This *Church* seemed like a mother who was no mother. A step-mother who threatened the children by chasing their mother away. Surely Aidan was mistaken.

'Ye wit, I'm sorry to say it, but I near gae to sleep when he speaks.' The voice was Mairte's, come down from Croft Intoch to the shareg's house to sew with Aileen and the other women who gathered there. Morag was among them. These days, she was willing to put her needlework over her shoulder and walk down the brae. Heads were nodding. Tongues were clicking. 'He's no like your man, Morag. Father Hugh, Ghea rest him, talked from where we are. This Father – I canna grasp what he says.'

'What's this *Mother Church* he speaks of?' Rhona asked. 'What's it do? It's all I can manage just to say it.'

Aileen spoke. 'I think he means to re-name the rondal.'

'Wi respect, A'Shar'g,' Sionag, the mother of Niall the dairyman, glanced up from her seat under the window. 'If this *cheurgh* –' she made it sound as if she were clearing phlegm from her throat '– is the Mother, he canna be meanin the rondal. The rondal's a house, like yours or mine, only it's holy. We know the Mother. She's the rock in the rondal, an the ground we stand on, an she's Ghea who holds us, birth to death. She's no wattle an daub.' She sat back, picked up her work and held it close before her rheumy eyes. Under her breath she muttered, so that only Morag heard. 'The man's a gowk.'

As the women were leaving, Aileen touched Morag's arm. 'Micheil's going to have a word with him – the priest, ye ken. He wanted you to know. He's worried. After all, the rondal's the centre of the town, and the Tollagh is where we all come together – the fishers, the shepherds, everyone. If he drives the people away, we all fall apart.'

But the next day Micheil arrived at Teigh Riseart. He kicked the snow off his boots at the door. The dark clouds looming overhead, barely clearing the peaks of Talor Gan, made the short day even gloomier. His mood seemed to match the day.

Morag took his cloak and hung it near the fire to dry. He slumped onto a bench and stretched his legs towards the flames. His boots began to steam.

'Oh Morag, Morag, Morag! Who has come to us in the place of your dear man?' He shook his head. 'Cattle I understand, and they me. Men I thought I understood. But this priest …'

The shareg took another pull at the warm beaker she had placed beside him. 'He wants to call the rondal something else; some fancy word he says the new arch-priest upholds. I can't make head nor tail of it. And he wants to name it after Saint Peter. What's Saint Peter got to do with it, I ask him. *It's because of the rock*, he says. He says Peter means rock. Does that make any sense to you, Morag? Cos I'm damned if it makes sense to me.'

Morag felt a tiny shudder pass through her. She thought of Robert's words, as they walked across the moor. She began slowly.

'I know the story he's using. When Ieshu called his followers, he did name Peter his rock. *And on this rock*, he said, *I will found the ones I call out.* That meant all the people who wanted to live by his teachings and look after each other.'

Micheil looked up, through the smoke and heat above the fire. 'Don't we do that?' he asked. Their eyes met.

'Hugh used to tell a story about what happened after Ieshu died. He said his followers scattered – north, south, east and west. Wherever they went, they took his teachings and ways and brought them to other peoples who saw their own traditions anew. As these teachings came to different peoples, they kept their own practices, but changed them as the Chrisht-light guided them. Each was different, but the same spirit shone through all. But then came a time when the High King of Rhuome declared that all lands under his sway must follow the Way of Chrisht, and must do it in the self-same way, as Rhuome decreed. Hugh said that this same-doing and believing was more important to them than either compassion or forgiveness, which were the hallmarks of Chrisht. Then, he said, the Spirit of Chrisht was driven underground.'

Micheil was watching her intently. 'I'm minded of what your Robert had to say about the new archpriest that day he came to my house.'

Morag nodded.

'And I'm feared,' he went on, 'this Father Aidan is the archpriest's man.'

He stopped speaking. They sat in silence, facing each other.

'I'm going to have to speak to him again,' he said, slowly. He gave her a hard look. 'I'm going to need you there when I do it,' he added.

Chapter 40

Iulgh, the longest night, fell on a Fifth-day. The people would meet in darkness in the rondal as the light died, having pushed aside the benches. The women would be there now, decking the place with bright-berried holly, placing the lanterns, while the men brought in wood for the fire. Of course, the priest would not preside. It would be a night for song and story. Morag would be called upon to tell a tale. Aileen was ready with her harp, to join with the crouth, the pipers and drummers. Only, for the second year, Hugh would not be there playing his pipe. All through the short day the town would be busy.

Morag went for her cloak and boots, hoping to return with a little meat for the Chrisht's Feast on First-day. As she passed the press, she noticed a little corner of cloth spilled out. She raised the lid to set it right. Someone – it must have been Sorcha – had rummaged through the contents. Why? She would say nothing: these things would most often explain themselves in time.

Most days as she walked out she would hear the men as they started work around the place. It was all looking so much more kempt and tidy than it had been when she and Sorcha first arrived. But today all was quiet. There was no sign of them. A mistle thrush churred from a windswept holly bush beside her path. The bird plucked a blood-red berry and burst into the air, leaving a tiny cascade of snow falling through the stiff leaves.

In the town they had slaughtered a bullock, and most of the wives had gathered round, hoping for a good cut if they were lucky, or at least a bit of offal for the coming feast. Outside the rondal Colin, Shareen's little boy, was playing with some others: a game of catch and run with a sheep's bladder stuffed with straw. A few geese skittered out of Morag's way, cackling.

When suddenly a loud voice rose over the hubbub, she knew it at once. Robert, an outrageous hat on his head, was teetering on a log set on end like a mounting-block, his arms in the air.

'Good people, come! And witness a showing of such egregious dichotomy, such habilious loquacity as eye has not heard nor ear beheld.'

What?

Slowly a ragged circle formed around the players. As Robert rambled on she scanned the other three. There were her clothes! And that was Iain inside them. Malcolm had draped a length of dark woollen cloth over his ample belly – where had that come from? – and belted it like a priest. While Duncan was wrapped in a splendid cloak fastened with a brooch fit for a shareg. With some misgivings, she stayed to watch, with many of the townspeople.

Now priest Malcolm hopped onto the large log. He was haranguing poor Iain in a torrent of incomprehensible words while Iain overplayed his woman's part, his knees trembling beneath his smock, his chattering teeth gnawing at his nails, until he clean fainted away into the arms of Shareg Duncan.

It was unfortunate that Aidan should come out of the rondal just as the player-shareg pointed his wooden sword at the player-priest, who was pouring down the wrath of heaven upon shareg and woman and all. Morag turned. In a moment, Aidan's placid face changed. He looked stricken, and sidled quickly into his house, like a crab disturbed from beneath a stone.

She watched the crowd, her sense of the priest's wounding surging through her. Who else had noticed what she had just seen? The crowd was looking at the players, not after their priest. She could not mistake

Shean's guffaw, but Leighan turned away, rather stiffly. She bit her lip.

Aidan sank down on his chair in the safety of the priest's house. But almost at once came a call at the door.

'Father.' A deep voice. Fearing what this might be, he was relieved to find only one of the fishermen standing on his threshold, looking quite unthreatening, a scrip in his hand. 'For you, Father. It came three days ago. I kept it safe until I saw you to-day.'

'Well, thank you. And remind me of your name.'

He was beginning to recover in the simplicity of the exchange. It was clear the man meant no disrespect.

'Targud Ma'Fengoel,' he answered. He stood, tall and straight.

'Ah! I know your father. A very good man.'

Targud nodded but said no more. Aidan thanked him again, and retreated.

He trimmed the lamp so that it shone more brightly into the mid-winter gloom. He opened the scrip.

Brother Moran, Scribe and Secretary to His Grace Feirgas Archpriest of Fincara, to Aidan, Priest Cairpatrick, Greeting.

His Grace thanks you for your letters, and instructs me to write in this wise.

It is the clear teaching of Holy Church, as received from the Blessed Apostles of Our Lord, that the worship of Stones, of Trees or Rocks, is a Pagan Vanity and against the Commandments given by Moses, saying, Thou shalt not bow down to them, nor worship them. His Grace is concerned that you should need to seek his guidance on this.

Aidan stared. He had not sought guidance. His intention had been to inform, as the archpriest had required. Had he forgotten?

285

Six weeks. Six weeks it had taken for a reply. And then it came not from the archpriest himself, but from a lowly scribe. Aidan remembered the man: running around after the archpriest, never saying boo to a goose until someone lower than himself in the order of things crossed his path, a kitchen boy or an urchin. Then the man might find his tongue, to set such running for him.

> As to the other matter, concerning the man you wrote of. You will know, Father, that the people of heathen parts such as remain in the far west and north of the Isle Fincara are given to all manner of vain imaginings as to Magicks and Powers. Does not the Apostle Saul write, *There will be terrible times in the last days. Men will be lovers of themselves, boastful, proud, blasphemers, unholy. But you, O Man of God, flee from these things and pursue righteousness.*
>
> Assuring you of our Prayers at all times in Christian Fealty,
>
> Moran

Then, in another hand – a junior clerk, Aidan guessed –

> Sealed with the Seal of + Feirgas Archpriest Fincara

Just what had the archpriest told his scribe Moran to write? Aidan could guess. He sat, his head in his hands, a vision forming in his mind of the archpriest's chamber in the High House at Mhreuhan. He had stood there once, as Feirgas sent him to his new living. He imagined Moran the secretary reading out the letter. Feirgas waving his long-fingered hand vaguely: *Answer it.* The secretary retreating, obsequious: *Yes, your Grace.*

He, Aidan, had obeyed the archpriest's instruction. And now, when he reached out to his superior for support, he received only this. This … worse than nothing. It was very clear that no help would be forthcoming from Mhreuhan. He was on his own, so far as the archpriest was concerned. Left to be rebuked by a junior. And here, in Caerpadraig, they were making fun of him in the streets.

Through the winter the warmth of the smithy was always a welcome meeting-place. Having done all that was required of them to prepare the rondal, several of the craftsmen gathered – Olan, Padragh, Tearlach the shoe-maker, and Dhion, while Shean presided. Murdogh had slipped in, preferring this company to the cold mud of the steadings. Leighan's new apprentice, Dillon, a pale youth, hung back in the shadows.

'Aye, ye should'a seen his face.' Murdogh was finishing his tale. 'When them whatje-callems finished, he went dark as a peat-pool an slipped awa jist as quick as he could.'

They all laughed. Most of them had been there, outside the rondal. Had seen the show, even if they had not all witnessed the priest's escape.

'He's a fool that canna laugh at himself.' Shean took a pull at his mug. Dhion smiled a wry smile.

Aidan stayed miserably in his house. He could not bear the thought of what was going on in the rondal as the people prepared it for the mid-winter feast. He felt shut out, while at the same time his church was being desecrated. Midway through the afternoon, he heard the widow-woman's call at the door.

'I've come early, Father,' she said. 'To get you something to eat before dark.'

'A'De, God's blessing. Thank you for coming.' He tried to put some warmth into his voice.

She made a little curtsey. 'Father, the peace of Ghea.'

He sighed. Had she not listened at all? Had no one been listening?

He sat and watched her bending over a pot on the fire. Shareen: that was her name. It was only in the week past that he had really started to talk with her, ask her about herself. Her husband had died a few years back now, she said. Another – like his foreholder – called to the Lord by the wasting sickness.

The smell of porridge made him queasy.

'Your meal is just now ready, Father.'

Could he face it? He must try.

'Thank you.' He sat at the board. She brought him a wooden bowl and his horn spoon. A thought crossed his mind. He looked up. 'Have you eaten?'

'Oh, Father, thank you. But we'll wait for the feast.'

Of course.

She turned as he ate, reached for the besom, began sweeping where some kindling for the fire had drifted across the floor. She bent low to catch a few twigs that had strayed beneath one of the benches. Her skirts rode up her legs a little, showing her thin calves.

'A'De.' She straightened at his summons and turned towards him. The lamp-light caught her cheek-bones. Her wispy hair was always awry. 'Do you believe in the goodness of God to provide?'

'Oh, to be sure I do. God and Ghea. Even though life has been hard since my Andy was taken, they have provided. Through the kindness of people. Only today Niall the dairyman brought a little milk for the children. He often does, you know, so that they'll grow up strong. The people keep us in good health, to be sure. Once Dhion, the Seaborne, ye ken, he saved my Colin from fire when he was wee. I never forget it. An then they built us a new house, right by my mam and da, so we can keep an eye on them, and they on us. An … comin here, Father. It helps us as much as you. So I have much to be thankful for. When I walk in the fields, I rejoice.

An do you know, I feel the rejoicing all around. The fey folk, ye ken. Merry and bright.'

He sat back. Unthinking, he laid down his spoon. This was what he was up against, this attachment to beliefs that had nothing to do with Mother Church, but which, apparently, supported these people. More than he himself felt supported in this moment. He took a deep breath.

'But you must not think of the fey folk.' He said it gently. 'They are no more than the deceits of the Evil One.'

She frowned. 'Do you think that, Father? Truly?' She looked crestfallen. It pained him to see it. But he blundered on.

'Indeed, I do.'

She said nothing for a long moment, her grey-green eyes searching his. Then she bowed her head. When she raised it again, she asked, 'How do you know it?'

He had not expected this. For just a moment, he did not know how to answer. But of course, his response was plain.

'It is written in the Book, woman. We are not to bend the knee to Principalities and Powers.'

She stared.

'Well,' she said at last, 'there's no princes hereabouts, thanks be. And I canna read any book. But I do know what I feel out in the field. And I'd rather have that. It's what my mam taught me, an what I want to pass on to my girlie.'

She was getting ready to leave now, placing her wrap around her shoulders. 'Won't you come after all to the rondal tonight, Father?' She was looking at him with what seemed an expression of concern. 'It'd do you good. We always have such a grand time.'

He shook his head. Waved a weary hand.

Her words had pierced his armour. The players, Moran's letter, and now this: a third wound. This one ran deepest.

Chapter 41

He knew it would be no good calling on the shareg the day after Iulgh. No one went to bed until it was time to get up. Not even Shareen appeared until after noon, and he had to fettle the fire from the glowing embers for himself. But he could expect the people to have recovered by the Feast of Chrisht's Mass. To his relief, enough gathered and worked with a will to restore the rondal to its proper order, and in the end he was rewarded by a good throng. It had not been easy to decide what to say to them after the events of Iulgh. He feared nervously that, in the eyes of some, he might have become ridiculous. Still, he preached his prepared homily on Mother Church as Guardian of the Light. But, on this day, when angels, beasts, the powerful and the humble all gathered to celebrate the birth of the Chrisht-child, he found he could not bring himself to shatter any more of Shareen's dreams.

The weather changed soon after. The wind that had been in the north-west veered round to the north-east. It blew the snow-clouds away, but instead cold grey sheets covered the sky. The wind scoured the snow from the peaks and formed a crust of ice over all. For man and beast it was a hungry time. From the shoulder of Talor Gan, the wolves howled.

'Father, I've brought ye a little salt beef from my manspeople,' Shareen greeted the priest as he came in from his daybreak prayer.

'Thank you, A'De. You've left yourself enough for your little ones?' He was grateful for the meat, and looked forward with relish to his midday meal and enjoying it with a hunk of her good bread.

making a little progress,' he said. 'But … I don't know if you heard about … ' He hesitated. 'Those players. Last week, right in front of … my house.'

The shareg sat back in his chair.

'I did hear something about it,' he agreed, evenly.

'Well …'

Morag saw her opportunity. 'I saw the players,' she said quietly. 'Though they live up at Teigh Riseart I had no knowledge of what they were preparing. And may I say, there has never been anything like this in the town before. I could see it must have been difficult for you, and I had sympathy for you. But they are good-hearted men.'

Indeed she felt concern looking at this man who had come among them, who seemed so lonely, so out of place. People had tried to welcome him, she felt sure, but any exchange she'd ever had with him felt awkward. Being his foreholder's widow as she was, she knew he might feel greater discomfort with her than with others. Yet it was clear his difficulty was wider than that. Still, from what Micheil had said, it seemed he was beginning to reach some. She wondered who they were.

Now he rather gaped at her words and she could see he had not expected her to speak. But she knew she must continue; must try to reach this unreachable man, help him see something of who they were here in Caerpadraig.

'Of course,' she said, 'the players are only newly come here; more so than yourself. But if I may speak a little for the people here, I see them struggling with this idea of church, which seems intended to replace much that we hold dear.'

Father Aidan was looking increasingly uncomfortable, and it occurred to her that he may never have spoken directly with a woman in this way. Perhaps the same thought had crossed Micheil's mind, for he turned to the Father and said, 'Ye may not be used to a woman

293

speaking out like this. Time was, I felt the same. But I have come to value the judgement of Mother Morag and I'd ask ye to hear her.'

Mother Morag? She shot a glance at Micheil.

'As you ask, Shareg.' Father Aidan appeared to be struggling to find his voice.

How to say this so that he could hear it? She must be clear, but also gentle.

'We have strong traditions here, Father,' she began. 'They go back to our ancestors, time out of mind. But when Rortan brought them news of the way of Chrisht, he did not bid them turn from what they already knew.'

'That is why Rortan's work was incomplete!' Aidan had at last found his voice. 'There is the time before Chrisht, and the time after. They are two different times.'

'Forgive me, Father,' said Morag. 'You will know more about these things than I. But my husband told me that at the School in Sharilland he used to study the tales of the ancestors of Ieshu, from the time before Chrisht. He said that these included chronicles and words of wisdom and prophecy, but also fables very like our own. It seemed to him that people could learn better from their own stories that they know and hold dear, than from those of a people far distant from them.'

'But, A'De, you must realise that what you call the tales of the ancestors of Our Lord are holy writ. All that people can get from their own folk tales is error,' the priest said. 'Do you not see?'

'Why so?' she asked.

'Because,' he said, looking as if he felt on surer ground, 'such tales are not of Chrisht. They are not of the Spirit.'

'But all contain wisdom, and some do point towards Chrisht to my mind,' she said. 'I can show you one in the Book in the rondal that speaks of a time when justice

294

and compassion will reign, and the leader of the people gives his life to protect them.'

'You can read, A'De?' His astonishment was plain.

'I do read,' she said. Out of the corner of her eye she glimpsed Micheil smiling.

Aidan stared.

'Father Aidan,' Morag continued. 'You seek to replace our tradition of the Mother with the idea of Mother Church, but this Mother Church does not seem – very motherly. As you speak of her she seems, not the helpmeet, but only the unquestioning servant of God the Father. May I ask, do you not think there is wisdom in the understanding we have here of God the Father and Ghea the Mother? A balance, as in all good marriages?'

Aidan looked as if he did not understand her. She was absolutely sure he had never given any thought to what might make a good marriage.

He shook his head. 'God is Father,' he declared, 'as you rightly said, and as your husband surely knew. And God is Son, and He is Spirit. That is all.'

'Is that what they say at Kilrivain?' she asked, evenly. 'Yet Father, you just now spoke of holy writ. My husband also told me that when scripture was first set down, in the tongues those scribes used, they wrote of the Holy Spirit as She. What do they say at Kilrivain about that?'

'What do you mean?' Aidan cried. 'Surely you do not imagine that, because the words used are in a feminine form, this implies anything at all about the nature of God.'

'But whyever not, Father?'

She watched him. At first his face looked stupid, as if he did not see. Then he began to bluster, but soon stopped. It was as if something passed across him: a dawning. But plainly not one he welcomed. She guessed he had not thought about any of this before; had received whatever line his masters gave him simply because they were his masters. What kind of rootless man was this?

It was Micheil who rescued Aidan from his confusion. Reaching across and offering him another mug of beer, he said. 'Ye mentioned *making progress,* just then. I wonder now – what kind of progress did ye have in mind?'

Aidan seemed to pull himself together, but it was clear he was bruised. He stammered, 'I think … I hope … that the people are starting to hear me. I believe … I am beginning to move them in the right way.'

'Hmm. Ye think we're in the wrong way, do you?'

There was an uncomfortable pause. Micheil leaned forward. 'All right. And this word, *church,* ye keep using … I still don't understand what a church is, nor why we need it here.'

Now Aidan seemed on surer ground. 'The archpriest would have us use the word,' he explained. 'It signifies a people called out from the world.'

'Called out of the world!' Micheil shook his head. 'How are we to put food on the table if we're called out of the world?'

'But … ' Aidan stared at the shareg, aghast. Morag could have helped him here, for she knew the special sense in which the words he had just said were meant. It was the world of mischief that Chrisht's people were called out of; not the round world of plain dealing. But she knew that now she must keep quiet and leave him to Micheil.

The shareg put his head on one side. Then, speaking rather slowly and distinctly, he said, 'Perhaps I need to make the point. That house there' – he leaned his head in the direction of the rondal – 'is not the archpriest's house. Neither is it yours. It belongs to the township. The township built it. And we call it, not a church, but the rondal.' He said it not unkindly, yet Morag looking at Aidan now saw a defeated man.

'It's round, like the wheel of the year,' Micheil continued. Like the wheel of life – birth, and death, and birth again.'

He paused, letting this sink in. In the silence, a tic disturbed the priest's smooth face.

'As you say, Shareg.' It was almost a whisper.

Chapter 42

Aidan retreated to his house. Fortunately Shareen had gone. He sank down on the chair and put his head in his hands. The shareg one side, the archpriest on the other. And that woman, the former priest's widow … What was he to do? If he kept to his teaching, he would lose the support of the shareg, and with him, the whole community. If he went along with what they were saying, he would be turning aside from his commission and the archpriest's favour. He licked his lips. The archpriest was far away. And, anyway, his answer to his letters had been an insult. The shareg was here, now. Whichever way he looked, there seemed no way through. The future was dark to him.

He rose from saying the evening office. That infernal rock! He could no longer see it as the ground of the church. It was there in all its primeval solidity, round, red, deeper than ground. Bedrock, clotted blood of the fire-veined earth itself. He had lost.

He looked towards the shareg's house. A few gaunt timbers for the new wheel stood over on the far side of the burn. The sight of it stung him as he remembered the archpriest's rebuke. A hoodie crow perched on a joist and gave a single throaty caw.

Smoke was rising through the roof of his house. Shareen would be there, making the meal. He pushed open the door.

The biting wind outside made the difference on entering his house all the greater. The fire was leaping under the blackened cauldron. The room, with the shutters up, was pleasantly warm. She was there, her back to him, stooping by the pot with a spoon in her hand. She glanced over her shoulder as he entered, her unkempt red hair rippling as she turned, catching the firelight.

'There ye are, Father. An here's yer meal, all pipin hot for ye.'

He sat on the side of the bed. Food – he couldn't face it just now. He leaned forward and rested his face in his hands.

He couldn't help it. A dull moan escaped him.

'What is it, Father?'

She lifted the pot and set it aside. In a moment she was beside him, an arm round his shoulder, her womanly smell all around.

'Ye can tell me, Father. No one else'll hear.'

What could he say? This young widow couldn't possibly understand. She no doubt worshipped that pagan rock the same as the rest of them. He shuddered for the second time that day. He felt her arm tighten around him, drawing him closer against her body.

He was back in Kilrivain. Brannan had been his name, a young probationary like himself. Their bunks were next to each other in the dorter. Most of them did the same: when the light had been put out, they would creep into each other's beds, whisper, tell each other their fears, the burdens that they alone carried, their passions that could not – could never – be consummated. *They must be mortified,* the sub-prior taught them, *transformed, brought into the service of the Lord.* But there, in the arms of another brother, they could, in a way, be held within what was bearable.

'Aidan.' She said his name. Not Father. Not Brother. Brannan had called him Aidan. His mother had.

He turned his head. Before him was her shadowed throat, moving up and down just a little. To his amazement, he realised she was sobbing too. Sobbing with him. He felt the sympathy flowing out from her and drank it in like a parched man. Her skin was red in the firelight. She rocked him.

He turned towards her. His hand felt for her free arm, lying in her lap. Her skin was warm, moist. He found himself tracing its smooth shapes up to her shoulder. Her leine was rough, coarse wool. She had untied it a little in the heat of the cooking fire. He pulled it open further. What was he doing? She did not resist. He felt her rocking him. 'There, my love, my little one. There there.'

Beneath her throat was a little hollow. Her collarbones met there, and the long, smooth sinews of her neck. He kissed it.

He could not remember afterwards how it happened that they were lying on the bed, together. He was a priest, sworn to the service of Holy Mother Church. But an irresistible force had swept over him. It boiled from his belly and flamed around his heart. And the woman seemed willing. She was warm, she was open, she was caressing him. For a moment he weighed the two: the sense of his duty and the fire that blazed in him. He could not weight the scales heavily enough – there was no comparison. He must give in, burn in its consuming heat. In a moment of decision, he knew he burned willingly. His hand pulled the coarse woollen cloth to the side. He bent, saw her skin shuddering to the beating of her heart. Kissed the warm, living skin.

He had not known, had not realised, the power of it; the sheer animal force of it. He lay with his head beside hers, his face buried in the deep red snakes of her hair. He turned to his side. It was dark. The fire had died down to embers. He raised himself and stood, straightening out his rumpled cassock. She turned, moaned a little, reached towards him.

He bent, lit the lamp. What had happened? What had he done? No – it was she. She had brought him to this. This Eve had brought him a poisoned apple. And he had eaten. He had bitten into it, and – God forgive him! – he had enjoyed it, had given himself to it. And now, would he be ever cast out, banished from God's garden? Was there no going back? Had not the Apostle written, *Put away the slave woman and her son*? This was the slave woman, lying upon his bed, and this was her offspring, this terrible, all-consuming fire. Put them away. *Come ye out from among them. Be ye perfect, even as your Heavenly Father is perfect.*

He shook her, rather roughly. Pulled her to her feet. She looked at him, a little dazed. She smoothed down her skirts, pulled the edges of her leine together, laced them once more. She reached for his hands.

He pulled away. Turned. Paced to the far side of the house, putting the fire between them. 'You'd better go.'

He felt, rather than saw, the look she gave him. He could not bear to see it.

'Yes, Father,' she said, meekly. And added, 'The children will be looking for me.'

She hesitated. 'Shall I come tomorrow?'

'No. No, you're not to come. You're not …' He could not turn to face her. He felt a terrible pressure bearing down on him. He could not bear it.

'Aidan – what is it? You're …'

'You're not to call me that. I'm the Father. Don't call me that again.'

'But, Aidan …'

'Get out. Just get out. You must not … Oh – Go away!' He grabbed an iron from beside the fire. He hurled it at her. She dodged. It clattered against the wall. She fled. And he collapsed on the floor in tears.

Chapter 43

The first moon after Iulgh is always the bitterest. The dark clouds bring little relief, and if the sun shows her face at all, it is only to draw away what little warmth remains in the soil.

Aidan felt the chill as he woke. It was First-day Eve, and still quite dark – not a glimmer from a rush-light, no glow from the fire-pot. The fire was out. He had neglected to take some embers and keep them safe for the morning. That was the woman's job.

The woman. God…

He recoiled at the blasphemy. *Thou shalt not take the name of the Lord thy God in vain.* That rock was infecting him, every part of him. It was beginning to show in his thoughts, his words.

And yesterday – which sin was greater? Did it matter? Sin was sin. And he had committed mortal sin: a grave sin, committed knowingly. Indeed it was the woman's fault. She had drawn him into it. But still he had given his consent. That showed it was more than the woman. Had it been only her, he felt sure he could easily have resisted. But the evil influence was all around: in the taunts of the players, the intransigence of the shareg. He knew where it sprang from, and he knew he could never move that. Round and round his mind went. The strain of it! Strain to breaking point. He didn't know what to do.

He doesn't know what to do.

Who said that? He heard the words as clear as if someone had spoken them two paces away. He looked round, peered from where he sat into the dark recesses of the house. Surely there was no one there. He wrapped his cloak around him, drew it close. But now there was another voice.

He's foul.

Yes. Very foul.

He jumped up. 'Who are you?' he shouted.

Silence.

No light. The fire was out and he lacked the skill to light it.

He lacks the skill to light it.

Lacks skill. Lacks skill.

'Who are you?' He blundered across the room, stubbed his toe, cried out, collided with the book-stand. Held onto it. His one thought was to find the door, throw it open, confront whoever was outside.

He couldn't find it. Somehow his groping had only brought him back to his bed.

He can't find the door.

Can't find it. Can't find it.

A man's voice, derisory, a Westerland accent.

No. And he's foul. A mocking voice. Superior.

'Go away! Go away!' He heard himself shouting. He huddled against the wall, pulled his cloak over his head, willed the voices to depart. He was shaking.

Dawn came slowly, so very slowly, greying the outline of the shutters, making a ghostly half-light. He had fallen into an uneasy sleep where he crouched. Now his body ached from cold.

He must find spiritual help. He looked around him. His precious book that he had brought with him: *On the Epistle of Saul the Apostle to the Hebrites.* He smelled the fine leather of its binding. There wasn't enough light to read by. Cautiously, he replaced the book, took down a shutter. Taking up the book again, he reverently undid the clasps, felt the texture of the parchment between his fingers. Squinting in the weak light, he let his eye fall where it would. He read:

Now when the Apostle writeth, If we sin wilfully after that we have received knowledge of the truth, he speaketh not of those who know not the truth, but of those that have heard the truth and have, as in the parable, sprung up joyfully to receive it. If such then wilfully and knowledge-fully sin, the Apostle saith, there remaineth no more sacrifice for sins.

He thought of Father Denys, who had written the commentary; given this copy to him personally. His soft voice with the foreign accent. How he would invite Aidan, as a promising student, to come to his cell. His hands.

He put down the book. The voices had not come again, but in his head he found himself repeating their words, over and over. He stumbled to the door. If he could open it, there would be more light. But now he dared not open it. *They* would be outside, would see him. Instead of throwing wide the door, he made sure the bar was firmly across. The shutter! He hurried back across the room and lifted it back into place. He checked the shutters were tight.

The house was very cold now. There was water in the stoop, skinned with ice, and oatmeal in the tub. He took a bowl, not very clean, put a small measure of oats in it and stirred in some water. His spoon: where was his spoon? No matter. With two fingers he scooped up a little of the thick gruel.

As he took his fingers out of his mouth he paused. Those two fingers – with those fingers he used to make the sign of blessing. He could do that no more. He knew he was contaminated, infected, unclean. Never again could he say the morning office. Not go out to tend the sanctuary light. Everything, absolutely everything, had come to an end. But still, he breathed. His body had sensation. And this was foul. And … he must relieve himself.

He sat, not knowing what to do.

> *Plead my cause, O Lord, with them that strive*
> *with me:*
> *Fight against them that fight against me.*

He began to mutter the psalm.

> *Let them be confounded and put to shame that*
> *seek after my soul:*
> *Let them be turned back and brought to confu-*
> *sion that devise my hurt.*
> *Let their way be dark and slippery:*
> *And let the angel of the Lord persecute them.*

He must go on. Keep chanting the words. Keep the holy words in his mouth. He must not cease.

Midday passed. He did not eat. While he was chanting, he could not hear the voices. He cringed from the everyday noises that drifted to him from outside. He had forbidden the woman to come; thankfully, no one else drew near. Compulsively, he checked the door and the shutters. The day waned. Evening fell. Outside there was silence. Aidan crouched by the wall. He had stopped chanting. He had stopped everything. His breath steamed.

Then he saw, quite clearly, flames flickering in the fireplace. He stared at them. He was transfixed by their leaping, dancing movements. And he knew these were the flames of purification, come to consume his defilement. They had come to make him clean again. He watched, fascinated.

It was then the voices started once more.

He must be made clean, said the first, a man's voice, reedy, high.

He must be washed. Another man, with a nasal tone.

In the sea. Now it was a whole chorus of voices. All men's voices.

In the sea. The sea. Only the sea can save him. He must be washed in the sea.

The voices rose to a crescendo. It sounded like plainsong.

He must go out. Out. Out. Go to the sea. The sea. The sea …

A figure stood behind the flames. A man, in a black habit. His cowl hid much of his face. The figure turned towards him. Spoke in Latin – good Latin, educated Latin, with that slight foreign accent. 'Father, you must go from here. They know you are here. They will come for you. Go while you may.'

'Who are you?' Yet, was not the voice familiar?

'Come, Father! It's been long since we met, but you know me.'

Of course. Father Denys, as he had been at Kilrivain.

'Do you come from the archpriest?' he inquired.

'Dear me, no, Father. You must know that this comes from further away than your little island. It is much more important than your archpriest. What you're about, Father, is so much more important.'

Well, yes. Indeed. It was. If only he could remember what it was.

'But now that you're stained, you must go from here, Father. Go while you may. Flee from *Them*. Tonight. The widow woman who soiled you, she will follow. She will follow your blood, Father. To stop her, you must wash, in the sea.'

'Won't she still follow me?'

'Not if nobody sees you. Go tonight. Make sure no one sees you.'

'Where must I go?' He heard himself say the words. They seemed to echo within him, repeating themselves after his voice died.

'To the coast. Walk south along the shore, Father, until you come to the Isle Talmey. In its holy waters you can wash yourself clean. The brothers there will receive you. They take vagabonds and lepers.'

Talmey. He knew the name from his boyhood, growing up in Midland. The isle filled a great bay, biting into the southern flank of the Island. He had never been there: to his memory it was only summer pasture for the herds. 'There are brothers there?'

'Indeed, Father. The brethren of the Holy Chalice. They receive the foul and the tainted. Only go quickly. Go tonight. Before the woman leads *Them* to you. Remember how important your work is.'

The figure seemed to merge into the gloominess of the house.

Away. Tonight. At least there would be no difficulty in finding the place. You just had to walk to the coast, turn south, and keep walking. No one must see him. If they saw him they would try to keep him. He would go tonight. Go towards the sea. The cleansing sea.

A chill wind was rising in the north-west. Aidan watched the gloom in the house slowly deepen. Sometimes he thought he saw Father Denys, like a great black bat standing in the shadows. The voices came and went. And always his thoughts – impure thoughts. As they returned, so did She. As he once more muttered the words of the psalms, so She subsided again.

The wind moaned in the thatch, a cold sound, making the cold house colder. It was dark, but he would leave his departure for later. There might still be someone going about by torchlight. He wrapped his cloak around him and huddled on his bed.

Now it was utterly dark. This time if he was going to escape he must find the door. He felt for the wall, and ran his hand over the stones. Guided by his touch like a blind man, he stumbled round the house.

'They will take me. The brothers. They will take me.'

He had never heard of them before. But he knew they would be there, waiting. Father Denys had said.

Here was the door. He lifted the bar and threw it behind him. He heard a crash as it hit something.

Outside it was bitterly cold, but a waning moon was swinging clear of Talor Gan, gleaming between dark clouds. Light enough to find his way.

'They must not see me.' Over and over he muttered this to himself. He feared to tread too close to the shareg's door, and skirted the house widely. There was the path that led up to the pass. Then the coast. 'They will surely take me.'

Chapter 44

Morag woke to a morning of cold, dark rain that slowly cleared to a brilliant, fragile sunshine. It was First-day.

Sorcha said, unusually, that she would stay and keep house that morning. Morag wondered, but said nothing. She set out for the Tollagh alone. As soon as she entered, she saw that the sanctuary light was unlit. The usual press of faces greeted her as she slipped into her seat among the women at the front, but the absence of the light disturbed her deeply. They were all waiting for the priest to enter. They waited, but he did not come. A murmur began. Fineenh, sitting near, turned to her and raised her eyebrows.

Now Micheil made his way to where Aileen was sitting. Morag could not catch what he said, but straight away A'Shar'g rose and left. Micheil remained, standing at the front.

'Let us wait quietly for the Father,' he said in his resonant, reassuring voice. A hush fell. But people kept half-turning, looking over their shoulders towards the open door.

It was Aileen who, in a little while, came through it.

She went straight to her husband, whispered something, and returned to her place. Micheil frowned. The hush deepened. The shareg spoke into it.

'I am sorry to say that we do not know where Father Aidan is.' He paused. 'I will lead the Tollagh today. It will be shorter. And there will be no breaking of bread. We'll begin in the usual way. Then we'll hold a short time of silence. And we'll send out our prayer for the Father.'

The people stood. They chanted the opening words. But Micheil could not light the great candle from the sanctuary lamp. It was like the time at the beginning of the Easter ceremonies, after the Day of Sacrifice; a time when the Chrisht was dead and there were no lights, no bells, no song.

A sense of solemnity hung over them.

Aileen found Morag straight after the Tollagh.

'Morag, the man's gone. It's as if he's just walked out and disappeared. And his house. It's in a terrible state.'

The two women went together to Father Aidan's door. They pushed it open and entered.

The first things Morag sensed were darkness, cold, and a tang of stale piss. She wrinkled her nose.

As her eyes accustomed to the dimness, she made out a scene of confusion. A stool was overturned, and the door-bar lay in the grey ashes of the fire.

She took down the shutters and let in the winter light and the clear, cleansing air. Beside the chair – her teaching chair – was a plate and a bowl with remnants of food on them. Beside the bowl was a rolled up piece of parchment. Wondering, she opened it out.

As she was reading, the shareg entered. Morag looked up. 'Micheil, something very bad has happened here.'

Aileen's voice broke in. 'I thought the other day when he came to us, how brittle he seemed. How alone. Friendless. He seemed to me a man who did not know his way. I ... have never known a mad person. But I wonder ... could the Father have gone mad?'

The shareg looked about him and shook his head. He sat on the edge of the bed, his chin in his hands. Then he said, 'If he's run away in this weather, he won't last the night.'

He stood. 'I'll talk with Duigheal Shepherd. But – we've no idea which way he's gone; and the day is short. No point at all searching after today.'

He turned at the door, puffed out his cheeks and let the air out in a sigh. He seemed on the point of saying something, but turned again and went out.

Morag watched him go. She still had the letter in her hands.

'Is there any clue there?' asked Aileen.

'Nothing clear,' she said. 'But it may be part of the picture, if ever we piece it together. It's from the arch-priest. And I don't like it.' She sank down onto the chair. She was shaking. 'I can't tell you how it feels to come into this house, where Hugh and I lived happily for so long, and find it like this.'

Aileen came to her and put a hand on her shoulder.

'Even for me it's bad,' she said. Then she added, 'What of Shareen? She must know something.'

'Was she at the Tollagh this morning?'

'I didn't see her.'

As this exchange was passing between them, there came a call at the door. It felt to Morag as if they had summoned the young widow by speaking of her.

When Shareen appeared she looked wilder than ever. As she surveyed the scene, her hands went to her mouth.

'Ghea help us!' she cried. 'The poor man must've gone out of his mind!'

'Have you any idea what's happened here?' asked Aileen.

Shareen stood, shaking her head, her hands still raised and clasped under her chin.

'Oh dear,' she wailed. 'I tried to help him. I thought it would be for the best. But it's all gone wrong! I've done wrong. Oh dear, oh dear!'

'Do you have any idea where he is now?' asked Morag. She could see there was a story behind Shareen's words, if ever she was minded to tell it. Now was not the time: as Micheil had said, the time was short.

Shareen seemed to recover a little at the simple question.

311

'That was why I came,' she said. 'I couldnae go to the Tollagh after what's happened. But when the people came away an were talkin about the Father being gone, I knew I must find ye an tell ye.'

'What?' asked Morag.

'It were early this mornin. You know Niall brings me a little milk when he can, bless him.'

Morag did not know. But she nodded.

'An there's no much to be had this time of the year. Well, he said, last thing afore he went to bed, he went back to Shareg's byre. One of the cows is sick, and he wanted to see she was all right.'

Shareen's eyes looked round and big in the dim of the house. The grey light made her face greyer. 'He were just finishin when he heard footsteps. You know how it's all muddy round the back of Shareg's, where the cows go. An then there was this voice. Mutterin it was, so's he could scarce make it out. But he caught a few words, an it seemed to be saying, *to the sea, to the sea*. It made no sense to Niall, an he went to the door to see who it was. By the time he got there, the man had passed by. But he could see him in the moonlight, going up towards the Pass of the Sea. He wore a long gown. It must've been the Father.'

They found Micheil who listened, chin in hand.

He sat for a moment in silence. Then, 'Damn. Niall was attending to that cow again at the time of the Tollagh, or he'd surely have let me know himself. Now I've sent Duigheal down the east road after him, and Tomas up the north, and both on fools' errands. I was sure he wouldn't go Fisherhame way. Well, we'll do what we can.' He turned to Morag. 'That son of yours: he can run. I want him, now, over to Fisherhame. See if there's any news there.' He almost shouted at Morag.

312

'Now! We've precious little daylight. I'll follow behind with whoever I can pull together.'

Morag declined Shinane's invitation to stay with them and wait for news. She was spent, and knew she had done all she could. Wearily, she climbed the brae to Teigh Riseart. Sorcha had a hot meal for her. She sank down, gratefully. When she had eaten, when she had related what had passed, Sorcha simply said, 'So it's come, Antie.'

Morag looked at her sharply.

'What?'

'Yer time. Ye'll be needed, don't ye ken?'

Chapter 45

Shinane sat by the fire listening for footsteps. The twins were asleep, and it was well after dark when Dhion returned.

'We found him.' Dhion sank down onto a stool as Shinane quietly rose. 'He was huddled under a rock on the shoulder of Talor Gan. The madman – he'd actually pulled off his cassock. He was only in a thin shirt and trews.'

'Is he …' Shinane put a steaming beaker in his hand.

'Yes, he's alive. But only just, I reckon. If we hadn't found him before the light failed altogether, it would have been a different story.'

'Where is he now?'

'We got him down to Shelagh's. It was a struggle, I can tell you. Fengoelan and Targud and Callen and myself. Shelagh's looking after him. It takes me back to when I was in his place. At least in Fisherhame they know what they're doing with that ill.'

'So he's been spared,' said Shinane, slowly. 'But what's it all going to mean? I think he'll have to stop priesting with us, don't you? He never really knew us. He was trying to make us into an idea he had in his mind.'

Dhion took a sip. 'You've put something strong in this,' he said gratefully. 'And I needed it.' Then: 'Long ago I thought of Morag as priest, alongside Hugh. I told her so once.'

Shinane nodded. 'She is a priestess anyway. Hugh made her one.'

'What?'

'It was the last thing he did,' Shinane told him. 'And he gave her his stole. I'm sure she'll still have it, up at Teigh Riseart.'

❧❧

Fourth-day. Morag looked out as a squall of snow blew bitingly across the braes of Talor Gan and cleared to a fragile blue. It was then that she saw the broad figure of the shareg with his rolling gait, stumping up the hill.

As soon as he was seated with a mug in his hand, she asked for news.

'Well. He's very ill. Still at Fengoelan's house, with Shelagh watching over him. Oonagh's been to see him and talked it over with Shelagh and Maureen A'Dhael. Though it's certainly a madness that's fallen upon him, yet they think he can recover from it in time, with care. But he won't be priesting for a long while, they say.'

Morag sat very still.

He shifted in his seat. 'That's why I'm here, Morag. I'm in a cleft stick. I canna turn one way nor else. I need you to help me out of it.'

It was quiet in the house.

'What is it you want me to do, Shareg?'

He gave her almost a shy look. A look, Morag could imagine, he'd last worn when he was no more than a lad. He opened his mouth.

'It's like this.' He tapped the side of his mug. 'I don't want to send for Mungo again so soon. He's enough to do. And anyway, we need a priest here, among us.' He paused, turned in his chair, glanced over his shoulder, then back to glare at the floor. 'And I don't want to send to this new archpriest for a replacement. I'm feared he'd send us another like Aidan. We can't be doing with that. So …' He drummed on his mug again. 'D'you think you could take the Tollagh for us – with myself, of course? D'you think we could do it together?'

Here it was: it had put on the form of spoken words. Morag took a deep breath.

'And how exactly would you want me to – take it?'

'Well, you've a good voice for leading the chants. And – you can read. And d'you think you could say a few words to us all after? And … bless the bread and the cup?'

It sounded like all of it. She closed her eyes. Cleared her mind. Into the space she saw faces, heard voices. Sorcha's voice: 'Antie, do ye no remember what the lady Amirah said? An the lord Guirman? This is your time.'

But could she, really? She held her breath. She would be stepping out into unknown territory. They all would, the whole community, to have a priest not sent to them by the archpriest. And a woman to boot. Yet now she saw clearly that this was what she had been pre-pared for all down the long years. First by Father Callen, teaching her to read. Then all the years with Hugh. And now, most lately, by the Guardians. All pointing in the same direction. She was the Daughter of the Priestess to Priests. And now the space had opened before her in a way she could never have imagined. Was it not her place to step into it, and deal with whatever followed? But still, it was so sudden. And she could not help thinking: would she be welcomed? How would she be supported?

She let out her breath again. 'Micheil, give me a day or two. What you say is right, and if I am to stand in for a while, then most will accept your word. But I've got to know in my heart that what I'm doing is right. Will you give me time?'

She watched him sit back, place his hands on his knees, a shareg to the core. He spoke. 'I will take the Tollagh again this First-day. Come to me when you've decided. They'll soon tire of me: not of you.'

It was cold out round the back that evening, and gloomy. Morag perched a lamp on a high shelf and found a couple of neeps from the dwindling pile on the floor. Leaving the door open, she went out to cut kale. She

316

had her knife with her, the knife that Shean had made for her. A good hunting knife. What was she doing, using it just to cut vegetables? But then, she never went hunting.

Bringing in an armful of cold green leaves, she placed them on the block to trim the stems. But now her fingers were cold and clumsy. She fumbled. With a clatter the knife fell to the earth. Scolding herself, she peered down into the darkness that cloaked the ground. And there it was, upright, its point buried in the floor, still trembling, right between her feet. Just as she had seen a knife nearly a year before, in Finneuchan's house.

Now would ye look at that! Finneuchan's voice, so far away. *Take it, an learn how to use it!*

She bent down and took it. *Knife speaks to knife.*

How does it speak? *It speaks in here, girl. An those that will listen can hear it.*

What could she hear – in there, in her deepest heart?

She straightened. It was the word she had been waiting for.

As she stood, taking it in, there was a small sound behind her. The door scraped softly open, and she felt a cold gust on her back. The *chock* of the door closing again. A small, silent shape standing beside her.

A long moment, and a hand reached for her hand. She looked into the girl's face. She made a small, word-less nod.

'Aye,' Sorcha replied.

317

Chapter 46

The little room at the back of the rondal always smelled musty. Here, in a plain wooden press, were kept the linens for the altar. Above, little boxes of fragrant herbs, lumps of resin to blend the incense. And on the opposite wall that separated the chamber from the rondal itself, so that they hung nearest the altar, the chesibles were stretched out on rods. High, out of reach of mice, and only three: they could not afford all eight of the different colours that full service required. Brown for funerals, like the earth into which the body would be laid; a creamy white embroidered with ochre and red for high days; and green for everything else.

Morag knelt on the little stool. 'In the name of the One; without beginning, without ending; in the name of the Highest Intention … '

She had asked Shareen to help her; now she was almost pressed against the wall in the tiny space, lifting the green robe off its hanger.

Morag looked round. 'No, not that. Today's a celebration. I'll wear the white.'

She stood. She had seen no need to change from her habitual gown, its blue clouded with grey like the skies of the Island. To wear her husband's cassock – the one that did not lie in the grave with him – would have been to mimic him. She would be herself.

First, the stole. The stole she had saved, not knowing for what purpose, only that it was right. She kissed the tiny cross at the back of the neck.

Shareen was now ready with the chesible. She held it out, its back rolled so she could easily slip it over Morag's head. Morag bowed, pushed herself through the collar, her arms through the open sides, and stood.

And for the first time felt the embroidered weight of it on her shoulders. Shareen's face before her was solemn.

A moment of silence. From behind the curtain that screened them from the people came a hushed murmur. Shareen pulled the curtain aside.

Morag stood in the rondal, Hugh's stole – now her stole – hanging from her shoulders. It was the full of the second moon of the new year: Imbolg, Candlemas. There were lights all around the rondal, the gleam of the sanctuary light falling upon the reassuring bulk of the Mother. The rock sparkled as Morag moved. So many faces, waiting, watching.

Before her were the people she knew so well. Micheil in his place at the front. Beside him, two paelchte, sentenced bondmen serving their time and under the shareg's cloak. The women's benches: Aileen, Fineenh and Shinane with the two wee ones. Shelagh, and Shareen. And behind them the men: red beards, black beards, grey, white. Dhion's dark brown beard. Leighan's shrewd face. Shean sitting back, arms folded.

They came to the point in the Tollagh where Hugh would so often tell them a tale. She sat where Hugh had sat, a story from the Old Book in her heart. The one she chose was that of Gelda: stolen from her mother as a babe, never knowing who she was until she found the Well of Truth deep in the forest one mid-summer eve.

Now it was time for her to speak to the people. She rose.

'I want to tell you my own story. All but our newcomers and the very youngest of you will remember the funeral of Mother Coghlane, and how people came from far and wide to honour her, so that we made a great feast of it.' This was how she began, and she went on to tell them the outlines of how at last she found her mother-line.

'Hugh used to go from time to time to visit Coghlane,' she finished. 'And all those years, I never knew he was meeting my own mother.'

She paused. Her tone changed.

'Hugh's last day, Shinane and I were sitting beside him. We all knew he didn't have long. He wanted to receive the *beannach*, so he sent me for the holy things. Then he had me give him the bread and the cup. He anointed me a priest.'

If there had been a fly, you might have heard the patter of its feet on the wall in the stillness.

She reached for her knife where it lay upon the altar, and dipped its point into the chalice. A drop of the fermented mead that served them for wine upon its tip, she made the sign of the encircled cross on the cup, on the bread. Hugh's voice was silent now. As she rose into herself, she knew he could rest.

She lifted the paten bearing the bread: *'Corp Criosd.'*

The chalice. She felt tall. *'Fuil Griosd.'*

Afterwards, the people surged around her. The sense of relief was evident. As the crowd thinned, Olan came to her. She turned to him.

'Mother Morag,' said he. 'I've got a nice lump of yew wood just waiting to be made into a thing of beauty. Once the wheel's working and I've learned some skill at the lathe – ' his eyes shone ' – I promise you, I'll make it into a cup and a plate for the bread and wine. A big one, for the rondal. And for you.'

Chapter 47

The elder bushes were decked with lacy blossom. The air was sweet. White daisies and golden celandines starred the green grass. Beltane came straight after Easter that year and, benefitting from the lengthening evenings, Morag was sitting by the loughside with Dhion and Shinane. Sorcha was plaiting daisy-chains and crowning the twins' curly heads with them, while the two girls, one after the other, pulled them to pieces with serious expressions on their little faces.

'Shareg has had a talk with me about Aidan.' Morag's glance took in her son and sonswoman. 'Having him back in the priest's house was what had to be while we all needed to care for him. But we've seen that where he lives isn't helping him to heal.'

When Aidan was well enough to walk the distance, he had returned from Fisherhame, and was for a time visited by Oonagh and cared for by all the wives of the town. Aileen kept control of who came and went so that there were never too many nor too few. Seemingly in his right mind now, only a shadow crossed his face if someone mentioned Tollagh, or Rondal, or Priest. He had asked the town to provide him with a plain leine and trews, same as the working men wore, and he laid aside his cassock.

Shinane nodded. She too had looked in on the man from time to time, bringing the twins as a diversion. 'Yes,' she added. 'The house holds difficult memories for him. I think, Mother, he's done with priesting.'

'I think so too. He seems all right now, in his way. But he won't go near the rondal. And there he is, right next door to it.'

'So...?' Dhion's voice was loaded with the question.

'Well, Micheil has asked me to go on holding the Tollagh.'

'The people are with you, Mother.' Shinane said. 'Even Catrean. She said the other day coming out of the rondal how she prefers you to hold it rather than Father Aidan.'

Morag looked down at her hands in her lap. 'We shouldn't call him that any more. It doesn't help him. When I asked him, he said he'd rather be known as Aidan the Bees.'

'The bees?' Dhion looked at her quizzically.

'Oonagh's been teaching him. It seems he's quite taking to it. A few stings, Oonagh says, never hurt anyone, and may do him some good. She says they're marvellous for people with rheumatism. As for ills of the soul, she says nature's the best healer. She's teaching him about herbs, too.'

'Tell 'em the rest o the news, Antie.' Sorcha turned from where she was sitting with the twins.

'What's that?' Shinane questioned.

'Well, now Duncan's taken Iain back down Caerster way, there's plenty of room up at Teigh Riseart. Micheil wants Aidan to move there. Oonagh's giving him some skeps to put in the orchard, where there's plenty of forage for the bees. Sorcha will keep them all in order. And Malcolm and Robert will be company for him. Now the man's keen to be off.'

Shinane smiled. 'Those two – they're a pair, aren't they?'

'Won't they... I mean, it was the players mocked him at Iulgh.' Dhion frowned.

'That's just it. While he's been ill Robert has been coming down to him and telling him stories to cheer him up. They've got on really well together.'

'Then that leaves the priest's house empty,' cried Shinane. 'And a priest's house needs a priest in it. Or perhaps a priestess. You're coming home, Mother Morag!'

Morag smoothed out an imaginary crease in her skirt, but could not hide her smile. 'Yes,' she said. 'I'm

322

coming home.' She turned to Dhion. 'I can move my things in next week, if you'll help me.'

She glanced up at Shinane.

The young mother's eyes were shining. 'Then Hugh's book must go with you,' she said.

Morag looked at her. 'I hadn't thought.'

'Wouldn't you like to keep the book that Hugh began?' Shinane asked.

Morag hesitated. 'Well … how do you feel about it?'

'It would want to go home. I've just looked after it when you needed me to.'

Morag looked into the young woman's eyes. Then, 'Thank you,' she said. 'Thank you for writing what I couldn't.'

There was a sudden wail. They all turned their heads, and Shinane's eyes widened at the sight of Lois. The little one had tumbled down a hummock, and her elder sister was rolling down the slope to fall on top of her.

Then Dhion's eyes widened, too, for beyond them a tall, strong man, was striding towards them.

Sorcha jumped up delightedly. Morag sat, unperturbed. 'I've been expecting you for some time, Wolf,' she said. 'Sit down, and meet my family.'

Epilogue

Now, when the Sidh of the Island spreads her wings of gold-brown and green and hovers, looking through the thatch of the priest's house, the head she sees lying on the pillow in the bed-alcove is one she knows well. They call her Mother Morag, down there in the town.

The Sidh takes wing and rises higher. Up above the town they call Caerpadraig, the burn still tumbles its way towards the lough. Only now some of its water runs to the great wooden wheel. Its new timbers are dripping as the water sluices down upon them, falling into the tail-race and back to the burn. She knows it to be the work of the seaborne one, who came from a place beyond the meeting of the worlds; who brings with him a knowledge of the powers of the Mother such that, should he let himself, should he be allowed, would set Her to work for him. Well, for the most part, he stays his hand. The people have taught him a little wisdom to leaven his knowledge. The wheel rises and, indeed, it sits well in its place. In time to come it will look as if it too has grown out of the earth.

Here in the Westerland and in the North, the Sidh can see the Island that is her body. And in the places where men and women do little but pass through, she remains at home with the care given her for all its peoples: the wolves, the seals and the geese; the tree-peoples and the rock-peoples; the folk of the little creeping things and of the tiny green things.

But now there are parts of herself she can no longer see. There in the great town they call Mhreuhan, in the archpriest's high house on the hill, she has been driven out. She can no longer hover low with her unseen wings, nor see in. And, more and more, in the towns of the parts they call Midland and Caerster, she with her sisters and brothers is being driven away, to hide and to sleep in the hollow hills that still hold them. Bit by bit, she is being banished from the Island that is her charge. Banished for all the time that will unfold before it will lie once more entirely in her care.

She rises, until the Island is no more than a patch of green and brown, of heather-red and lichen-gold. A patch in the limitless ocean that is forever washing her shores. A tiny oneness, held in a fierce love.

Acknowledgements

When a book has been in gestation for as long as *The Priest's Wife*, it begins to rest upon the creativity and artistry of many people. My good friend Plaxy, in her Radnorshire farmhouse, provided welcome solace during the Pandemic and read for me an early draft. She was the first of three mothers who gave me searing criticism of the 'birth chapter,' with their direct experience that I cannot have had. To my sister, Mary Coles, a big thank you for many helpful comments on the phone and for pages of hand-written notes, leading to numerous revisions.

Being a much more interior book than *The Seaborne*, I am indebted to my friend Isabel Clarke, author of several books, including *Madness, Mystery and the Survival of God,* for sharing her deep insight into the processes of spiritual emergency and psychosis. She read the whole typescript with a critical eye for the descriptions of such processes there, and we discussed them over dinner and during walks on Southampton Common.

I was fortunate to have the expert advice of Maggie Hamand, author of *Creative Writing for Dummies* as well as of her own novels. This did much to help shape and develop the plot from an earlier, unsatisfactory ending to something altogether tighter, truer, and more dramatically satisfying, and to bring out the essential themes in the story. Once more Richard Danckwerts' indefatigable wit helped spot detailed errors and implausibilities.

As in *The Seaborne*, in my descriptions of the traditions and beliefs of the Island people, I draw deeply on my time with the Céile Dé, to whom I owe much for my own spirituality. My friend Gelda MacGregor, on the shores of the Moray Firth, has given much input there down the years, and it has been good to talk over Gaelic names with her and to know where I have deviated from the correct and the plausible, so far as this, non-fictional, world is concerned.

My gratitude to the team at Publishing Push who prepared this book for printing and distribution. You have been meticulous. And at a fairly late stage in the book's development I was enormously encouraged and grateful when *The Priest's Wife* received the backing of Cyngor Llyfrau Cymru, the Books Council of Wales.

I save my greatest thanks for someone who has believed in this story from the beginning, tolerated my tantrums and burned the midnight oil on my behalf, implacably arguing away weaknesses and tirelessly hauling the whole text through the wringer, not once but countless times, until it is just about as good as we can make it. My wife and editor, Gillian Paschkes-Bell, works collaboratively and creatively with me to arrive at the final expression of my narrative. While mine is the act of first creation, there is much passing to and fro of different versions before we arrive at the final telling, for which I take responsibility.

A.G.Rivett

The People and Places of the Story

As in *The Seaborne*, I've grouped these names first by their home, and secondly by their family relations. In brackets, I've provided a simple guide to pronunciation, where this isn't obvious.

As a general rule *ch* is pronounced as in *loch*, never as in *church*.

Bh and *Mh* both sound like our *v*. *Dh* is simply *h*.

Gh is silent, as in English *though,* or it's a glottal stop. *Ph* remains like our own *ph*.

As in other Celtic languages, initial consonants of names can change under some circumstances. So Morag is the wife of the priest (*an Padr*), and so is known as *A'Phadr*. Similarly, the daughter of Catrean is *Mi'Chatrean*. And as in so many languages, this change is not always consistent, especially in place-names. So you might expect the central town of the story to be *Caerphadraig* (or even *Dunphadraig*). But it isn't. Beh' Mora is not Beh' Mhora, except, maybe, to some pedants in Caerster, but somehow Beh' Bhica has kept its lenition. That's languages for you!

Beings of Otherworld

The Sidhe	(*Shee-eh*)
The Sidh	(*Shee*) of the Island

At Caerpadraig

Morag	Wife of Hugh; also A'Phadr
Hugh	Priest, son of Colm
Dhion	(*H'yorn*) Their adopted son, formerly John, also known as Ingleeshe and the Seaborne

Shinane	Dhion's wife, daughter of Shean and Fineenh
Regan	(*Regahn*) Their infant daughter, twin sister of Lois
Lois	Their infant daughter, twin sister of Regan;
Shean	Blacksmith, Shinane's father, son of Ronal
Fineenh	Wife of Shean
Micheil	(*Michale*) Shareg of Caerpadraig
Aileen	Wife of Micheil; also A'Shar'g
Tamhas	(*Tarvas*) Their son
Seamus	(*Shaemas*) Their son, Tamhas' twin
Doirin	Seamus' wife
Leighan	(*Lee'an*) Carpenter
Catrean	(*Catrean*) Wife of Leighan
Olan	Their son
Moira	Wife of Olan, and Shinane's friend; also Ag'Olan
Bran	(*Brahn*) Their infant son
Dillon	Leighan's apprentice
Duigheal	(*Doo'eel*, loosely, *Dougal*) Shepherd
Shareen	Widow
Padragh	Potter
Rhona	Midwife, wife of Padragh
Tearlach	(*Cheerlach*) Leather-worker
Murdogh	A labourer
Oonagh	(*Oonah*) Herb-woman
Siocan	(*Shocan*) Farmer, daughtersman to Rhiseart
Odhran	(*Oran*) Siocan's wife's sister's husband
Tomas	Siocan's son

Aidan	Priest

The Guardians
Wolf
Fearánn   (Fear**ahn**)
Freia   (***Freya***)
Guirman   (***Gear***mahn)
Tearlach   (***Cheer***lach)
Amirah   (*Am**eera***)

The Players
Robert   Horse-dealer
Malcolm   Shoemaker
Duncan   Tailor
Iain   Son of Duncan

The Isle Fincara Trilogy

The island of Fincara, or Finchaighe, exists in Irish myth, fated to be cast beneath the waves by druidical spell, where one day a deep-diving hero finds its stalwart ladies continuing unhindered in their tasks.

Using the conventions of the portal fantasy and a parallel world, A G Rivett's Island has a different fate. Out beyond the Western Isles, in the ocean we call the Atlantic, and remaining solidly on the surface, it is visited by an unwitting time-traveller from our own day.

Such a scenario lends itself to the exploration of some radical questions.

- Did humanity take a wrong turn when we ceased to see ourselves as part of nature and set ourselves apart?

- Have science and technology created greater problems than they have solved?

- "*Without a vision, the people perish.*" What is the new story for our times?

When the Roman Empire adopted Christianity as its state religion and Church was married to State, the alliance actively suppressed pagan cults. While *The Seaborne* presents a picture of a harmonious fusion of spiritual world views, the second and third books of the Trilogy explore the tension generated when a State-endorsed Church sets itself against other expressions of spirituality. These tensions extend to the present day.

Gillian Paschkes-Bell
Editor
4th September 2023

Pantolwen
Press

Also by A G Rivett

The Seaborne

First book of the Isle Fincara trilogy

A novel of Celtic quantum time that asks us to consider the ways in which we are all born strangers, living between worlds. A parable for our particularly torn times.   Damian Walford Davies

John Finlay is fleeing from failure. His engineering business has failed, his relationship has failed. His flight from debts leads him to disaster—and to the Island, where he must learn to live anew.

Dermot, pulling a body, barely alive, from the water, has never seen anyone so strangely dressed. His Celtic island knows nothing of debt, nor engineering. Where has this man come from?

John struggles to accept that he has been carried across time and into another world—both like and unlike his own. How he got there is a mystery. But John the foreigner must turn slowly into Dhion the Islander. Still, he brings with him unfinished business that must be faced, and ideas that may not always be welcomed. Meanwhile Dermot, consumed by a growing jealousy, develops his own deadly agenda. The whole community finds itself caught up in what becomes a matter of survival—or transformation.

A tale of discovery and reassessment, in which John/Dhion must struggle to find himself, his role, his love and his place in this new, old world.

Published by Pantolwen Press

Pantolwen
Press

Coming in 2024

𝒱𝓊

by Kenneth Sinclair

Summoned by the Princess Scheherazade,
a tale to take your breath away

Gabriel, a twentieth century English storyteller, is abducted while journeying in an unnamed land. He is summoned to narrate to the Princess Scheherazade, who occupies an imaginal world not bounded by time or place. His narration spans more than two thousand years, told over twenty evenings. It is a many-layered tale, in which poets, painters and players jostle with explorers, sages, and scientists, hurtling towards the silver screen and the apprehension of string theory.

The last word is given to the birds, who fly through the narrative, calling us to attend to them and to the natural world in which, and against which, all human striving takes place.

The piercing cry of a peacock calls from the starlit garden.

— Time to begin, she said.

And so that night, the black hulls of the Greeks already on the blue Aegean, bound for Troy. The long sea oars drip diamond drops that flash in the noonday sun. In all beginnings there is a magic force.

Published by Pantolwen Press